A Rampage Of Chocolate

A journey to womanhood through the ministry of chocolate

Anne-Marie Alexander

authorHOUSE®

AuthorHouse™
1663 Liberty Drive
Bloomington, IN 47403
www.authorhouse.com
Phone: 1-800-839-8640

© 2011 Anne-Marie Alexander. All rights reserved.

No part of this book may be reproduced, stored in
a retrieval system, or transmitted by any means
without the written permission of the author.

First published by AuthorHouse 5/25/2011

ISBN: 978-1-4567-8094-4 (sc)
ISBN: 978-1-4567-8095-1 (e)

Printed in the United States of America

This book is printed on acid-free paper.

Because of the dynamic nature of the Internet, any web addresses or
links contained in this book may have changed since publication and
may no longer be valid. The views expressed in this work are solely those
of the author and do not necessarily reflect the views of the publisher,
and the publisher hereby disclaims any responsibility for them.

This book is dedicated to my beautiful children:

Eve
Thomas
Phoebe

With grateful thanks to:

Joy Maddison, the editor, for her supportive style and encouragement.
Barbara Coffin for her last minute proof read and her belief in this book.

FOREWORD

One of the hardest things on our journey through life is coming to a place where we value ourselves. As we meander down the path that we've been given, we get battered and bruised by things and people along the way. Sometimes we lose so much of ourselves in the process that we look to others to fill the gaps.

I was one of those people born 'accident-prone' with often hilarious consequences. Of course I've had to learn to shoulder that hilarity because with it often came great humiliation. For me there was a journey, a path to tread that took me to a place where I could stand firm, no matter what my situation threw at me; knowing that I was still a precious individual who was loved. Life is to be enjoyed, if only we can secure our hopes to the right place.

A Rampage of Chocolate is a journey of (mostly) my disastrous experiences lived out through a fictional character - Anne Rosetta Booth. This is her story; her journey.

Although all of the characters and situations in this book are purely fictional, many of the thoughts, fears, dreams, hopes, disasters and bizarre situations are ones that I myself have enjoyed on my life journey. I will leave you to decide which ones…

Enjoy reading. Enjoy laughing. Enjoy the journey.

Anne-Marie Alexander

The Tender Years...

Chapter 1

In The Beginning

It is fair to say that my life has been dominated by 2 main themes: clumsiness and chocolate. The 'ministry of chocolate' has been essential in patching up the external and internal wounds received through the knocks of life. For the most part the chocolate was successful, achieving its purpose, but occasionally more was required. All things have a beginning; all things have a purpose. The purpose of chocolate and my association with it as a comforter was made at a very young age…

My life began in a flat in Hounslow. By all accounts it should have been an ordinary start to life, had it not been for the passion that my parents held for the environment and for their rights. They were part of the freedom movement in

In The Beginning

the 60s, always marching and campaigning for the right to live according to their choice.

It was after one such protest march - the right to free contraception for women - that Mum discovered she was pregnant. My Dad clearly wished that he had protested sooner because he did the only thing that any self-respecting hippy would do - he packed his bags and scarpered!

He left a note, which read quite simply:

Davina

This world is no place to bring up a child. I'm off to change it for you both. I trust you to raise this child, so trust me to fight for your environment.

My love always,

Dave
x

He didn't go far to change the world; just down the road. It would appear that he felt the battle would be best fought with a student nurse; a curvy lady named Rita.

In the 9 months that followed, Mum ditched her headband and her principles and instead turned to capitalism and hard work. The only clue as to her former existence was her colourful dress sense and her somewhat random thought processes.

We were a pioneering duo, defying all odds. The combination of a working mother with an illegitimate child was an unpopular one to most of society, but it suited us. She had rejected all the proposals and offers of adoption at an early stage, choosing instead the road of life together, yet alone. A tough choice, but one for which I would be eternally grateful.

Mum was great. She was conscientious and loving, always ensuring that I had the best that she could afford. This included a good seat on the new sofa, propped up between 'Bunny', who became my treasured possession, and 'Edward Bear' (a knitted teddy), who never made it past the first 18 months when his stitching gave up and all his stuffing fell out. Secure in the knowledge that I was safe, Mum trotted off to get a bottle of milk to stave off any potential crying. It was all going so well - the idyllic flat with its modern, flock wallpaper and patterned carpet, Mum in her red, flared trousers and yellow top and me on the chocolate-brown velvet sofa… Until the fateful 'Thud!'

Mum dropped the bottle and ran back into the lounge.
"Aagh!" she exclaimed as she scooped me off the floor with a tender, loving arm. "Are you okay? … Shhh don't cry… Mama's here… Silly Mama; I shouldn't have left you on the sofa. Look, have a bit of chocolate. It's Mama's favourite… There! That's better isn't it?"

And so, nestled against my mother's breast, lump of chocolate in my mouth, melting and oozing on my tongue, the recurring theme of my life began:

First the bump, then the chocolate!

Chapter 2

Kitchens and Children Don't Mix

Mum coped in the best way she knew how. After all it couldn't have been easy to look after a child as a single mother in the 60s whilst holding down a full-time job. It didn't seem to faze her though. She still looked amazing. She had dark olive skin, jet black hair and never wore any make-up apart from a shock of red lipstick. All the men loved her because of her curvaceous figure and easy manner, or at least they 'loved' her until they realised that she came as part of a package. I sorted out the time wasters for her, mainly because of my fondness of either vomiting on their trousers or knocking a drink over them.

I'm not sure why it happened so often; it just did and was somehow always timed to coincide with the obligatory, but never heartfelt:

Kitchens and Children Don't Mix

"How nice that you have a child. She's so beautiful, just like her mother." (Even Mum was never taken in by that lie - I had blonde hair, blue eyes and pale skin. It hardly reflected her Mediterranean beauty). "What did you say her name was?" Most of them didn't wait around long enough to find out the answer. Had they done so, they would have found out that it was 'Anne', which means 'grace'. I can only assume that my mother was either dazed with post-delivery euphoria or just applying her mischievous sense of humour when she named me! Whichever it was, the irony of her choice would accompany me for the rest of my days!

At first it was easy for Mum. She would take me to work in my carry cot, which she would stand on the big chest freezer in the corner. This then left her free to perform her duties as the 'Banqueting Manageress' and head chef at the local Pavilion. All she needed to do was to satiate my desire for milk and say the odd 'cooing' noise, whilst stirring vats of soup and preparing all manner of other delights. However as time moved on, so did my ability to move around and 'help'. I always considered myself to be very useful, priding myself as a vessel of some importance in the workings of the kitchen - a veritable asset to Mum in the flurry of all her culinary activities. I liked to go wherever she went and observe whatever she was doing, sticking my finger in anything open and gooey as I went.

I had 2 favourite places in that kitchen. The first was the store cupboard. This was very special to me because it was where they kept the boxes of chocolates and crisps; row upon row of boxes containing packets of chocolate, chocolate bars, individual chocolate biscuits and every conceivable flavour of crisps. Walking through that door was like entering my seventh heaven. Occasionally, if I knew that no one had

A Rampage Of Chocolate

spotted me going in, I would help myself to a chocolate covered biscuit. However, with 4 types to choose from, it was often hard to decide which one to have; and so I felt forced to stay inside until I had sampled all of them. After much deliberation I would then chose my favourite and eat that one again! For the most part I was not caught, although occasionally my squeals of glee and the sound of my troughing would attract the attention of a passerby and I would be hauled out of there with chocolate around my mouth and silver wrappers in my hand. Shamefaced I would be dragged towards the soup section where I had to face my Mum. She would look me up and down, purse her red lips and with total predictability exclaim:

"Honey what on earth were you thinking of? You know that we don't eat chocolate; it's for special occasions or when we get hurt. Just for that you are not going to have any more chocolate for a whole week."

Her threat always came as a great relief! By that point, my stomach would be starting to react to the furtive and overly-hurried consumption of 5 or more chocolate bars and I was invariably feeling quite unwell.

On one such occasion, I was stood in front of the soup pot receiving the all-too-familiar ear bashing, when I heard the door go. I looked up and saw a tall, handsome, dark-haired man enter the kitchen. My heart leapt with joy. This was David the crisps salesman. He had a real soft spot for my Mum (like so many), but he was my absolute favourite. I think this was largely influenced by his big smile and the fact that he always gave me a packet of potato hoops. Secretly I hoped that he would marry my Mum and become my daddy since I couldn't imagine anything better than a house with a mummy, a daddy and lots of crisps. I ran towards him with open arms. Of course, when you're feeling unwell after 5 chocolate biscuits, running is perhaps not the best activity to engage in; it can cause an internal chain reaction. By the time I realised what was happening, it was too late; I was upon him and so were my chocolate bars (albeit a liquefied version). We didn't see David much after that.

The second place I enjoyed in the kitchen was the fridge. This was no ordinary fridge, this one you walked into! I used to love following my Mum in there and just standing and gazing at all the delights that awaited the guests of that night's banquet. From Dublin-Bay prawns to glazed lamb cutlets with little chef's hats on the ends, it was a feast to the eyes. Sometimes I reached out to take something that caught my eye, but for the most part I was rooted to the spot, mesmerised by the delicacies on offer.

It was, as I say, a big fridge. Well actually, it was a giant fridge to me. One busy afternoon, my Mum popped in there to get out a half-opened tin of grapefruit. She didn't notice me follow her in. I in turn didn't see her leave, but instead stood rooted to the spot in my usual state of mesmerisation. On this occasion,
when I finally peeled my eyes away from the goodies in front of me, I found myself all alone.

Now, if you've ever wondered about the light in a fridge and whether it really does go out when you shut the door, I can confirm (as an involuntary observer), that it does *not*. At least not in those giant fridges. The light does not go out until someone switches it off outside. Thankfully that enabled me, a lone, frightened fridge-ranger, to see my way to the 'emergency door release' handle. A long, spring-loaded lever, it was easy to find since it stuck proudly out of the door with a big, red knob on the end. I attempted to pull it, but found that a 4 year old's strength was not sufficient to pull it back far enough to open the door. Several attempts failed, leaving me frustrated and cold.

By now I was starting to get a little panicky and the previously tempting food had completely lost its appeal. My only focus was getting back to Mum at the stove, so I put my left hand on the door to give myself something to push against and with my right hand I pulled for all I was worth. As the door opened, I released the lever in relief. Now I think I mentioned that the handle was 'spring-loaded', well the combination of that and my left hand still being on the door turned out not to be a winning one. As the handle was released from my right hand, it trapped my left thumb with its full force and I found myself being catapulted with a yell out of the fridge still attached to the door. I had for a single moment in time become a flying fridge-ranger!

Mum abandoned the grapefruit and came running.
"Oh my goodness! Annie, are you okay?... I am so sorry... How long were you in there?... Let me see your thumb... Oh! You poor thing! Let me get my jumper and wrap you up, you're so cold." She scooped me in her arms and took me to the store cupboard. "Here, have some chocolate. It will make you feel better." So I sat in a corner by the big chest freezer - a heroic, if somewhat hypothermic adventurer, swaddled in Mum's rainbow jumper, my left hand in a pot of cold water and my right clutching a bar of chocolate. I let the chocolate melt on my tongue, gently swishing it around my mouth until my whole mouth was coated. Then I sat back to enjoy the rest of the bar and to let the troubles of a 4 year old's day pass me by.

Kitchens and Children Don't Mix

Of course an industrial kitchen is not an ideal place for a 4 year old and the combination is not without its humiliations. You see, my Mum was not the only person to work in that kitchen. In fact when they were getting ready to serve, there could be as many as 20 people - 8 from the kitchen and 12 waitresses ready to serve the baying crowd. The waitresses would hang around waiting for their serving dishes to be filled. And so it was, one fine July afternoon, (not that we could see that it was fine, for the windows in the kitchen were all opaque). Mum was busy co-ordinating everyone, going over the final details of the serving plan.

"Julia, I want you on table number 1 with Peggy. Please be especially careful of Mr Humphries at the head of that table; he is very particular about where you put his potatoes." Julia and Peggy giggled at this and I overheard them muttering something about where they were going to put his potatoes, but I wasn't quite sure I heard right because it didn't sound like a very sensible place to put them! Anyway, I thought I would ask Mum about it later when she wasn't so busy. As it was I was happy sitting, playing jacks.

Just at that moment the jacks' bouncy ball leapt away from my grasp and I ran after it. Now running in kitchens is never sensible, particularly when the floor is wet and when there is the tendency for the odd spill here or there to be left until later. That is exactly how it was this particular day, as I found myself running across the terracotta tiles. It was only a little wet, but that was just enough to take the little legs from under me and send me flying backwards into the assembled line of pots waiting to be served. I landed bottom first in the vat of peas with green sludge missiles spitting out in all directions like some kind of monster, volcanic sneeze. I

A Rampage Of Chocolate

screamed. I guess it was shock, mixed with embarrassment; after all there were 20 faces looking at me as I sat there with my bottom immersed in an extremely large saucepan of peas. Alerted by my piercing screams, Mum ran as fast as she could, determined to minimise the burns that I was sure to have received. With that in mind, she grabbed me out of the saucepan and, without another thought, pulled down my white tights and pants and ran my naked bottom under the cold tap, in front of everybody.

With 20 faces staring at me and my naked bottom exposed for all to see, humiliation washed over me and I began to cry. Only at this point did someone think to check the water in the saucepan.
"It's only lukewarm! You can stop now. She'll be okay."
Mum was both relieved and irritated and deposited me in a little pile in the corner with a tea towel to dry myself. Still sobbing, I opened my hand as a bar of chocolate was thrust into it. So I sat in the corner sucking the chocolate off the biscuit as I patched up my pride and watched the surviving peas from the pan being scooped into the serving dishes and sent out to the unsuspecting guests.

Now I am not going to blame these kitchen traumas for any of my personality traits, but I do think that it is fair to say that there was always a theme. First there was disaster then there was chocolate. If it hurt then chocolate worked and if it was embarrassing chocolate worked. So through the 'ministry of chocolate' I managed to overcome all of the evils of the kitchen. School, on the other hand, was not so easy. There I was expected to endure countless humiliations and all without the comforting arm of chocolate…

Chapter 3

A School for the Genteel

When I was 9, Mum had gained enough money to put me into private education. I should have realised that public school was going to be a very different experience because even in the beginning there were signs that my 'unique qualities' were not going to be an exact match to their requirements.

The brochure stated proudly:
'St Ethelreda's is a peaceful environment uniquely suited to nurture the daughters of the genteel. With many distinguished former and present pupils, we have a heritage which will be an asset to any child. We nurture our girls in order to unlock the greatness within and to enable their unique qualities to shine.'

So there it was, an unlikely match by any stretch of the imagination. In fact I was never quite sure how I even got an interview. After all I don't think my 'heritage' exactly

A School for the Genteel

qualified me as a 'daughter of the genteel'. My mother was a hippy (albeit quite a moderate one by now), who had a penchant for brightly coloured clothes, pillar-box red lipsticks and lurid wallpapers. As for my father… well… he was… just a hippy. I don't believe that he had a purpose in life other than to… just… 'be'. There were no society weddings in my background and no peerages in the family line. We were middle class through and through - apart from some distant relative, who was apparently a pirate!

And then there were my 'unique qualities'. I suspect that whoever wrote the brochure had things like poetry and art in mind, maybe even sport or the ability to debate and lead. The trouble is that none of these 'nobler' talents were ones that I would necessarily associate with me. In fact, when considering myself, there was only one 'unique quality' that immediately sprang to mind and that was clumsiness: the ability to put the left foot where the right one should be both physically and verbally. This was certainly not a quality St Ethelreda's (plum in mouth and book balanced carefully on head) would want to unlock or cause to shine. As far as I was concerned, the longer that particular 'quality' remained hidden the better!

And so it was that I went for my interview, dressed in my smartest blue sailor's dress. Actually it wasn't mine. It was borrowed from our next-door neighbour because all of my clothes had been selected on the basis of the various colours of the rainbow, with particular emphasis on bright yellow and red. My usually tousled hair was tied into a bun to give the impression of a neat child with an orderly mind. The whole outfit was finished off with a pair of white tights and patent black leather shoes. My mother was so impressed by the instant transformation from tomboy to St Ethelreda's protégé, that she took a photo to remind herself of the child that she could have had, had she chosen my father with a little more discernment.

As for my mother, well that was the greatest transformation of all. Gone were the rainbow clothes, platform shoes and shocking red lipstick and in their place was a simple, black dress, a string of pearls (borrowed from Auntie Sylvia) and a beautiful pair of black, kitten-heeled shoes. Even her red lipstick was toned down for the occasion. With her hair pinned back into a neat bun, my mother looked the image of Audrey Hepburn. I was very proud to be her daughter that day and thought (for the first time ever) how beautiful my mother looked.

The head mistress, Miss Chartridge, was clearly taken in by our charade for she smiled sweetly at us as we entered her office. There in front of her desk were 2 wooden chairs, one large and one small. With a simple gesture she indicated that we must choose our preferred seat. Even with my limited intelligence I knew which one to take and hopped on to the only one with a cushion. With a gentle sweep of her arm my mother gracefully transferred me onto the smaller chair, smiled at the headmistress and said:
"Anne has aspirations of greatness!" They both roared with laughter and their connection was made. Thereafter the conversation flowed easily between them and my place at St Ethelreda's was assured.

As the 2 of them conversed I sat there looking around the room. On the wall I noticed some signed photographs of previous pupils, all of whom were now famous. I imagined Hilda Rayburn, now the Chancellor of the Exchequer, sitting outside the office awaiting punishment. This was followed by thoughts of Princess Gertrude having tea with the headmistress, maybe even sitting on this very chair. As my eyes glanced around the room they settled on the glass cabinets. There were 3, of which 2 were within easy sight and one was just off to my left. The first contained various silver trophies all reflecting Miss Chartridge's personal achievements. As I sat there reading the various plaques, I realised that she excelled at darts and the shot put. Whether the contents of the cabinets were genuine or fake did not matter, they had achieved their purpose. Faced with the veiled threat of a shot-putting headmistress, I resolved to be a model student. I wondered how many other applicants had come to a similar decision whilst seated in my position!

As I bored of the first cabinet, I let my eyes drift over to the second. I couldn't help but stare as I realised that it contained a collection of pipes. These ranged from the ordinary, brown, walnut pipe that I had so often seen my grandfather smoke, to the white, ornate, carved pipe which was clearly only for ceremonial occasions. Her array of pipes was fascinating. My mind was racing now with visions of Miss Chartridge smoking a pipe whilst throwing the shot put. The image I conjured up was neither reassuring nor conventional: Popeye, only in a skirt!

I could hear my mother and Miss Chartridge chatting and was aware of the occasional glance from them to me, but on the whole I couldn't be bothered to listen. I was, after all, on strict instructions not to speak unless I was spoken to and so my mind drifted to the third cabinet. The fact that its contents were just out of sight made it all the more intriguing. Now I knew that I wasn't allowed to move, and shuffling and wriggling were definitely not acceptable behaviours. A toilet break was out of the question and a

A Rampage Of Chocolate

request to leave my chair and walk over to the cabinet would almost certainly get me expelled before I had even been enrolled. I needed a tactic to turn around, so I started to exercise the mathematical side of my brain. I worked out what I considered to be the exact angle of lean required in order to get sight of the contents of the cabinet. Given the contents of the others, this third cabinet was sure to reveal another interesting facet to Miss Chartridge. After all, if I was to survive as an 'Ethelredian' then I needed to know what to get her for Christmas. So far I had worked out that tobacco and tickets to the athletics were probably the assured favourites.

Having estimated the tilt, I started to lean my body sideways. Of course I had forgotten that leaning generally leads to tipping - the tipping up of my chair. I felt the sudden lurch and snapped my legs and bottom down sharply to stabilise the situation. Even I knew that falling off a chair when you are supposed to be sitting still would not be appreciated and I did not fancy finding out exactly how strong Miss Chartridge's shot put arm was. So I was relieved to discover that all 4 chair legs were safely back on the ground and my mother and the headmistress had not even noticed, let alone paused for breath.

I allowed a couple of minutes to pass, just to be certain that they were still engrossed, then I shuffled my bottom back into the centre of the chair. As I did so I felt a gentle tug on the back of my leg. I tried to move again and found that I couldn't. Unsure as to the reason, I resigned myself to sit where I was until they had finished. I didn't have long to wait. With an,

"Oh goodness me, is that the time? We mustn't keep the Hamiltons waiting. They have come all the way from

A School for the Genteel

Shanghai; he's the Ambassador there you know." Miss Chartridge drew the conversation to a close. "Anyway, it has been lovely to meet you both," (well that was a joke because she never even spoke to me), "and I look forward to receiving Anne into St Ethelreda's in September."

With one final sweeping gesture of the hand Miss Chartridge indicated the door. We both got up, or at least my mother did. I unfortunately remained attached to the chair; or was it that the chair was attached to me? I looked up at my mother and over at Miss Chartridge and knew that it was extremely important for me to leave this room… and therefore this chair. So I decided to just go for it; believing that if I pulled hard enough, then whatever was holding me to this chair would release me; or so I thought. With a lunge and a (worryingly extended) ripping sound, I landed in a heap on the floor with the chair upended beside me. Dangling from the chair (or rather from a protruding nail on the chair) was a significant portion of my tights and a strip of blue skirt. I looked behind me to see my tattered skirt and a ladder in my tights that reached from my bottom to my ankle. I was devastated. I had ruined my tights and my neighbour's outfit in one motion, and so I did the only thing that a child facing the shot put and dart-throwing squad could possibly do… I howled!

Now I am not sure whether it was the noise of the howling that affected Miss Chartridge so much, or whether it was her concern for my damaged clothing (and potential lawsuits), but at this point I found the compassionate side of her, whilst also discovering the contents of the third cabinet. She rushed over to the cabinet and drew out a huge box of chocolates, which she promptly thrust under my nose. Instantly my attention was diverted from my situation and

A Rampage Of Chocolate

all of those reassuring associations of melting chocolate started to form in my mind. I knew this situation would be alright. I just had one further question to ask before I could take my chocolate and embrace the moment…

"Have you got the menu card?" I asked (very politely of course).

Chapter 4

Round Pegs and Square Holes

I would like to say that chocolate was offered at the school on a routine basis, but it would be a lie. The fact is that my first experience in the headmistress' office was the one and only time that chocolate was administered to me in the whole of my school career. Like all good promotional material, it was just not representative.

School was actually a much harder place than I had anticipated. The warm welcome that I had received from Miss Chartridge at my interview was never again to be repeated. Instead it had been replaced by an icy demeanour and a frosty glare. Her message was clear: 'Do not approach me! I shall tolerate your mother, but I will not tolerate you.'

Being rejected by the headmistress (and as a result by the teachers) was not an issue to me because acceptance comes from your peer group. Unfortunately, that acceptance was not forthcoming either. I had joined St Ethelreda's at a strange age (my mother had come into an unexpected inheritance and so was suddenly able to afford to send me to Public School), hence I was the only new girl in my class that year. Everyone had already formed their circle of friends. The trouble with a circle is that it has no gaps; no entry points; it is sealed at both ends. I was different to the other pupils in my background and in my approach to life. Mine was very straightforward, whilst theirs had airs, graces and frilly bits that I didn't understand. Consequently I didn't naturally fit in. I was an oddity, more of a mascot than part of the team.

I drifted from group to group, never seeming to settle. Friendships were fickle and not long-lasting. My home-clothes were different, my attitudes different and so I was different. These differences seemed to matter and prevented friendships from forming properly.

In my snatched moments of acceptance, it felt great to be part of a group, but most of the time I felt so isolated. Thankfully my humour got me through. I started to notice that my popularity with the whole class increased when I made people laugh. The fortunate thing was that I was so clumsy physically and so thoughtless mentally that I often achieved laughter without even meaning to. Unfortunately when you are the class clown, people start off laughing with you and end up laughing at you. Before you know it, you have crossed over the line from popularity into ridicule. So that was the path I trod at St Ethelreda's, from the day I joined at 9 to the day I left at 17. Everybody liked me, but nobody loved me. I was always set apart.

A Rampage Of Chocolate

I used to muse on my differences at home, generally whilst chewing on an ice-cream sandwich or a chocolate biscuit. I could never quite put my finger on what it was that stood between me and total integration. My background was no longer the barrier to my acceptance. I had to face the fact that the only barrier was me and who I was. It is a bitter pill to swallow when you come to that realisation. I found it easiest to take that pill in the form of chocolate - liquid or solid. Every day when I got home from school, I would run to the cupboards and scavenge for my salvation. When I found some, I would sit and let it melt in my mouth. However it was never quite enough to overcome that emptiness inside; that dead feeling. So I decided to up the dosage to 3 chocolate bars a day. Surely that would be enough to overcome the pain? It wasn't. It made me feel sick, but at least then I was distracted. It was a coping technique.

Chapter 5

Can't Cook. Shouldn't Cook

The more I embedded myself in the school, the more I found myself accepted for who I was. Or rather I found myself ridiculed for who I was. It seemed that no matter where I turned, everyone thought that they were better than me at something. When I was invited to join a group it was normally for one of two reasons: either out of pity, or for their own amusement - a bit like a cat playing with a mouse. I was always so hungry for acceptance that I generally jumped at all invitations, ever hopeful that my standing was about to change; a hope that was nearly always followed by disappointment.

My whole situation was made tolerable by 4 things: the fact that my mother loved me, totally, unconditionally, and to the detriment of all her male suitors; my Uncle Paul's frequent humorous visits (including the £5 notes that he generally slipped into my hand as he left); my academic gifting which meant that I was now accepted by my teachers; and the fact that I consumed vast quantities of chocolate in the safe-haven that was my bedroom.

Now I said that I was academically gifted and that was true. In comparison to my peer group I shone. However when you go to a school for the genteel, you find that there is actually little, or no emphasis on achieving academically. Obviously every school needs to have a few scholars in order to validate its existence, but the main purpose of St E's (although they never publicly stated this) was to transform the daughters of the genteel into ladies suitable for marrying the gentlemen of society. (In other words it was little short of a dating agency). I was 13 when I grasped this concept and realised, to my horror, the conversion process to which I was being subjected. In fact I got to wondering why on earth my mother put me into the school. My unorthodox beginnings could not be more at odds with the criteria for St E's. Surely I was destined to be part of the backbone of Britain - someone who would contribute to the workforce and use my brain, not someone who would be a dab hand at profiteroles and know how to sit without flashing their knickers! It struck me that in one of my mother's rainbow moments (as she used to refer to her hippy schemes), she had simply got it wrong. Or maybe it was just her sense of humour. Maybe I had annoyed her one day and this was her way of reeking revenge and teaching me a lesson. So I asked her...

"Mum? I was wondering something..." Mum turned around, she was whisking meringues and appeared to be wearing much of the mixture on her lime-green, yellow and pink jumper. She was currently seeing the pork-scratchings man and he had a penchant for lemon meringue pie, so we ate it twice a week and had done for the last 6 weeks. She put

A Rampage Of Chocolate

the mixing-bowl down, rubbed her hands on her electric-blue trousers and gave me her full attention. Uncle Paul (or Uncle P as I liked to call him) seized the opportunity to stick his finger into the mixture. Mum in one single motion and without turning around, slapped his hand and moved the bowl. Unfazed by his 18-stone rugby player frame and determination to annoy, she concentrated on me whilst Uncle P made faces behind her back. I giggled.

"Erm, you know how you've always told me that choices in life are very important?"
"Yeeees," she replied, tilting her head and wiping the egg white off her red lipstick.
"Well... I'm intrigued to know why you chose St E's for me? After all it doesn't strike me as the obvious choice. I mean, I know that they have great facilities and that you get on very well with Miss Chartridge, but why there?"
My mother was a great one for unpredictability and so I had imagined many different responses to this question, but nothing could possibly have prepared me for the actual answer that I was about to receive:
"Because they wear red."
"Because they wear red?" I repeated.
"Yes. Because they wear red." She said it slower this time, as if it would make the interpretation easier to absorb, followed by a 'doesn't-that-make-sense-to-you-because-it-makes-perfect-sense-to-me' sort of look.
"You are joking? You chose my school on the basis of the colour of their uniform?"
"Why yes. It's my favourite colour. You've always looked great in red, and I know how awful it is to have a school uniform that you can't stand. Mine was dark brown and I hated it. It put me off school for life... You know how I like to wear bright colours. Anyway, I wanted you to

Can't Cook. Shouldn't Cook

enjoy school so I picked a school uniform that you'd like. I thought about putting you into Clangdon Manor, after all they are renowned for their academic achievements, but they wear grey and I just couldn't face the thought of such a drab uniform. Can you imagine how dreadful it would be to turn up at their presentation days and look out upon a sea of grey? How awful! It would remind me of Blackpool on a stormy day. The only other option was St Bedlam's and they wear black. Well that would be like attending a funeral parlour. There was no way that I would send you somewhere as depressing as that! So St Ethelreda's was the obvious choice. It was easy really." With that she turned around and continued whisking. The matter was now closed.

I looked at Uncle P who simply shrugged his shoulders and made a 'don't-worry-she's-just-a-bit-bonkers' sign with his hand. Then, winking in my direction, he said with mock-seriousness,
"Makes perfect sense to me! Dark blue suits you too, so I think you should consider a career in the Navy." I muffled a snigger as Mum looked perplexed, unsure as to the source of our amusement. Uncle P simply grinned and then seized his chance to take a huge swipe of cake mixture from the bowl. He headed in my direction with a playful roar. I squealed and ran out of the kitchen for cover. I was no match for Uncle P in speed or size; he effortlessly swept me up from behind and proceeded to try to smear cake mixture across my face. He succeeded in part, although I managed to transfer much of it back onto his beard. We both laughed and declared the 'battle of the batter' a draw. Mum on the other hand was looking to start a new battle - a battle over who would clear up the mess in the lounge. Uncle P put me down and like 2 naughty children we surveyed the damage. Lots of little batter spots covered Mum's new aqua blue sofa

A Rampage Of Chocolate

and bright orange carpet. I cast my eyes to the ground for fear of laughter, but I needn't have worried; Uncle P was here. He was always my defence.
"Leave her alone Davina, the girl's got enough to worry about. I'll do it." Then he turned to me with a big grin and quipped, "Off you go Little Red Riding Hood." I screwed up my nose at the reference to my school uniform, but gratefully left the situation while I had the chance.

As I headed to my bedroom, I was at least smiling and tomorrow somehow looked a little brighter. My big bear of an uncle always knew how to transform my circumstance, if only for a moment. His very presence brought me safety and hope. I always knew how to rest when he was around.

I opened the door to my room and flopped onto my bed. I lay there smiling somewhat bemused but at least now enlightened as to the reason for my presence at St E's. I realised at this point that my lot was not going to change, so I decided to embrace the ethos of St E's and take solace in the fact that the uniform suited me. With that in mind, I took up 'Domestic Science' (cookery to you and me).

Mrs Percy was thrilled to see me in her class.
"Oh Anne, I am delighted to have you join us. You will be such a welcome addition to this class. Now girls you want to watch Anne she comes from good stock…" Everyone looked amazed at this comment, myself included, until she explained: "Anne's mother is the Banqueting Manageress at the *Radstock Hotel* and I have eaten there several times and each time it has been a delight to my tongue. That woman knows how to cook! I stand in awe of her skill. Her

Can't Cook. Shouldn't Cook

ratatouille is something to behold and as for her swan éclairs! Well, what can I say? Except that they looked so elegant floating on a white chocolate sea... Mmmm." For a moment there was silence as Mrs Percy relived the flavour of those meals. Emma giggled and it brought her back with a start.

"Ah yes, now where was I? Over the next 6 weeks we are going to focus our efforts on perfecting the art of desserts and cakes. It is very important when entertaining to have a masterpiece: something that stuns the eye, stimulates the taste buds and provides a talking point. This week we will start with profiteroles. You will learn both how to make them and how to present them. For the benefit of those of you who are just starting out, I shall teach you how to present a tree of profiteroles; a living sculpture. You will also each make 6 swans to swim around the base of your tree. I am sure you agree that this would be a stunning feature at any dinner party." With that Mrs Percy produced a circular, silver platter with a cake stand in the middle. On the stand was a cone of profiteroles neatly placed in perfect symmetry. Each one was an exact replica of the one before. On the platter at the base of the stand were 6 elegant swans. Their long, graceful necks protruded out of the back of some larger profiteroles which had been split open to ensure that they looked like wings. The swans swam on a sea of dark chocolate sauce and everything was delicately dusted with icing sugar. We all gasped. It was beautiful.

For the next 30 minutes Mrs Percy waffled on about methods, mixing and timing. With plenty of instructions and useful tips we were dispatched to our kitchen stations where our bowls, tools and ingredients awaited us. I was so excited at the prospect of producing something so beautiful and set to work, humming away to myself. With a flurry of flour, milk and butter I produced a seemingly perfect mixture. Mrs Percy looked over my shoulder and smiled. I beamed back and reached for the piping bag. Now the thing about a piping bag is that it is all about the consistency of pressure that you apply. The trouble is that consistency was not one of the things that I was renowned for, but what I lacked in consistency I make up for in enthusiasm.

I squeezed. Nothing! I squeezed again. Still nothing. I looked over at Veronique, 6 swan necks already arranged on the baking tray, her mixture smoothly flowing out from her piping bag. I looked over at Emma. She winked. She had 8 perfectly formed profiteroles. So I squeezed again. Well actually, I didn't so much squeeze as wring the bag. In fact I had to wring very hard indeed - so hard that the nozzle shot out with a loud 'pop', turning the heads of the girls closest to me. They all saw as the bag split down one side, mixture cascading over my hands. A giant pile of slop lay in the centre of my tray. Swan swamp. I don't know which was worse - the dishevelled pile of mixture, the stifled sniggers around me, or the deflation and disappointment that I felt inside.

I looked up. Mrs Percy was busy helping Penelope and hadn't noticed my disaster, so I helped myself to a new piping bag, scooped up as much mixture as possible and started again. This time I managed to get the mixture out in a relatively even flow. In fact now I had a different problem - stopping the flow. So my swan necks were not S-shaped but M-shaped and my profiteroles were not neat little balls but lumpy, misshapen snowmen. Due to these extra appendages and also the mixture that had been lost in the original explosion, I wasn't able to complete as many structures as required; only about half. Still, I popped them into the oven. Maybe they would improve with filling...

There is only so much that filling can salvage and if you press too hard with the cream in an attempt to smooth out the bumps, then the profiterole splits and the cream escapes. At least, that is what the next leg of my baking experience taught me. By now most people had created their structures and were taking them over to the main table for Mrs Percy to review. I looked at mine... I didn't have enough profiteroles to make a cone shaped tree; mine was more of a stump. My troupe of 6 elegant swans had been reduced to a paltry gathering of 3 and as for my chocolate sauce, it was so runny that it was positively tidal! My mutant swans actually looked okay, apart from the cracks where the cream had leaked through (I had managed to submerge the extra bends into the body, so only the correct neck shape was protruding). So with a more-than-generous dusting of icing sugar, I finished my creation and sheepishly placed it before Mrs Percy.

I looked into her face, hoping to see the earlier warmth and encouragement. It was there! She smiled at me and with a burst of enthusiasm said, before the whole class,
"Now, let's see what your mother has taught you." AND THEN SHE LOOKED DOWN. In that one moment everything slipped - first her eyebrows; then her smile; then her shoulders; and then the swan's head (revealing the extra mutant bend on its neck). My heart slipped also, down into the pit. My platter was not the peaceful scene that I had aspired to. Instead it looked more like a nuclear survival scene. Without a doubt I had created a talking point, though perhaps not in the 'stun the eye and stimulate the taste buds' way that Mrs Percy had anticipated.

A Rampage Of Chocolate

Alison was the first to giggle, then Pippa and then, like most unwanted, contagious infections, it spread until the whole class were unashamedly laughing at my production. Mrs Percy regained her composure first, after what seemed an age. 60 seconds of their laughter felt like an hour of humiliation to me.

"Now girls, that's not ladylike behaviour. Anne's obviously had an off day." She turned to me with a reassuring, but slightly false smile. "Don't worry. There is always next time. Now go and sit down with the others."

Unfortunately my next time was no better. My scones were like bullets. The time after that, my Victoria sponge came out flat with icing (that should have been neatly piped on the top) running over its sides, forming yet another chocolate puddle. Mrs Percy always rooted for me and encouraged me, but even she had a threshold. One day as I presented her with a sunken soufflé she exclaimed,

"Oh dear, Anne. You are just not like your mother!" With that one damning comment, her expectation of me was lowered and I was written off as just another no-hoper, not destined for success in society.

At home my cooking was a real success. Whatever I created worked and was always readily consumed by my mother and Mr Pork-Scratchings. It didn't always look quite like the pictures in the recipe books (mine often had a more rustic feel), but it always tasted great. It is funny how so often we can be successful at home, yet not in public. In fact I had successes 4 or 5 times a week at home, always to rapturous praise. I only had to endure my cookery class failures once a week. So why is it that the once a week failure seemed so much more important? Why is it that my 5 successes never

Can't Cook. Shouldn't Cook

felt as big as my 1 failure? I don't know why. They just did. The mathematics of life is cruel; I hadn't yet learnt how to overrule it.

Chapter 6

An Identity at Last

Failures sometimes bloom success. It was one such conversion that resulted in my friendship with Darcy:

We had first met in the cloakroom as we were hurrying to change into our school uniforms after PE. Her peg was close to mine, so our things quite often overlapped. Our first major encounter was when I was endeavouring to place my legs into my skirt at great speed. In my rush I lost my balance and fell over, knocking Darcy flying. She ended up in a ginger-haired pile on the floor, her lanky body spread-eagled like a giant 'X'. I remember being consumed with dread, fearing the backlash that would ensue. After all St E's was not exactly renowned for its grace. Most of the students would switch effortlessly from a friendly smile to disdain whenever you 'let the side down'. Judgement was rife and I was normally the recipient. I had seen Darcy laughing many times, but that did not reassure me that her reaction would be any different from anyone else at St E's.

"I'm so, so sorry!" I grovelled apologetically, reaching out a hand to pull her up.
"Don't worry," she laughed, wrinkling her freckled nose. "I have 3 brothers and 2 sisters and they do much worse to me. At least yours was an accident. Actually, it was quite funny watching you getting changed in such a rush; I mean, have you realised that your shirt is on inside out?"
"Erm, no I hadn't." My heart sank yet further and I started to consider my failings and to wallow in my own ineptitude, but I wasn't able to stay there for long because Darcy hadn't finished.
"Yeah! You're just like me… Look at my socks - they've got completely different patterns on. I was in a hurry this morning when I put them on. And last week, well that was really amazing - I managed to come to school in odd shoes. Anyway, I'm Darcy. It's Anne isn't it?"
"Yes. Although Mum calls me Annie."
"Annie it is." She beamed at me and we exchanged smiles, my failures forgotten; I had moved into forgiveness and acceptance.

So that was how it began; a friendship built on ineptitude, honesty, mercy and grace, with lots and lots of laughter. We had much in common it seemed, for our values were very similar and we both loved baking, playing and enjoying life. There were differences though, but they were about our character and outlook, so they never impacted on our friendship. Darcy didn't seem to care what anyone else thought of her and on that point we differed greatly. In fact she never even seemed to care whether she was alone or in a group, for she flowered wherever she was.

A Rampage Of Chocolate

As time went on, we became firm friends. In fact I became her best friend. So there it was… I had an identity at last. I was accepted. It was all there in the title, for anyone to see: 'BEST FRIEND'. Anne Rosetta Booth was at last valued.

Chapter 7

Darcy, a Friend Indeed

Darcy was lovely; one of the few, truly genuine people in my class and probably in the whole school. She expected nothing from you and gave everything to you. She never laughed at you, just with you and boy what a laugh she had - the most infectious giggle I've ever heard. Sometimes she would laugh for 5 minutes without stopping (she called it 'getting stuck'). She seemed to accept me for who I was, warts and all. It was great. With her I was free to be me. With her I could relax.

There was no fear in trying new things with Darcy. If it worked out she smiled and if it went pear-shaped then she laughed. For a season (2 years, until boyfriends made an appearance) we were best friends. I cherished the times at her house spent in her company. Her family, although more orthodox than mine, were just as chaotic. With many family members there were many voices to be heard, so they had a

Darcy, a Friend Indeed

system - if someone is talking just talk over them, but louder. Somehow this chaos made my life seem more normal.

Her father was originally a baker, although now he worked in the city and they lived in a huge mansion - an inheritance from his grandfather's estate. With sprawling gardens and a view out over the nearby hills it was breathtaking to behold. So we spent most of the time outside playing hide-and-seek with her brothers and sisters or simply lying on the grass musing about life. Lunch was often outside too - platters of cakes and bread and jam all piled up on their wooden table. When her mother called 'Lunch' we would all sprint to the table and dive to get a seat on one of the benches. It always felt that there wasn't quite enough seating for us all, but we managed to squeeze up tight and fit on anyway. Eating would then prove to be the next challenge. It was impossible to lift your arms without affecting your neighbour on either side, so we developed a Mexican wave type action, as the person on the end raised their arm to eat. After a while we learnt to cooperate with each other and even count down to the ripple effect:
"Ready? 1… 2… 3… go!"

It was on one such occasion when we were sitting outside at the table, tucking into platefuls of meat and salad that Darcy complained,
"Oh Mum, you forgot the bread and butter!" Mrs Pottington-Smythe disappeared back into the kitchen to retrieve the forgotten plate. After a couple of minutes, she returned looking somewhat perplexed.
"Well I know I did it… but I can't find it… In fact… I'm sure that I brought it out."

We all looked around expectantly hoping to find the missing

A Rampage Of Chocolate

bread and butter. Suddenly George let out a shriek and then, pointing at me, descended into peels of laughter.
"What?" I said, suddenly feeling very self-conscious. I shuffled in my seat; uncomfortable with all this attention because now even Carolyn (Darcy's 3 year old sister) was pointing and roaring with laughter too. As I shuffled, I heard a 'clanking' sound. With absolute dread and horror I looked down and, lifting one buttock cheek, revealed the very squashed plate of bread and butter. I peeled it off and placed it in front of me. Everyone was laughing now, even Mrs Pottington-Smythe. No-one cared at all, they just thought it hilarious. Even in my red-faced state, I started to chuckle and then to laugh. No-one minded. It didn't matter. Honest!

The next time I visited Darcy's house was equally as eventful:

After several days of torrential rain, finally the sun shone. It wasn't dry enough to lie on the grass, but the weather was definitely okay to go for a bike ride. When Darcy suggested this I didn't exactly jump at the suggestion, mainly because my last memory of riding a bike was one of being forced off by a car. Although I was technically okay, my confidence and my bike had taken a hammering that day. Still, 3 years had gone by and I felt sure that the time had now come to get back on a bike and overcome my fears. So after much reassurance that we would only be riding on narrow country roads, where we were unlikely to meet any traffic, I mounted her mother's butcher's bike, complete with pannier on the front. It was a pretty tall bike for me, but I could just about reach the floor, so off we went.

Darcy, a Friend Indeed

We set off cautiously and my nerves welled up. I found myself wobbling all over the road, but as I got into my stride everything started to settle down and I began to appreciate the beautiful views. As I looked out, it was as if all of creation was set before me: lush green pastures; animals grazing; birds singing; the sun shining and the breath of the wind gently caressing my face. I started to smile and to enjoy it. At last I had peace; at last I had overcome my fears.

"There's a hill coming up in a minute," shouted Darcy from ahead.
"Right O." My muscles were starting to ache but I felt there was enough power in them to overcome any hill. After all, if I had managed to get on a bike and come this far, I was certain I could get up any hill.
"Yeah, you may need to use your brakes a bit, 'cos it's quite steep and you'll end up going too fast otherwise."
Steep? Brakes? Too fast? All of a sudden the realisation hit me… This was not an uphill approaching, it was a downhill and if I didn't get it right I would crash. Again!

Panic welled up inside me as I went over the edge to start my descent. I started to go fast, to go faster still.
"Too fast," my brain told me. I hit the brakes. Hard. Too hard. The bike stopped dead, but I didn't. I flew (in what seemed at the time quite a graceful and slow motion arc) right over the handle bars, landing face and arms down in a manure-filled, muddy puddle. Yuk!

"Oh my goodness! Are you okay?" Darcy was leaning over me now, not laughing just concerned.
"Yeah, I think so," I replied extracting my face from the mud and spitting puddle as I spoke. I lifted my limbs from the

puddle with big squelching noises. Slowly and tentatively I stood up. Nothing broken. Nothing hurt. Nothing but my pride that is. I turned to face Darcy and as I did so she took one look at my face and doubled over with a snort, closely followed by noiseless shoulder shaking. I knew from experience, this would lead to at least 5 minutes of her 'getting stuck' in laughter. I stood waiting silently, mud dripping off my nose. For some reason she found that even funnier and so her knees buckled from under her and she rolled on the floor for an extra minute.

When Darcy finally recovered enough to speak, she resumed her role of encourager and friend:
"Oh, if only you could see yourself, you look hysterical." I frowned. "Oh don't be so serious! People pay good money to be covered in mud. You just got it for free." Then she stood a bit closer and caught a whiff of the 'mud' that I had fallen into. She laughed again. "I think you may have got a bit extra for your money! Still, if it's good for the fields then I'm sure it will do wonders for your face! Although I suggest you don't smile... or it might crack!" With that final quip she descended into peels of laughter again and I waited patiently for her to recover, all the time feeling the tightening of the mud on my cheeks as it dried.

She looked at my face again and appreciated my sense of humour failure. She apologised.
"Sorry, I shouldn't laugh." I heard a suppressed snigger and frowned at her (or at least I tried, but the mud no longer allowed free expression). "Come over here to this puddle and look at your reflection," she suggested, leading me over to the other side of the road, where I peered into the somewhat cleaner water. I had to admit, it was very funny - half of my hair was flattened due to the 'mud' (for that is what I prefer

Darcy, a Friend Indeed

to call it) and the other half was sticking up as a result of the wind. The mud had covered my forehead, nose and cheekbones just like a Roman soldier's visor, with an extra blob that looked like a goatee or a floating chin guard. I couldn't help but laugh and as I did so I felt the ripple effect as my entire mask cracked, giving it an even more grotesque appearance.

Just then 2 little boys peddled by (more proficiently than me) on their bikes. Their necks were craning to maximise the opportunity to stare at me. Maybe it was because I looked so different, so inhuman, that they did not try to conceal their stares, but whatever the reason, it annoyed me. I didn't mind Darcy laughing at me, but I was not going to provide a spectacle for these 2 little pip-squeaks. So I opened my mouth and bellowed the first thing that came to mind. "10p a look!" They screamed and peddled off as fast as their legs could carry them - presumably heading home to tell their parents about some awful swamp monster that had just roared at them. Darcy and I fell about laughing. In fact we laughed about it the whole walk home and then some more as we recounted the events to her mum.

Mrs Pottington-Smythe laughed with us too and then quickly found me some alternative clothes to wear. She sent me up to the shower (for everyone's sake; even the dog wouldn't come near me) and set to work preparing some hot drinks to complete my recovery process. When I was all clean and washed, I settled down in the sitting room in front of the fire; dipped my homemade biscuits into a mug of hot chocolate; snuggled under a blanket and relaxed. All was well again.

Chapter 8

Disaster Looms around Every Corner

I'm not actually sure who was the clumsiest, me or Darcy, but either way it didn't matter. What was irritating to the rest of the class was laughter fodder for us. My mother and the teachers did not always view it in the same way, but they did at least realise that our clumsiness was regretful not wilful. So long as we stuck together, it felt okay.

Darcy and I were often the last ones out of the classroom, not because we were slow but because we were talking. It seemed that no matter how long we were together, we always had more to say. Annoyingly the rule at St E's was that the last person out of the classroom at the end of the day needed to place all of the chairs on the desks. Sadly that was usually me! So on a typical afternoon, at the end of a day, I found myself lifting up the chairs. 30 chairs is a lot to lift, but at

Disaster Looms around Every Corner

least with 2 of you the load is halved. So after 10 minutes of chatting and lifting our task was complete. 30 chairs stood in proud formation upon their desks.

"Fantastic, let's go home!" Darcy shrilled and throwing her bag over her shoulder, she went towards the door.
"Just one sec!" I said picking up my bag and throwing it over my shoulder too. However, I, unlike Darcy, was not in a free space. I was at the back of the room and as I threw my bag over my shoulder it caught the chair beside me. The chair rocked forward catching the one in front. Darcy and I turned back at the sound and watched in wide-eyed terror as the classroom transformed before us into a life-sized Domino Rally. The chairs toppled forward one after another, like nine-pins, until the penultimate chair crashed down hitting the front desk so hard that it split the desk lid in half.

I stood and stared. I knew what this meant - a trip to the staff room to confess my deed. I could see it all now in my head: Miss Geyser's angry red face, her grizzled mouth pursed up like a cat's bottom… and then… THE BELLOW! I even knew the words that she would use so well, for I had heard them so often before:
'Irresponsible'; 'thoughtless'; 'clumsy girl'; 'stupid girl'; 'useless girl'; 'not fit for anything'. She had spoken those characteristics into my life on many an occasion, so I braced myself and set off towards the staffroom, mentally preparing myself for the battering. Just as I started to descend into dread, Darcy laughed and said,
"You should see your face! Is that really the best you can do? If that's your sorry face, then I reckon you ought to just act clever instead. Let's face it… you'd have to be an amazing engineer to achieve what you have just achieved!"

A Rampage Of Chocolate

I looked back and laughed. The fear left and I knocked on the staffroom door. I was in luck. Miss Geyser wasn't there, so Miss Twopot dealt with the matter… and even she had to admit that it was pretty unlucky and quite clearly an accident. Her parting words to me (which were to become a familiar part of my life) were:
"Don't touch anything else on the way out."

Actually what she really should have said was,
"Don't ever touch anything at all," or, "Anne, you are big and tall and strong and most things on earth aren't, so please be careful!" But actually no-one uttered those words of advice. In fact most people just waited until the inevitable happened and then exclaimed, "Oh Anne!" in an exasperated tone, before rolling their eyes and shaking their heads in dismay, or in the very worst case, making a very pointed and public exit in disgust.

Unfortunately, I didn't always find my disasters disgusting, but instead I found them downright hilarious and so, often failed to look contrite, which always made matters worse. Like the time when I was racing Darcy to get changed for PE so I kicked off my shoes in an attempt to beat her. Actually it wasn't just your average kick, more of a goal-scoring-can-can-extravaganza sort of kick. The result was that my right shoe flew off, arced through the air like some graceful swan, only to crash-land through the cloakroom window. On another occasion Darcy and I thought the laboratory door was stuck, so we heaved it together with our shoulders, only to find that it hadn't been stuck at all, but locked… and was now… very… very… open, complete with mortise lock lying on the floor!

Both of these escapades started out in total innocence,

Disaster Looms around Every Corner

ended up in disaster and laughter, closely followed by… a detention (clearly the school couldn't see the funny side). I am not really sure whether we received the detentions for the crimes we had committed, or for the fact that we giggled and sniggered our way through our apologies. Either way the sentence was passed.

Only on one occasion did I avoid sentencing, but I think that was just a sympathy vote. I was dripping with blood at the time, and it really did look quite dramatic…

You see, Darcy was the door monitor for our class, which basically meant that she would stand outside the classroom until the teacher appeared and then she would dutifully open the door for them. A good door monitor was worth their weight in gold because they would stand outside and, if they could see any teacher approaching, they would knock to warn you to return to your seats. That way you could mess around to your hearts content, but when the teacher entered the room it was just like entering a Buddhist temple - a sea of calm (with no signs of the world War III that had actually been taking place only 5 seconds before).

Darcy was the best door monitor we had and she took her role very seriously, which occasionally meant that she would walk off in the middle of a conversation to fulfil her duty. So it was this day… We were discussing 'the relevance of TV in today's society', or rather, I was trying to justify why I should be able to watch programs after 9pm (especially those containing Arnold Schwarzenegger or George Clooney). It was at this point that Darcy walked off. Only I hadn't yet won my point, so I decided to continue my debate through the glass in the classroom door. Darcy was having none of it. She held the door firmly closed, so I tapped on the glass, but

A Rampage Of Chocolate

she refused to acknowledge me. I tapped again, somewhat irritated; it achieved the same result. There was nothing for it other than to escalate my tapping to a knock. It was an obvious but fateful mistake to make.

I had managed to temper my annoyance with Darcy, but in doing so, I had clearly forgotten to temper my knock. I misjudged its strength and so watched in horror as my hand continued on through the pane of glass. I winced as I felt the shards puncture my hand and arm. However my pain was short-lived, for it was quickly replaced by fear… The fear of Mrs Denver-Smith. She was due at any moment and she was notorious for her uncontrolled outbursts of temper. I looked at Darcy, who was stood frozen to the spot, mouth open, eyes bulging. She seemed to be transfixed by my arm, which was still protruding through the window only inches from her nose. I removed it carefully. Very carefully!

"Quick, quick, the glass!" I appealed to Darcy, but she stood rooted to the spot. As a captain clings to a sinking ship, so she refused to abandon her damaged door. I looked at the debris and panicked, desperate for a way out of my predicament. I racked my brain for ideas, but all I came up with was the ostrich approach: "If we leave it, do you think anyone will notice?" No-one replied. They were all just staring at my bloodied arm. We could hear Mrs Denver-Smith's footsteps in the hallway. Time was running out. They sat in stunned silence, like rabbits caught in the headlights. Everyone, without exception, processing the full horror of the situation.

I got on my knees and started scrabbling for pieces of glass, like a woman possessed. I wanted to clear away the evidence. Just at that moment, Mrs Denver-Smith swept into the

Disaster Looms around Every Corner

classroom. She took one look at me with blood dripping down my arm, selflessly clearing up the glass (for that's how she interpreted my actions) and screeched,

"Aagh! Don't worry about that! Just get yourself off to Mrs Jacobs. She'll deal with your arm." The mixture of relief at her unexpectedly kind words and the adrenaline of the preceding moments caused me to burst into tears. This only helped my case, as Mrs Denver-Smith put her arm around my shoulder and led me out of the classroom, instructing Darcy, "Come now Darcy, you go with her and make sure she's alright. Please let me know if you need anything." Wow! Not the reaction I had expected.

Thankfully on this occasion Mrs Jacobs was equally sympathetic, I had severely tested her patience and compassion over the preceding weeks with my frequent visits, however the copious amount of blood trickling down my arm clearly pulled at her heart strings. With many soothing sentiments and maternal clucking noises she set about cleaning my arm. Her sympathy soon waned when she realised that all of my wounds (and there were quite a few) were superficial. Given the quantity of them, she felt it would be easier to swathe me in a single bandage rather than 15 sticking plasters. It looked very impressive when she had finished!

When I finally returned to the classroom, I felt like a hero. Everyone wanted to speak to me because no-one could believe the reaction (or lack of it) from Mrs Denver-Smith. This time my mistake didn't feel too bad. I didn't feel stupid because everyone was so very kind. At least, that is, until I got home… Mum was entertaining her new squeeze, the butcher (Frank I think his name was, but it is so hard to remember because he wasn't around for long). She took one

look at my arm and with every maternal instinct she could muster said,
"Oh no. Not again!" My heart sank as it joined her disappointment.

And so my school life continued - a combination of academic studies mixed in with a generous helping of disasters. With each cocktail of experiences I held my breath and awaited the reaction of my peers. When it was positive then I was fine, but when it was negative then I looked to Darcy, for she held the casting vote. And so I hung on in there with my self-esteem almost intact.

The Teenage Angst...

Chapter 9

All Change!

For two years I had a position in life; for 2 years I could relax. I was 'Darcy's best friend'.

I had long since been ignored by the 'in crowd'. They now pursued bigger things - designer outfits and boys. I had neither the looks, inclination, nor the money to compete, or even to keep up, so I stayed separate, safe in the innocence of my friendship with Darcy.

It was subtle really, the change within myself. I no longer relied on anything or anyone. Chocolate had naturally been relegated to an occasional treat and loneliness no longer featured in my life. I had even survived the wrench of Uncle P moving away to the seaside because now I got most of my laughs through Darcy. I still loved him and missed his visits (I used to enjoy watching him wind Mum up) but any void that he'd left had been seamlessly filled with my new friend.

All Change!

I was still aware (painfully so) of my clumsiness and social ineptitude, but as long as Darcy was with me I didn't feel rejected. My reliance, my identity, were found completely in her. Thankfully for me Darcy never abused her position, for she was a great encourager, but the risk was always there. Still, while we were both into making hideous mistakes (particularly at school) neither of us were in any danger of taking the higher ground.

At 14 I had never been to a party. One of the reasons for that was that I wasn't invited, but neither was Darcy. We didn't mind too much because it wasn't what we enjoyed doing. It was just that it would have been nice to be asked. At least then we wouldn't have felt unpopular. That all changed in June during the last couple of weeks of term.

"Do you fancy coming over to mine this weekend? Mum and Dad are out for most of it, but George is there so I can still have friends over, so long as we cook for ourselves… Let's skip the main course and just do lots of puddings and chocolate!" I smiled at the concept.
"Actually I can't. We're going away for the weekend - off to see Uncle P; he's not too well at the moment, so Mum wants to go down and look after him. It shouldn't be too bad though because he lives by the coast, so at least I can go down to the beach."
"No probs. Another time. Maybe I'll do the pudding thing anyway and bring some to school on Monday."

I was a bit disappointed that I couldn't go because I loved spending time with Darcy. It was always so relaxing at her house. Ours was a bit strange at the moment because Mum had taken up with the salami salesman and he had a penchant for bright colours too. Sometimes the combination of the 2 of them was like looking at a psychedelic rainbow, only brighter and smellier. Thankfully, he was not coming with us this weekend because Uncle P was apparently really very ill and their combination might have been enough to send him over the edge!

When we finally arrived at Uncle P's I was shocked. Last time I had seen him he had been full and ruddy faced; not fat, but definitely big and chunky. Now he was skinny and gaunt, pale and sallow; his eyes were sunken and hollow, not the bright treasures that normally greeted me. So much deterioration in just 6 months. I hadn't appreciated the seriousness of his condition and now, as reality dawned, I was fearful of his outcome. I felt a tight knot rising in my throat. I just wanted to hold him and not let go.
"Alright Little Red Riding Hood?" he asked and winked, but his voice didn't fit the familiar greeting. There was no longer any force behind it. Usually his booming voice could be heard in the crevice of any house, but today it wouldn't even travel the length of a room.

I didn't speak I just hugged him. Tight. Too tight. I felt bones. My stomach churned. I felt a panic rising inside of me; like when a mother searches for her lost child. Only in this case it wasn't a child I was looking for, it was my big bear of an uncle.
"Careful!" he protested as he tottered backwards, his frailty showing. "I do break you know." I saw the wry smile on his lips, an insight into the humour of the man that still existed under this ravaged exterior. I looked up and we exchanged loving glances. This was my uncle whom I loved. He felt very precious to me. In a short space of time our roles had

drastically reversed - I was the strong one now, not him. My mind struggled to process this new order. I found it disorientating. It was as if my whole world lay broken around me, only I didn't have the instructions to rebuild it.

I felt a weight in my chest as my heart ached. Its beat was dull and erratic, like the death throes of a fish out of water. I longed for peace. I longed for the familiar. I longed to turn back time. Memories of the times when he would toss me carelessly over his shoulder and carry me off around the garden rose to mind, but they didn't bring hope or peace, instead they just added to my loss. Where was my bear? The man before me would not be capable of that right now. He was no longer the Uncle P that I had known. I felt the constriction of my heart. It was excruciating.

I struggled to suppress my thoughts and emotions, but they came too thick and strong. I felt the dam begin to break; a tear trickled down my cheek. I blinked back the flood. I swallowed the fear. This time was precious; to be savoured. We followed Uncle P through to the lounge and sat down. It felt awkward. The silence was deafening. Uncle P understood. So he filled the air with witty observations about my mother's clothing, until he made us both smile.

Now that we had absorbed the shock of his appearance, we started to relax and to enjoy the time. We talked lots and reminisced over all the good times, making sure that we didn't miss any out. We laughed as we remembered his practical jokes and smiled as we remembered those family occasions of which he had been such an integral part. Then there was silence. Normally at this point a conversation would move on to the plans for the future, expectations and hopes, but that wasn't possible. At least not today, for that

A Rampage Of Chocolate

would have been irreverent. Uncle P was an intelligent man and it was obvious from his face that he knew how sick he was. Unfortunately, now I knew too.

The rest of the weekend passed more easily, with lots of good food, prepared by Mum, and a few (very slow) strolls along the promenade. I didn't go down to the beach, because I wanted to stay close to my Uncle P. I didn't want to waste a minute. For much of the afternoon all we did was snuggle up on the sofa and watch TV, but even that felt important. It felt like time well-spent: a moment shared; a moment to be stored.

Saying Goodbye was hard. I felt a wrenching in my heart as fear gripped me. I was desperate to see him again, so I said the only thing that I could:
"I'll be back very soon. Wait for me. I love you." And then we got in the car and left. Silence filled the air.

When I got to school on Monday, all I wanted to do was to share my emotions with Darcy. I wanted her to hear and understand the pain I was in. My insides felt flat. I felt deflated and most of all, I felt very alone. I knew that she would stick her arms around me and give me a huge hug and that warmth would fill my soul. Ordinarily it would be a mother's job to comfort her child, but my mother needed her own comforting at the moment and anyway her hugs were currently reserved for Pepperoni Pete - a close friend of the salami salesman and thankfully slightly better smelling.

So I found myself sitting on a sofa in the school common room, listening to all the commotion around me. I could

All Change!

hear 2 girls chatting in the corner about their exploits on Saturday night and others were in a heated debate over their history homework. To me it was all just background noise. None of it mattered. None of it was important. All that counted was that Uncle P would survive.

Suddenly the door burst open and Darcy rushed in. Her head shot from left to right, eyes darting around the room in a desperate search for me. I felt her energy. My heart began to lift. I knew that she would help me out of this hole of misery. Relief started to wash over me. I started getting ready to speak…

"You are never going to believe what happened to me this weekend!" she blurted, without even stopping to notice my disposition. She was obviously hideously excited, so I thought that I would be gracious and listen to her news first. "You know how George was going to be looking after me this weekend? Well he did. Sort of… Well anyway, at the last minute on Saturday he got invited to Wolfie's party."

('Wolfie' was Wolfgang Amadeus Smith, a boy from St Hubert's whose parents adored Mozart and had great pretentions of grandeur. His mother, Mary, and dad, John, had always been unhappy with their straightforward names and so felt that they wanted to set their son apart by giving him a name more befitting of his status and ability. Despite their affectations, the truth was that all of their money was inherited and Wolfie was actually exceedingly stupid. He was a bit of a class clown and completely tone deaf, thus unable to play any musical instrument - not even the triangle!).

Darcy continued:

"George realised that the only way he was going to get to go was if I went too. Well you know how I feel about parties, let alone dressing up, so when he suggested it, I just screwed my face up, and marched off. So he tried again. Eventually we came to a deal - I would go to his party with him on 2 conditions: the first, that we left by 11.30 (he wasn't best pleased at that one I can tell you); and the second, that he took me out on his quad bike the next day. I knew that he only wanted to go because Samantha Egret was going to be there, so I knew that he would agree to my terms and he did! Actually, thinking about it, I should have asked for more… but I didn't…" At this point Darcy paused for breath, wrinkled and twitched her lips and then gushed some more. "So when we got there it turned out that Samantha was ill, so George was gutted!" She laughed, reliving the moment, "but he got hooked in with his usual crowd leaving me standing at the door.

Not knowing what to do, ('cos I certainly didn't fancy dancing) I made my way to the drinks table and poured myself a lemonade. There were straws there too, (which I think were for the communal punch bowl), so I took one and started amusing myself by blowing bubbles. Just at that moment Felix Green came over. Well you know how I have always admired him, particularly his brown curly hair…" Darcy paused for a moment, her eyes misted over as she was clearly lost in wistful thought. She jolted as she came back to reality, "So I was really shocked to find him in front of me; in fact so shocked that I coughed… into my straw… and ended up blowing lemonade all over him. He thought it was hysterically funny because he's not at all stuck up like I thought. So we got talking… and he likes all the things that I do. So…" she made sure that she had my total attention, "he is taking me out this weekend on a proper

All Change!

date! In fact, he is also meeting me after school today and we were on the phone all last night… So how about that? I Darcy Pottington-Smythe have a boyfriend!" She grinned. The biggest grin I have ever seen. "So what do you think about that?"

What a question to ask me. What did I think about that? Was I pleased for her? Actually, no I wasn't. Why did she need a boyfriend, she had me? Where would I stand now? Didn't she know that I needed her right now? We always spent the weekends together (nearly all of them) and already that was changing. I didn't want her to change. I needed my world to stay the same right now. I needed stability. I needed… I needed… I needed… The school bell went. It was time to go to the first lesson, so we got up and left. I never answered her question. She never noticed. I never got to tell her about Uncle P or how I felt. She never saw my pain.

From that day on Darcy and I drifted apart. She was totally focused on Felix and failed to see anything else around her. Every weekend was now spent with him, so our friendship was now restricted to school times and even that was diluted because she had started to hang out with Lorna, who was dating Felix's best friend. They were often together at the weekends as part of a cosy foursome, so it was only natural that they should spend time together at school too.

Our friendship, it seemed, had been for a season, not for a lifetime. It had been easily formed and was easily abandoned.

So where did that leave me? Nowhere really. Friend to all and friend of none. Likeable but different. With no identity.

A Rampage Of Chocolate

I drifted from one group of friends to another, never quite fitting in. Occasionally I got invited to a party, but even then I didn't have the inclination to go. After all what was all the fuss about?

Chapter 10

A New Identity

For a long time I watched as week in and week out my friends did the 'dating thing'. They always seemed so excited, but I still didn't have the confidence to join them. The thought of further rejection was too huge and actually I didn't feel ready to embark on a relationship. I had seen my Mum flit from one man to another - one day floating on air, singing their praises and the next day lying in a crumpled heap on the bed, rueing the day she had met them. The trouble with not joining my friends on 'the circuit' was that I was being left behind. I knew that something had to change. I had to find my niche. I needed an identity. I wanted my loneliness to end. Uncle P was fading fast. My world was crumbling around me and if I wasn't careful I would crumble with it.

I looked around at all my peers and I could find value in all of them: Darcy was so sweet and friendly; Emma had great

A New Identity

style and finesse; Tessa was a totally awesome cook and Tanya was quite the best tennis player I had ever seen. The list was endless. No matter who I looked at, they had something to offer; something that set them apart; something that made them acceptable and worthy. Of course there was Humpy (real name Humpfrieda Dawson). When I got to her, I did have to think very hard. Her portly body and lack of personality didn't immediately spring forth revelation of the giant within, but more squeaked of a mouse trapped in an oversized body. Then I remembered her stunning poetry. The whole class was reduced to tears when she read out 'an ode to my dead cat Billy'. She could also hit a rounders ball so hard that it would leave the playing pitch. One day the ball had actually reached the school building, smashing Miss Chartridge's window in the process! Even she scored a rounder that day (although none of us envied her trip to see Popeye afterwards)!

I considered myself… I excelled in my studies but for some reason that counted for nothing. No-one seemed interested in academic excellence. In fact, it actually worked against me. When you are too clever, you are labelled 'swot' or 'nerd'; so I had to work hard to keep my intelligence under wraps so that no one would notice. It was strange really because if I had the equivalent talent in sport then I would have been hailed as a hero and lauded by the class. As it was I couldn't run or indeed connect a bat to a ball. Those who excelled at art, cookery or sewing were again honoured for their talents and gained in popularity as a result. So why didn't physics or chemistry count? After all, they were just as useful, if not quite so glamorous!

I tried a variety of different avenues. My musical days were short-lived - I took up the violin for a term, but the

A Rampage Of Chocolate

screeching noise caused such a rumpus with my neighbours at home, that my mother begged St E's to let me drop out early. I tried to join the choir, (at least half of the class were in it, so I thought it would be a good place to be), but Mrs Harris soon had me out at the front trying to get me to sing a note in tune. In the end she announced,

"Well Anne, I think it's clear that your singing capability is somewhat limited! Obviously, we would *love* to have you as part of this choir - you have such a pretty face and such a lovely smile. My one request is that you always stand at the back and you don't ever sing in our public performances... Just mouth the words... No one will ever know."

Mum paid for me to have private tennis lessons. She had been an ace tennis player in her early twenties and had even qualified for Wimbledon. Unfortunately, she had never had the money to pursue it fully, so I think that all of her hopes and unfulfilled dreams were hinged on me. She secretly hoped that I had some latent talent that would emerge in these lessons and that she would be able to produce a budding tennis star as a result. Sadly, as per all of my other sporting attempts, it ended in disaster. Not only did I find myself incapable of hitting the ball, I also seemed to find it impossible to hold onto the racket. Whenever I served, both ball and racket would fly through the air... into... the net! I was a danger to both myself and my opponents. After a term, and a very heated discussion between my mother, the tennis coach and a rather-overworked Mrs Jacobs, we all gave up!

In fact, I gave up altogether. I finally realised that I was never going to actually fit in with any of the groups at St E's; so I decided to forge a life outside. With that in mind I got myself a job. I became a waitress. Now I had an identity.

A New Identity

Now I was a groundbreaker. No-one else in my class had a job. I was the first. Now I had a niche and even better… I had money!

There were many perks to being a waitress. I got to meet lots of new people, some of whom made me feel very special. The little old ladies who came in for their lunches referred to me as 'sweet', 'so lovely', 'pretty', 'how polite'. From time to time, some of the men would make me blush with their comments and occasionally they would ask me out, but they were all far too old for me. Still it was nice to feel wanted.

Of course, I wasn't the best waitress in the world because I was far too clumsy. Thankfully very few people minded because of my humour and my smile. The tea room, where I served, was a most forgiving place and I soon found ways around my skills, (or rather the lack of them). I no longer brought teacups out on the saucers (customers used to stare at me in horror as I poured the slops from the saucer back into their cups), but instead allowed the cups to sit in a flood on a tray before placing them carefully on a dry saucer. I was careful to only ever carry 2 plates at a time (my colleague Sarah could carry 4, at various positions along the length of her arm. I tried it once with crashing effect). If I was pouring sauces, such as gravy, I would do so in the kitchen where it was safer. It saved on the dry cleaning bills!

I was also quite nosy and would occasionally get so engrossed in people's conversations that I would forget what I was doing. Once I stood stationary halfway through folding a serviette. Sarah, mildly amused, came over to me and coughed in my ear to bring me back to awareness. It was truly stunning though to hear what people were prepared to discuss in a public arena. It appeared that there was a different etiquette:

whilst you would definitely not discuss your own piles at the table, it was perfectly acceptable to discuss those of your elderly friends; the more graphic the better! Occasionally the receptionists from the doctor's practice came in and they seemed to believe that confidentiality was preserved so long as they only discussed things directly with one another (even though half the tearoom could also hear). Gradually, over the year I got better at my job, which was clearly reflected in my tips. I really enjoyed the work and it was an interesting diversion from school life. I didn't conform, but then *The Fractured Teapot* didn't require conformity. There was plenty of room for my brokenness.

Chapter 11

Pretty in Pink

By the time I was 17 there was a real commotion in the town because a new venue was opening up. Some people were in favour and others were staunchly opposed. The notorious playboy, Jonathon Green, had opened up his mansion for 'private parties and functions'. There was a lot of speculation as to the nature of those parties and I was intrigued. For the first time in my life I wanted to go to a party. The only trouble was that I wasn't invited. Then the answer came, in an advert in the local paper:

HIGHPOINTS
Part time waitresses required for local establishment.
Hours varied. Uniform provided. Good rate of pay.
To apply, please contact Paul Dunsford on…

I held the advert in my hand a long time before I plucked up the courage to pick up the phone. I could feel my heart

Pretty in Pink

thumping inside. I heard the ringing tone. I held my breath. What would I say? Was I too young? Someone picked it up.

"*Highpoints Manor.* Can I help you?" a lady with a very sweet voice trilled.

"Yes, I'd like to speak to Paul Dunsford please. I'm ringing about the waitress position." By some miracle I had recovered my poise. I was calm, clear and confident. I was smiling to myself.

"Certainly, I'll put you through." So far, so good.

"Paul speaking." His deep, harsh voice triggered something in my heart.

"Um… I… Erm. I am rrrringing about the wwaitress position." All of a sudden I had lost the ability to speak and had no confidence in my skills as a waitress. All manner of questions flew through my head. Would I need to go and show him how I carried things? What if he required me to do silver service or even worse to carry 4 plates at a time? Panic filled my thoughts.

"How old are you?"

"17."

"Okay, so I won't put you in the bar area then. Main areas only. Are you available this Saturday at 6 o'clock?"

"Erm. Yes."

"What is your name?"

"Anne Rosetta Booth."

"Anne Booth," he said in very rough tones. (I was sad that he dropped my middle name, Rosetta was my favourite part).

"Fine. Come to the kitchen entrance; ensure that your hair is tied back and that you wear black shoes and tights. The rate is £8 per hour. okay?"

"Ummmmm. Yes."

The phone went dead. So that was it. I was hired. There were no questions. There was no interview. They were

A Rampage Of Chocolate

indiscriminately hiring. It was easy. The deal had been done. At 6 o'clock this Saturday, I would get to see inside the parties of the rich and famous. I was smiling, but I was scared.

On Saturday I went to the tearooms as usual. I couldn't wait until 4 o'clock closing. I shot home and jumped in the shower, determined to look nice for my new job. I knew that I was getting a uniform, so I put on a black skirt, red roll-neck top and black shoes with only a small heel. After all waitressing could be hard work. I applied my make-up and a squirt of perfume (Mum's, but she wouldn't mind). Then I was ready. Mum on the other hand was not. She was chatting to her latest squeeze on the phone - Dodgy Dave (real name Dave Henderson), a man of dubious origins and of 'varied career'.

I stood in front of her tapping my watch, feeling like the parent not the child.
"Okay. Look I'm going to have to go... Annie is making all sorts of faces at me because she's got some sort of job to go to... You know... Up at *Highpoints*..." I could hear Dave saying something on the other end of the line. Mum's face contorted and she scowled at me. "My Annie is not like that, as well you know! I'll thank you to keep remarks like that to yourself!" She slammed the phone down and stood up. She looked me up and down, studied my face intently and then, seemingly reassured, she smiled at me. "Come on, let's go. Are you sure you want to work at this place? It's not like your tearooms you know?"
"I know Mum. And yes, I think I do want to go. If I don't like it then I won't go again."
"Fair enough." She smiled, and with a gentle arm around my

Pretty in Pink

shoulder she led me to the car. Well actually, she wobbled me to the car - she had some new platform wedges on and she hadn't quite worked out how to walk in them.

I got in the car and strapped myself in. My stomach churned. I looked out of the window. It was strange really… almost as if I was saying 'goodbye' - goodbye to my old self. It felt as if nothing would ever be the same again. This was it. This was my coming out. Today was the day that I was going to join the rest of the world; the day that I was going to embrace the party circuit. I was going to gain knowledge and understanding. Maybe I would even work out who I was. So much rested on this one evening. I took a deep breath and sank back in the seat.

Mum started the car and put her foot on the accelerator. We shot off at great speed down the drive.
"Bloody wedges! Can't possibly drive in these!" She screeched to a halt, unstrapped them and I watched as the pair of orange wedges sailed past my nose landing on the back seat. "Right. Try again!" With that we left and drove out to the edge of town, arriving at the awesome black gates of *Highpoints*.

The security guard came out… dressed in pink. An unusual choice of attire for a security guard, but I felt it unwise to comment since he was wider than I was tall and was clearly designed to flatten anything in his path. I noticed the initials 'HP' on his lapels so I figured it wasn't his choice anyway. I would have loved to have been at the meeting where the guard was first presented with his uniform. I sat and imagined his face. Whoever it had been, (maybe Jonathon Green himself?) they must have been very brave.

My concentration was broken as the guard came to my window.

"Name?"

"Anne Rosetta Booth. I'm a waitress tonight. I'm due at the kitchen entrance at 6pm."

He scowled at me then referred to his list.

"Okay. Go ahead. Down the drive, left; green door." A man of few words. With that he pressed a button and the gates parted, revealing the tree lined driveway.

We drove ahead very slowly and as we did I surveyed the glorious gardens. They were so beautifully kept that they looked almost manicured in their appearance. Nothing wild or free, everything predetermined and positioned. It was a shame. There seemed no freedom for nature to express its full glory. It was so contrived that I wondered if wildlife was allowed to live here too, or whether every bird would have to check in at the security gate!

As I was musing on that thought, we arrived at the house. It was an old red-bricked mansion with the statutory ivy climbing up the walls. Nothing exceptional. I was almost disappointed. We drove around to the green, kitchen door and I got out.

There was a marquee behind the house and people were busily running between the two. Awnings, flowers and decorations were going up. A man with a water spray was putting the finishing touches on an ice sculpture - a majestic eagle - and a lady was scurrying around positioning pink bows on the back of every chair.

I turned my back on all the activity and entered the green door, as I had been instructed. I looked around, searching for

Pretty in Pink

someone to guide me, when my eyes found an unexpected sight… There standing by the wall were Kate and Joanna, from school. I wasn't sure how I felt. Part of me was pleased to see 2 familiar faces, then the rest of me wanted them to leave. This was supposed to be my experience. It was not for sharing. I put aside my jumble of thoughts and approached them.

"Hi guys! I didn't know you were working here too?"
"Yeah," Kate spoke first, (she was always the spokesperson. Joanna was too quiet). "We saw the ad in the paper and thought it would be good fun. After all, tonight is the launch party for *The Tentacle Brother's* new album. All of *Dynamo Box* and *Spandex Bully* are expected to attend. The whole of London is talking about it. Working here, we'll be paid to party! Shame about the uniforms though… Pink is so not my colour."
For the first time, I stopped to survey the uniform that they had been given (and that I would be wearing too). I winced. The short pink skirt was not too bad, nor even the little back apron that went around it. The problem was the pink T-shirt. Although plain in nature, it had *Highpoints* written across the chest in big black letters. Clearly someone's idea of a joke (just not mine). At that moment, a lady walked past wearing a black leotard, fish net tights, a pink jacket and pink top hat.
"She's one of the hostesses," whispered Kate. I looked at our uniform and I was grateful in comparison. It could have been so much worse. My thought train was broken…

"Right everybody gather round." An extremely short (4ft), plump man, with orange perma-tanned skin, stood on a chair in the middle of the room, wearing a pink T-shirt and

A Rampage Of Chocolate

black trousers. He reminded me of an Oompa Loompa; probably from the marshmallow section. I started to smile. "I realise that most of you are new here, so for those of you who have not already met me, I am Paul Dunsford. I am responsible for making sure that tonight goes smoothly. In a minute I shall allocate you all a uniform and an area where you will be stationed. Your role tonight is to ensure that all of the guests are treated like kings. You're to bring the food and the drink to them. If they have to hunt for you, then you have failed.

Michelle is in charge of the drinks section. Those of you reporting to her will be going around with bottles of champagne, topping up glasses. I want you to be generous and make sure that every guest has a full glass. The more they drink the happier they will be."

My excitement was no longer excitement. It had turned to angst. There was something unhealthy about this place and I was already becoming aware that I didn't fit.

"Pierre is in charge of food. Those of you responsible for food will be carrying around trays of canapés. Ensure that you keep these coming and keep an eye on the buffet table to make sure that it's fully stocked. The first sign of a food fight let me know (*Dynamo Box* are notorious for them) and we will bring out protection for the other guests. The party begins at 8pm. Make sure you are all set up and ready."

With that Paul stopped talking, climbed down off his chair and started handing out uniforms .
"Name?" he demanded as each of us stepped forward. He checked his list and then allocated us to drinks or food

Pretty in Pink

distribution by barking one word - either "Michelle!" or "Pierre!"

So that was it. I found myself dressed in a ghastly pink uniform, standing with Kate and Joanna, assigned to Pierre. Thankfully Pierre was slightly more human than Paul, even if he was dressed in a pink chef's uniform!

By the time 8 o'clock came I was really looking forward to seeing the guests. This promised to be a star-studded event. What an amazing first party to attend. I even forgot my dissatisfaction with my uniform. Instead I stood with a beaming smile, holding a tray of canapés. My adventure into a new life was just about to begin!

Chapter 12

High Points and Low Points

I watched as the first guests entered in. Each one of them made an entrance. Subtlety was clearly not the flavour of the day. The women were spectacular, if a little under-dressed, with an array of sequined outfits most of which appeared to be missing their skirts! The men, on the other hand, seemed to wear bright coloured shirts and garish shoes, with trousers that were so shredded that they looked like they'd been through a meat slicer. I wondered how it was possible for some of these garments to remain on, for it appeared that there was so little substance to them. I was so mesmerised that I forgot my role and so Kate and Joanna were the first off the blocks. They swanked straight up to the new guests with their trays, clearly revelling in the opportunity to mix with the rich and famous.

I started to offer my canapés around; all the time observing the guests. The men did and the women didn't (eat that

High Points and Low Points

is), but they all wolfed down the champagne. I started to wonder how long the champagne would last at this rate. Surely it would run out before midnight and if that was the case then I didn't want to be around to face this crowd. So I considered my emergency exit strategies. It is always good to plan ahead!

Just then my concentration was broken… Justin Edwards, the lead singer of *The Tentacle Brothers* walked in. He was a sight to behold. He had a curly mop of blonde hair trailing down his back, piercing blue eyes highlighted with mascara, and a silver and blue spandex suit which clung (so tightly that I now understood how he hit such high notes) to his sparrow-like thighs. There was no mistaking his entry or his presence.

"Do you think when he looks in the mirror, he thinks that he looks good or ridiculous?" I whispered to Kate. A somewhat deeper-than-expected voice replied,

"That is none of your business! As far as you are concerned, Justin is a God and he is paying your wages for tonight, so get your butt over there and serve him." I spun around and saw that it was no longer Kate who stood beside me, but Paul Dunsford. I felt my cheeks flush hot and red, putting the brightness of my T-shirt to shame, and scurried off to distribute the canapés.

I got to the entrance just as *Spandex Bully* were arriving. Unlike the *Tentacle Brothers* they had been on the scene for years and no longer had anything to prove. They were dressed in nice, well-cut clothes; understated but none-the-less impressive. Somehow I was not so afraid of approaching them. Or at least not too afraid until I spoke. Sometimes it just pays to think before you open your mouth and let the words tumble out.

"Toast?" I offered as I held out my tray of canapés. Sean Blaster, the saxophonist, spun around to see who had made such a ridiculous offer. I felt my cheeks burning (they hadn't yet recovered from my faux pas with Paul). I prayed that something would happen to remove me from this situation, 'Beam me up Scottie', was all I could think. However I needn't have worried because as his soft brown eyes met mine, he grinned from ear to ear.

"Toast eh?" he teased. "Don't mind if I do! Got any jam?" With that he reached out one arm and touched me gently on the shoulder. "You're very sweet you know. What's your name?"

"Anne Rosetta Booth." I was overcome. No male had ever paid any attention to me and now here I was with Sean Blaster calling me 'sweet'. I could feel my heart pounding. It was all I could do to stand upright.

"Pleased to meet you Annie," he whispered, drawing a little closer. As he did so the smell of his fruity chewing gum wafted under my nose. It smelt great. "I don't suppose you could do me a favour could you? I really *would* fancy some toast, now that you've mentioned it, with loads of butter and some jam. I don't really go in for all this fancy stuff."

"Sure, I'll see what I can do," I replied in a purposefully husky voice. It wouldn't have mattered what he'd asked for in that moment, for I was smitten and would have done my best to accommodate any request. It was pathetic really. All he had done was to touch my arm and say nice things to me, but that was enough. That was all it took.

"Thanks Annie," and with that he kissed me gently on the cheek. That was the signature I had required to hand over my heart - one fruity-smelling kiss! I shot off to the kitchen to find some toast.

Kate was hanging about in the kitchen waiting for her tray

to be filled. I spoke to Pierre about Sean's request and then rushed over to her.

"Kate, Kate, you're just not going to believe it… Sean Blaster just kissed me on the cheek and he said I was really sweet!"

"Oh!" she replied nonchalantly.

"'Oh!' Is that it? 'Oh!' It's only the most important moment of my life and all you can say is "Oh!"." She grimaced and shrugged her shoulders.

"Toast is ready!" Pierre called, so I picked up my tray, complete with toast and headed off to find Sean, my stomach churning with expectation.

As I entered the marquee I saw him… kissing Joanna on the cheek… one hand on her shoulder. My heart sank. So I wasn't special after all. This was how he treated everyone. He was quite simply charming and I had been charmed. I felt stupid and silly, and worse still I had to face him again to give him his toast! You would have thought that I would have been used to disappointments by now. It was just that this was a new area for me. The only boys that I had ever really interacted with were Darcy's brothers, and they were just… well… boys. My heart had never even so much as skipped a beat with them - not even with George. After all it is hard to fancy someone when you have seen them picking their nose and heard them trumping at the dinner table. No. This was different… My first foray into romance. My first taste of attraction. My first heartbreak! It had only taken 10 minutes. From now on I resolved to guard my heart.

The rest of the evening passed with very little upset. I kept hold of my tray, didn't drop anything and smiled sweetly

A Rampage Of Chocolate

at everyone. I even took all the outrageous comments, behaviour and clothing in my stride. The truth was that this kind of event was not really for me. At one point a youngish girl (in a very skimpy gold dress) came to me to ask for a canapé.
"What exactly's on them?" she asked in a broad cockney accent. The truth was that I didn't know. Pierre had never said. So I peered at the tray and named them (with all the confidence I could muster).
"These ones are smoked salmon," (that at least was obvious), "and these ones are redcurrant jelly and those are blackcurrant jelly."
"Oh!" she trilled, helping herself to a redcurrant canapé. I watched as her expression transformed into a grimace. She let out a shriek of disgust, gagged and fumbled for a serviette to spit into; quickly following through with a large swig of champagne. I made a hasty exit, latching onto the nearest unattended guest. I didn't want to be around when she regained her composure. It was clear that I had made a mistake.

"Pierre? What exactly is on these canapés?" I asked when I next went into the kitchen.
"Smoked salmon, Beluga caviar and Red Caviar."
"Ah! Not quite as I thought." I decided to give the lady in gold a wide berth after that!

By the time midnight loomed I wanted to leave. My feet were aching and I was fed up with the drunkenness surrounding me. Just then Steve Sweet, lead singer of *Dynamo Box*, tapped me on the shoulder. I turned around and was dazzled by his white teeth.
"Could you pass me the plate of profiteroles off the table love?"

High Points and Low Points

"Sure," I replied without thinking; quickly returning from the main buffet display with a plate brimming with profiteroles which were covered in gooey chocolate and oozing with cream. I expected Steve to take one, but instead he took the plate and shouted to the other end of the marquee:

"Oi! Justin! Great party! Am loving the food!" and with that he hurled the cream-loaded missiles across the room. The first was a headshot aimed at Justin, who pulled his head out of the way at the critical moment, leaving Bianca, Justin's glamorous girlfriend, to receive the gooey profiterole squarely in her face. It exploded on impact, splattering all those around her. She wiped the cream from her eyes and scowled at both Justin and Steve. However, her annoyance soon transformed into a raucous laugh as Steve's second shot hit its intended target, leaving a trail of cream and chocolate down Justin's spandex suit. Justin, overcome with humiliation and vanity, and clearly irritated by Bianca's disloyalty pushed her into the giant cheesecake on the buffet table. He walked away, leaving her kicking her legs in the air with her bottom sliding all over the table, trying to regain an upright position. Then he spied the tray of cream-filled meringues. Within seconds they were flying with intent across the room in retaliation. Soon the whole room had descended into chaos - a mass explosion of food. Some guests had escaped to the gardens or to the main building, but most had stayed. Cameras were snapping and flashing everywhere. I knew that this was going to be all over the magazines next week. The worst part was that I felt responsible. I had provided the weapons, despite Paul's earlier warnings. Duped yet again!

Out of nowhere, Paul (now literally covered in marshmallow, looking even more Oompa Loompaish than ever) appeared. He started handing out umbrellas to the guests and then

A Rampage Of Chocolate

to us. Clearly he had faced this situation before! I on the other hand set about distancing myself from the main areas of carnage. I hoped that the level of chaos in the marquee would be too great to trace the profiteroles back to me. As Paul thrust an umbrella into my hand he seemed oblivious to the link. He misinterpreted my frozen look of guilt as a sign of fear at the hysteria surrounding me. So he held my arm high, forcing the umbrella open, thrust a plate of canapés into my hand and commanded,
"HOLD YOUR POST!"

And so I found myself dressed in a ridiculous uniform, with one arm holding an umbrella aloft, and the other stewarding a tray of canapés, which in turn were being used as missiles, whilst a sea of food rained down on me from above. I felt, for all the world, like a musician on the Titanic, stalwartly playing my instrument to the end, as the *Highpoints* marquee sank around me. No noble thoughts crossed my mind. All I could think was,
'Give me *The Fractured Teapot* any day. At least I go home with my heart intact and my clothes clean.'

Two hours later when the last smear of cream had been wiped off the marquee; I stepped over the drunken bodies that littered the floor and carefully made my way out to the kitchen. I picked up my mobile phone.
"Mum? Where are you? I'm ready to come home now. This isn't where I want to be."

As I waited for her arrival, I mused over my anticipation of this evening. I had felt that something was going to change in me. I had felt the need to say 'Goodbye!' and now I understood to what. That night I had said 'Goodbye!' to my innocence, for now I had been exposed to the shallowness of the world. I had also said 'Goodbye!' to my unguarded heart.

I sat on the step outside the green door waiting for Mum and rummaged in my bag. I pulled out a chocolate bar. As my teeth sank in, the chocolate cracked and then melted on my tongue. I was relieved to find that some things hadn't changed. Some things still satisfied. If only for a moment.

Chapter 13

The Last Chapter

By the time Monday came I was suitably clean and had recovered from the shock of entering the 'real' world (or was it unreal - so hard to tell). When I went back to school everything seemed the same, except for the fact that I was just a little braver. Darcy bounded up to me,
"So I hear you had an interesting weekend! Did you enjoy it?"
"Sort of..." was all that I could reply, after all there were elements that I had enjoyed about *Highpoints*. It was just that I had placed so much expectation on the experience, and for a moment that expectation had been realised, but only for a moment. The one thing that I was definitely sure of was that I was not cut out for the life of the glitterati.

"Well how about I introduce you to a more normal night out. Something just a little cleaner. Something where you don't need to take an umbrella!" She laughed. Obviously

word had got around about the Saturday night events. Kate or Joanna had clearly blabbed, since they too hung around with the same crowd as Darcy. I felt a pang in my heart. I missed our friendship. Darcy continued, seemingly oblivious to my pain: "A whole heap of us are going out to the pub this weekend, (the bouncer doesn't mind our age so long as we behave and don't draw attention to ourselves) and I reckon you'd enjoy it. So what d'you say?" My heart lifted again. Maybe she wanted to resurrect our friendship too.
"Yeah, Okay. That would be nice." I heard myself saying it; I'm not quite sure how the words slipped out; they just did. Clearly my heart spoke before my brain had time to engage. So that was it; I was committed.
"Great!" Darcy looked delighted. "I'll pick you up at 8pm." With that she went to class and I was left musing on this next footstep into life.

By the time I got home I was mildly optimistic. Maybe life wasn't so empty after all. I mean, I had my job at *The Fractured Teapot* and all my customers seemed to love me - particularly the little old ladies; Mum for once was single (3 weeks now, the longest ever) so she had some time to spend with me and I was even being invited to join the others for a night out. Acceptance comes in many forms and this for now was my little package. I checked my heart. It felt lighter; not quite so disheartened. Smiling, I opened the door.

Mum was sitting at the dining room table staring out into the garden. Her curvy frame silhouetted against the rainbow wallpaper.
"Are you okay Mum?" I asked, but as she turned around to face me, I could see that she'd been crying.
"We need to go and see Uncle Paul. They've moved him into a hospice. He hasn't got long left. Are you okay if we

A Rampage Of Chocolate

leave tonight? That way we can be there for him in the morning."
"Sure." I said. I checked for my heart, but this time I couldn't find it. It had sunk too low. I looked for my new package of acceptance, but found that it had crumbled inside me. It seems it had little foundation after all.

The journey down to the sea was long and silent. Nothing seemed important enough to discuss right now. This was a time of life and death. All I wanted to do was to keep my promise to Uncle P. I had said that I would be back, but life had overtaken me and I had not gone. Now life and time hung in the balance and I didn't know which would win.

We checked into a lodge near the hospice. It was a bit run down, but we didn't care. All we needed was somewhere warm and dry to sleep for a few hours. The owners, the Greens, were nice enough and were very sympathetic to our situation. They simply showed us to our room saying gently,
"If you are hungry then breakfast is between 7 and 8am. It's always best to eat before you go there. If you can." With that, they closed the door and I glanced around the room. There were rainbows on the walls! It was just like being at home and I was thankful for the small comfort that gave. I smiled; then got ready for bed.

That night I dreamt that I was Alice in Wonderland chasing the white rabbit. The trouble was that I never caught the rabbit and all he kept saying was that I would be too late. By the time that my alarm went at 7am I felt like I had done 10 rounds in the boxing ring - a combination of all my tossing and turning and the prominent bed springs. I also felt just a

The Last Chapter

little damp - the result of sweaty nightmares and waterproof sheets. I was glad to get up.

As I walked down the stairs to the dining room, I could smell the fried breakfasts and they smelt glorious, but the thought of eating one myself just made my stomach churn. Instead Mum and I opted for toast and a cup of tea. The good old British cuppa… It solves everything; although maybe not this time.

The hospice was walkable and I was grateful for the fresh air. Somehow its purity and freshness seemed important to me. I was worried about what I would see and smell inside, so I wanted to have a fragrance to hold onto - something to get me through this ordeal. We turned a corner and saw the battered green sign: 'Welcome to Mighty Oaks'. The small letters below read: 'A peaceful setting where mighty oaks can lay down their branches'. I winced at the thought of Uncle P laying down anything. I wanted him just as he was. I wanted him to find energy; to find new life.

We walked down the gravelled drive until we reached the house. *Mighty Oaks* was a big, sprawling house set in beautiful gardens. There were roses growing in the front borders and various shrubs all around. A bird table stood in the centre of the striped lawn, with various feeders draped off the sides. The birds (mainly magpies) were having a feast, oblivious to the contents of the building. I'm sure that the birds were a welcome distraction to the residents that looked out of the windows. As we stepped forward, I trod on a stick which snapped very loudly, causing most of the birds to fly off. I looked at the lawn again; only 1 magpie was left. My stomach lurched at this superstitious omen. I searched the lawn and skies for another magpie, praying for the comfort

A Rampage Of Chocolate

of a flock, but I found only the one. A sense of loneliness and dread engulfed me.

Mum and I nervously held hands as we stepped through the front door. The automatic doors closed behind us, sealing us in. There was no turning back now.
"Can I help you?" greeted a gentle lady with green-rimmed glasses and a bun.
"Yes please. We're here to see Paul Booth?" Mum said it falteringly. She said it as a question and I understood why. She too wondered if he had made it through the night.
"Ah yes." the lady said with a reassuring smile. "He's in *The Dorset Suite*. Pearl will take you there." With that she beckoned a rather large African lady towards us. Pearl bustled over and welcomed us with a huge smile, her teeth glistening under the fluorescent light.
"He'll be pleased to see you," she said warmly. "He's just had his breakfast. A whole weetabix!" She said it so proudly. Little did Pearl know that in his heyday Uncle P could eat 4 shredded wheat!

She guided us down a corridor, past lots of rooms with stately names: *The Gloucester Suite*; *Buckingham Suite* and *Sandringham*. I smiled to myself… Uncle P would like this. He always had aspirations to hobnob with royalty. On one occasion he had done - well sort of. He had served the princes a pint over the bar one day. Apparently he had also saved the public purse by supplying them with a free bag of nuts. He had then cracked some joke about popping one under a few mattresses to find the right princess. He said they laughed, but either way it wasn't quite enough to get him invited to the next garden party.

"Here you go. He's waiting inside. Call me if you need

The Last Chapter

anything." We watched Pearl walk off, her big buttocks swaying in a gentle rhythmic motion.

Mum and I stared at each other and with a deep breath we entered in. Even the creaking door was not enough to distract from the shock of all the wires and machines that we saw. My uncle was thin last time, but now he had wasted to nothing. Oh, why hadn't I come and seen him sooner? I pulled up a chair and sat down.

Uncle P opened one eye and smiled.
"You came back then?"
"Of course I did. I promised didn't I?" He smiled again and pointed at the wires.
"Don't mind if I don't get up. I don't want to get in a knot." I laughed. Well it was more of a snigger actually. I wasn't really up to a full blown laugh. Mum shuffled in her seat.
"Hello Dave," he said warmly. (He had always called her that, ever since they were little and he had found out how much it irritated her). "I'm pleased you came. You always cheer me up, and if you don't, your clothes do! What are you wearing this time? Pyjamas?" I sniggered again. Clearly his sense of humour had been unaffected by his disease. Mum scowled and muttered,
"It's a chiffon trouser suit! I'm going to get a drink. I'll be back in a minute."

I looked at Uncle P and he looked at me. He smiled with his mouth, but his eyes winced with pain. There was silence at first as I wondered what to say to this living skeleton and then I realised that Uncle P was still there… just in a different body. I tried to remember all of our history together; trying to resurrect the memory of the man who lay before me. I spoke the first thing that came to mind.

A Rampage Of Chocolate

"Do you remember when I was 3 and you rescued me from your frog pond? You saved my life."
"Actually, I didn't. It was your padded anorak that saved your life. I just found you floating and had the pleasure of fishing you out and wiping all the frog spawn off your coat!"
"Yuk! You never told you me that bit before!"
"There are many things I never told you, like just how gorgeous you are. Don't try to be what you're not Annie. I've watched you over these last years, trying to fit in with everyone else. The fact is that you don't need to try to fit in. You already do. You are you. That's it. You *are* good enough. You *are* lovely and you don't need to change. No-one can give you what you already have." With that he squeezed my hand and shut his eyes to sleep. I wiped the tear off my cheek.

He woke again only once or twice, just long enough to smile or share some small pearl of wisdom. Just long enough for me to tell him how much I loved him. Just long enough for another squeeze of my hand.

The last time he slept, Mum and I talked. We reminisced about the good times spent with him. She even laughed about the first time he had called her 'Dave'. Apparently they were up in a tree house at the time.
"My name is Davina!" she had shouted back crossly, and then had pushed him so hard that he fell out of the tree. He spent the next 6 weeks with his left leg in plaster. Not to be beaten, Uncle P had written 'DAVE DID IT!' on his cast as a constant reminder.

We were so busy reminiscing that we didn't notice the moment that Uncle P left this earth. We never saw his line

turn flat. We just felt the coldness of his hand and saw his face - peaceful, creamy and waxen. I leant over and kissed his cheek.
"Goodbye Uncle P. I love you."

As we stepped out into the fresh air, I inhaled deeply, again and again. All the birds had gone, which seemed somehow fitting - a mark of respect, a symbolic absence. It mirrored the disappearance of my Uncle P. I knew that his body lay in the hospice behind me, but this was just a carcass. It was not uncle P. He had gone, and just as with the birds, I had no idea where. All I could feel right now, beyond the immediate numbness and disbelief, was a vague sense of emptiness. I felt disconnected with reality. The world was still ticking over around me but it seemed dimmer. The air was still fresh, but the smell had changed. Something was missing - the sweetness, the purity, the light. In this half-lit world around me everything was tainted by the stench of death.

A piece of me died that day. An important piece. A piece that was loved and cherished. A piece that accepted me as I am. Part of my hope and future ceased to be; or so it seemed.

Chapter 14

First Impressions Count

"I'm sorry about your uncle," said Darcy on Monday giving me a big hug. "How are you?"
I shrugged. She tightened her grip and all of a sudden I melted. It started with a quiver, then a pressure behind my eyes and finally the uncontrollable shaking as the floods erupted. I wept and wept, all the time sensing the absence of Uncle P; the void. Even as Darcy held me, I knew that whilst she was here for me now, in a second she would be gone, back to her new friends. At that very moment I realised that I was totally alone. *The Fractured Teapot* was not enough. I needed more. I needed to know that I was okay. I needed someone bigger than me to hold me and take care of me. The trouble was that there was no-one around me who could meet that need. That position was currently vacant.

When I had recovered sufficiently, Darcy tried to distract me with thoughts of the future:

First Impressions Count

"Well, you missed a good evening on Saturday. We had loads of fun. Tiffany accidentally spilt a drink over Edward, which was hilarious, although he didn't see the funny side because he stormed out! Felix was brilliant as always and had us in stitches with his impersonations of the teachers. Emma and Jonathon really hit it off together, so they are going out on a date on Friday. Anyway, there was way too much to tell you about now, except to say that we're planning to do it all again this Saturday. So why don't you come? What d'you think?" The truth was that I couldn't think. My mind was all foggy. All I knew was that something had to change, so it was worth trying something different. What harm could it do?

"I think I'd like that very much."

"Then it's a deal!" Darcy beamed. She was still as beautiful and enthusiastic as ever. Maybe this would reunite our friendship. Maybe the position of 'Best Friend' would be filled once again. It is funny the way we cling to the thinnest threads of hope in the caverns of despair. We rarely wait for something solid to come along, instead grasping the first thread offered and then we wonder why it snaps.

There was much anticipation and preparation in the run up to Saturday. First I had to get permission from Mum (although that was never going to be a problem), then I needed to sort out what to wear. Now this was tricky for me, never having attended a night out in a pub before. Mum no longer picked my clothes; so I had long-since ditched the rainbow colour scheme and resorted to jeans and plain T-shirts. That was how I felt most comfortable, but I understood that I would need to up my game to be accepted. Should I go casual and scruffy, or maybe understated elegance, or even high fashion?

A Rampage Of Chocolate

I never once considered who I was or how I liked to dress. I only thought about what other people would think of me. I looked for clothes that would make me acceptable to them. I was desperate to be liked. Desperate for acceptance. In the end I plumped for jeans, a pink striped shirt, a studded belt, a bright pink jumper and cowboy boots. I decided to borrow Mum's gold hooped earrings and her gold chain. All in all it looked really good. I had never dressed like this before. Looking in the mirror now I smiled. I knew that no matter what the others wore this outfit would hit the mark. I wanted to be noticed but not to stand out. I figured this would achieve my goal.

Mum was brilliant. She was so pleased to hear that I finally wanted to go out that she turned her entire make-up case over to me. We sat down in front of the mirror that Friday afternoon and tried various effects. I immediately excluded the yellows, greens, purples and oranges in her portfolio. Noah I was not, and I certainly didn't want any kind of rainbow on my eyelids! So we decided to experiment with blues, pinks and browns.

The sparkly blue eye shadow was too extreme - it made me look like a young Barbara Cartland, with not even a hint of me. Relatively speaking, the brown was more successful, although its colour was too reminiscent of my bike ride with Darcy! Our final attempt was the pink. This was subtle, but made my eyes look sore! 2 hours later, I decided on the simple effect of eyeliner and mascara.

Then it was the turn of the lipsticks. Mum looked overjoyed at this prospect - she was renowned for her garish red lips. I saw her eyeing up the post-box red. I cut at her off at the pass, just as her hand was swooping down.

First Impressions Count

"Pink I think, Mum. Don't you?" She cocked her head to one side, winced slightly and then agreed. So there it was, the final outfit, all ready and waiting for Saturday night. I put my jeans and T-shirt on, rubbed the make-up off and went downstairs

It seemed an age until Saturday night, but finally the grand moment came: my first step onto the social circuit as an invited guest. By the time I had arrived home from the tea rooms, I had 2½ hours to prepare for this great event. It was only just long enough! I spent a full hour soaking in the bath, followed by an hour styling my hair. I spent ages ensuring that it was curled to perfection so that it appeared totally natural and unstyled. Finally I finished it all off with the make-up scheme that Mum and I had devised.

I had just put my shirt and jewellery on when the doorbell went. It was Darcy. I grabbed my jeans off the floor (where I had left them the previous night), pulled them on and threw my jumper over my shoulders. I was ready! My jeans were a little tight in the leg, but that couldn't be helped (or so I thought). Anyway, I would fiddle with them in the car and rearrange them.
"Bye Mum!"
"Bye Annie! Have a great time. Don't do anything I wouldn't do!" It left me a wide scope. I smiled, shut the front door behind me and jumped into the back of Darcy's car.

"Annie, this is Felix," Darcy said, pointing to a curly-haired, boyish mess in the front seat.
"Hi!"
"And this is Gordon, Felix's cousin. He's just moved into

A Rampage Of Chocolate

the area." I turned and saw beside me a guy with green eyes and a mop of blond hair. His cheeks were fairly ruddy and he had mischief in his smile.
"'Right?" he ugged.
"Yeah." With the pleasantries over we all settled back in our seats and I started to (very subtly) fiddle with the leg of my jeans, tugging gently on the material (and in particular a lump) until it loosened its grip of my thigh.

As we meandered through the country lanes, I was aware of my every movement, both inside and out. My heart was beating so loudly that I was sure the whole car could hear it and I tried to regulate my breathing so that it was subtle, gentle and quiet. But the reality was that my excitement showed. Every time I was asked a question, I seemed to shout with enthusiasm. It was as if someone had turned up my volume control. I was also acutely aware that Gordon was staring at me, taking in my every move. I had never been scrutinised before (or at least not since my first day at school) and I didn't like it. It was hard to be natural, so I was very grateful when the 'Slug and Carrot' appeared at the top of the hill. At last I could escape.

Darcy parked the car in the car park (that was no mean feat, having only recently passed her test) and we all got out. I started walking towards the door, my heart beating wildly. What was inside? What would it be like? Who would be there? Would they like me? Was I dressed okay? Would I have anything interesting to say, or even worse anything that the others would want to hear? Terror gripped.

Just then I heard Gordon's voice call out,
"Annie, are these yours?" I swung around, irritated, my concentration broken. Didn't he know how much courage

First Impressions Count

I needed to step inside? How could he interrupt me at such a critical moment? With those thoughts (and a huge scowl) I faced him and took in the full horror of what he was holding, high in the air, arm outstretched for all to see… My pants from yesterday!

My mind raced to explain my predicament and a series of images flashed before my eyes… The hurry I was in last night when I got ready for bed, when I took my jeans and pants off in one motion; the rush I was in tonight, never noticing the offending article still inside when I put my jeans on; the tightness in my jeans; the lump on my leg; the freedom in the car as the lump released its grip. It all made sense now!

There was only one thing for it… I marched over, grabbed my rainbow briefs out of his grasp and said,
"Yeah. They are. Thanks!" I stuffed them into my bag and then marched to the door at full pace, ignoring the peels of laughter from behind.

I was aware of the burning in my cheeks, but I opened the door anyway and cast my eyes around the room until I found the table with our friends on it. Thankfully Kate and Joanna were the only ones there, giving plenty of time to recover. I ordered a drink and went over. The others came and joined me. Felix and Gordon could not contain themselves. Every time they looked at me they smirked or giggled. I felt the size of an ant, only without its strength. I sat back in my chair and picked up my drink. Unfortunately I missed my mouth and poured it all down my front. Felix and Gordon, now crying with laughter, disappeared onto the floor under the table. Darcy smiled. I glared. The door opened and the rest of the group walked in.

A Rampage Of Chocolate

I made my excuses and left the table, heading for the toilets. When I got there I just leant on the sink, staring into the mirror.

"Ridiculous!" I said to my reflection. "You have made yourself look totally ridiculous." I splashed myself with water (to wash away the coke) and disappeared into the cubicle. Just as I did, I heard some familiar voices. It was Vicky and Kate. I held my breath and pretended not to exist. I didn't want to be found. Not just yet. I was still looking for my dignity.

I needn't have worried. They seemed oblivious to my presence.

"I didn't know you smoked!" I heard Kate exclaim.

"Oh?" Vicky replied, "I don't!"

"But you've got a cigarette in your hand."

"Oh this? This isn't a cigarette! It's a cocktail cigarette."

"I don't understand?"

"You don't smoke them; you just hold them!" I stifled a snigger, not wanting to give my presence away. "They come in lots of different colours, all with gold ends. I thought this purple one would compliment my outfit." Kate just grunted and I heard the banging of the cubicle doors on either side of me. I came out of mine smiling. I had forgotten my predicament and returned to the table, all the time musing on Vicky's vanity and crass stupidity.

The table had also forgotten me and were all deeply engrossed in a discussion about the validity of guys wearing jewellery (that's a deep discussion when you are 17). Darcy was on the phone, as was Charles, closely followed by Vicky. Within half an hour the whole table were on the phone either due to

First Impressions Count

calls received or calls made. I sat there wondering what the point of meeting up was if no-one was going to interact.

Gordon was the first to come free and, with no-one else to talk to, he came over and started chatting. It turned out that he wasn't quite as irritating after all. In fact he was almost quite nice. I had long since given up on the idea of impressing him, so I just resorted to being me and chatting about my likes and dislikes and life in general. Conversation flowed and apart from one small incident where I choked on an ice cube and accidentally spat it into his lap, I survived the evening relatively unscathed.

When the time came to go I was quite sad. I had enjoyed the evening and it hadn't been too stressful after all. I hopped into Darcy's car and wondered if I had passed the test. Would they invite me back again? Only time would tell.

Gordon leant over and whispered,
"I've got 2 tickets to see *Spandex Bully* on Friday. Would you like to come?" I could hardly believe what I was hearing. Was it a joke? Maybe he was after revenge? But he was smiling and his eyes were kind. Given that I hadn't said anything yet, he went a little redder in the cheeks and continued, "I think you're really sweet and I would like to get to know you more."

My heart started pounding, sometimes missing a beat. I tried to find my speech, but all that came out was a nod and a squeak.
"I'll take that as a 'yes'," he said.

Chapter 15

Guard Your Heart

As I stood in the arena watching *Spandex Bully*, I felt victorious. Sean Blaster may have been the first man to break my heart, (albeit that it only took him the sum total of 10 minutes) but there I was standing watching him with someone who really did like me. I had been vindicated. The process that had been started by Sean had been completed by Gordon, or at least that was my hope. I looked over at Gordon. He had made a real effort in dressing up. He had a pink striped shirt and new jeans (I knew they were new because they still had the label attached). He had even put on aftershave just for me. (Actually he had put on quite a lot of aftershave, so I found it hard to stand near him, but I did appreciate the sentiment).

The journey to the arena had been flawless. We had chatted easily and I had even established that we liked the same favourite foods - curry and sweetcorn. It may not have been the most scintillating conversation, but we had to start somewhere and it was the best I could come up with at the time.

The performance started with a loud explosion and *Spandex Bully* launched into their most famous song. I felt myself being carried away by the music, singing at the top of my voice. I didn't always get the words right, but it was close enough. I looked over at Gordon and found him staring at me, smiling. He reached out and took my hand. At that moment, simultaneously, a firework went off in my heart and on the stage. I forgot to guard my heart. I was smitten.

On the way back to the car Gordon stopped and turned to face me.
"You are very beautiful you know." He held my face and leant over and kissed me. My first ever kiss. I read so much into it. Pictures of our wedding and children flashed through my mind. Our future was sealed.

As we drove home, I stared out of the window marvelling at the city lights and the new-found softness of my surroundings. I was deliriously happy. I checked my heart, but I couldn't find it - it had gone into orbit.

The rest of my school days were perfect. I was dating Gordon and Darcy was dating Felix. By now Lorna had split up with Oliver so that left just us 4. I had my best friend back and a boyfriend, both of whom valued and liked me. I felt prepared to take on the world. Even my A'levels, which had been looming like mountains, now felt like mole-hills. I felt worthy and confident. There was no stopping me.

Now I could attend any party or pub knowing that I was supposed to be there; I had the seal of approval - Gordon's and Darcy's.

My exams passed effortlessly (apart from setting light to the bench in my Chemistry practical), leaving me free to spend the summer with Gordon. We had such freedom. With no restrictions on time, we meandered through the summer, lazily picnicking by the side of the river, ambling through the woods or cycling around the lanes. (Yes, it was true, Gordon even gave me the confidence to get on a bike again. Only this time there were no muddy puddles awaiting me, only summer fields and loving embraces).

One of our most memorable days was spent punting on the river Cam. With so little money between us, we used our leather jackets as a deposit for the punt and launched out into the deep. Gordon, with his muscly arms and good balance, was more than capable of the challenge. He guided the pole with ease and the punt moved freely, safely passing all the other river-traffic. I laid back enjoying the feeling of being steered through life, all responsibility abdicated to him. With the sun warming every freckle on my face and the gentle rippling of the river, I experienced a level of relaxation that I had never thought possible.
"Your turn Annie. I reckon you'll enjoy this. Just remember to keep an even pressure and not to push down too hard." He smiled at me and I felt capable.

We swapped places on the punt (no mean feat I can tell you - the boat was wobbling so much that I had to resort to going on all fours to reach the platform). Gordon laid back, arms behind his head, looking up at me, grinning. I took my position; feet stabilised, pole in hand and pushed off.

Guard Your Heart

Or at least, that was my intention. The reality was that as I pushed the pole into the water it got swept up by the current and never quite made it to the bottom. I tried again, this time with a lot more force and with a better appreciation of Gordon's strength - he had made this look effortless and yet here was I pushing down hard with 2 hands and yet the pole was only just reaching the riverbed.

Steering with purpose was my next challenge - I was heading directly for the bank. I looked to Gordon for direction, but he was too busy laughing to be of any help. Frantically, I moved the pole to the other side of the boat and pushed down with all my strength. Relief flooded me as we started to turn away from the bank, swiftly followed by disappointment as we continued turning and ended up facing the opposite bank. Clearly steering was a more delicate balance than I had considered. I tried again and our boat was redirected down the river.

"Full steam ahead!" Gordon said, smiling.

"Aye aye Captain!" I saluted, accidentally letting go of the pole. I watched in horror as it sank into the river. I gulped - a gulp that started in my mouth and went all the way to the pit of my stomach. I looked to Gordon, who was staring at the trace of bubbles left on the surface. We both plunged our arms into the water in the desperate hope of making contact with the metal pole. Of course that did mean that we had both simultaneously moved to the same side of what was already a finely-balanced punt. That understanding only came to us as we were both tipped unceremoniously into the depths!

I gasped in surprise as I was deposited into the murky depths. As a result I inhaled copious quantities of green, slimy, river water. (And a tadpole or two)! All of a sudden my leisurely

A Rampage Of Chocolate

punt along the river did not seem quite so romantic. So I turned my attention instead to the river bank, and headed to dry land; leaving Gordon to right the boat and retrieve the pole. After a few dives into the water he succeeded and swam to the shore, dragging the punt behind him. He ushered me back into the boat and I reluctantly complied. With no consultation, but with my full relief and blessing, he once more took the helm and steered us back to the docking station.

And so it was that we returned the punt - both of us dripping wet, clothed in sodden garments, with remnants of the river embedded in our clothing. We were wet but happy. This was one day we would never forget.

As we stood on solid ground, Gordon stuck his arm around me, causing a stream of water to ooze from my T-shirt. He grinned at me and said,
"One thing I can say is that life is never dull with you Annie!"
With that he kissed me on the end of my nose. I melted into acceptance, all feelings of failure and disappointment swept away with one embrace.

The summer was a heady time: a time of perfection; a time of relaxation and a time of fun. Gordon and I grew close. I understood what made him laugh and he embraced all of my quirks. With him there was no embarrassment. What should have been disaster always became a shared experience of fun. He professed to love and cherish me. He told me that I was beautiful and that I made him smile. I believed it all, received it all and it made me soar.

Guard Your Heart

I had assumed that when Gordon and I went to university we would stay together. Birmingham and London weren't too far apart to see each other at weekends. But you know what they say about assuming -
"It makes an 'ass' out of 'u' and 'me'."

A week before Gordon left for Birmingham, he took me out to dinner. A wonderful meal, at my favourite Italian restaurant. As we waited for the dessert menu he reached over the table and held my hands. I looked into his soft green eyes and melted yet again, drinking in their safety, comfort, approval and love.
"I have loved spending this time with you. You are so precious to me. You will always be precious to me. I know that we will be friends for the rest of our lives." He spotted the confusion in my eyes, so he continued. "I hope that you get everything out of life that you want. Maybe we can still get together in the holidays. That way we can keep in touch. I'll ring you from time to time, just to check that you're doing okay."

So there it was, with no warning: the conclusion. In his mind at least, love was temporary; affection for a season. He was entering a new chapter in his life and it didn't involve me. I was part of his foreword, not his main book.

Once again I felt stupid and worthless. How silly of me to believe that I was good enough for a lifetime. I started remembering all the mishaps that we had shared; all the clumsy episodes. I guess you wouldn't want to be around them forever.

The trouble with a heart that goes into orbit without any guard is that it can be shot down easily with one targeted

A Rampage Of Chocolate

missile. Mine had received a direct strike. It was currently re-entering the atmosphere. I could feel it burning up. I could feel it breaking on re-entry. This time it wasn't going to survive.

"Oh!" I said in a fumbled whisper. "Right… Erm… I don't think I want a pudding… Could we just go straight home?"

We drove home in silence. I bit my quivering lip very hard. Numbness overwhelmed me. As I got out of the car, he came around to meet me and kissed me for the very last time. This time I didn't respond. This time my mind stayed still, locked in a dark, empty void. This time it was pain, not love, that washed over me.

The University Challenge...

Chapter 16

University Days. University Ways

As I stood on the campus for the very first time, watching my Mum drive off into the distance, I felt totally alone. This was it. I had no support. Mum was gone. Darcy was on the other side of the country and Gordon… well he was no longer part of my life. Even my dog was not here to comfort me. There were no cuddles; no words of encouragement, just a sea of new faces. So I did the only thing I knew how to do… I dug deep inside myself, walked into the building and smiled!

I soon got to know people it was true. Vacuous relationships were freely on offer. Everyone was in the process of friend collection. The more people you could be seen with, the more likely you were to establish yourself as popular from

University Days. University Ways

the outset. It was 'dog eat dog' and your friend-count mattered.

I watched around me as groups and cliques formed and morphed into mini-nations. I observed as a spectator not wishing to join any group until I understood their values. I didn't want to be with people that were cruel or bitchy, just with people who enjoyed life and cared. I was so busy watching that, before I had realised, I was nationless. No identity yet again. A few others were in the same boat as me and we all swam to shore together and formed our own mini-nation; not because we had lots in common, but because we were all left out.

Harpreet (Reeta for short) and Heather were genuinely lovely and very good fun. They were just a little shy that's all. Dominic was strange, to say the least, with his androgynous appearance, railway track braces and childish sense of humour. There weren't many people that could relate to him (myself included). Finally there was Sally, an academic in the truest sense of the word. She constantly had her head in a book and was always up for a debate, although she found very quickly that none of us were worthy opponents (it was obvious from our confused, screwed up faces each time she stepped below the first level of depth on any topic).

'Freshers' Week' promised to offer many opportunities to branch out, meet new people and to try new activities. I was excited at this prospect so went along to sign up with some of the societies. I entered a room full of trestle-tables covered in fliers. Each one had a banner identifying its particular flavour. As I surveyed the range I was disappointed. I couldn't see any that would suit my palette. I immediately ruled out the sporting activities on the basis that I wanted

A Rampage Of Chocolate

to win friends not embarrass myself. The remaining tables fell into 3 categories - academic, religious and alcoholic. The drinking societies were lightly disguised with names such as 'The Business Soc' (which organised a visiting speaker every month followed by a 24 hour drinking party), 'The Wine Soc' (which promised to introduce you to cheap wines to fit your budget), 'The Pub Soc' (okay, so that one wasn't even slightly disguised) and finally 'The Curry Soc' (the advertisement for which read: 'We frequent all the curry houses which offer cheap food and cheap beer').

I knew that I had to choose at least one society in order to integrate, so I enrolled with the Curry Society. Reeta signed up for netball, Heather for rugby (she later admitted to me, that it was only because she wanted a rugby player for a boyfriend) and Sally did a clean sweep of all the academic societies, even trying to start a debate with some of the stallholders, much to their amusement.

Just as I was about to leave, a tallish girl entered the room in a hurry, carrying another table, closely followed by an entourage. I waited to see what flavour they were bringing to the event and noticed that, even before she had fully set up, she was inundated by female students. Now I was curious, so I headed over to the table. Then I smiled. A big banner read quite simply, 'Choc Soc.' Finally a society that was suited to me (and Reeta and Heather). I signed on the dotted line. I was engaging in university life at last!

My days at university consisted of a barrage of lectures and forays to the student union bar. With over 100 people at each lecture and the union bar full to capacity, I found it hard to cope in such large groups. I always wanted to meet people, but never knew who to approach. After all, what if

University Days. University Ways

they didn't like me? How would I know? I would hate to be the person that they talked about behind my back. So I tackled my fear in the only way that students do - with alcohol. With several drinks inside of me I would fearlessly take on any group or clique. The trouble was that I never really remembered what happened, or what was said and often found the conversation going above my fuzzy brain. I never made any real friends that way, but often made a fool of myself - falling off my chair was a regular occurrence, as was smoking. Often I missed my bus home and would have to walk in the bitter cold. I persuaded myself that I was having fun, but the reality was very different. I was more unfulfilled now than I had ever been; more desperate for acceptance.

My lowest point came one Friday night. I had spent the evening in the student union and had drunk my full quota of cocktails. (They called them 'cocktails' but the truth was that they were just an excuse for students to drink as many different shots as possible, without anyone counting. Each cocktail had a name and a recipe. At this point the deception ended, for they unashamedly served them up in plastic pint pots, with not a straw or an umbrella in sight). I had long since lost count of the number I had drunk, but realised that it was too many because I could no longer stop smiling and my cheeks were beginning to ache as a result. A spotty student called Dave had recognised my vulnerability and had sat down beside me droning on for over an hour about his love of mathematics. Given that I had long since lost the power of speech, I was unable to voice the fact that it was not a love we shared. Instead I had smiled (unable to stop) and he had assumed that I was enjoying his monologue. I was so grateful when Ethan behind the bar hit the gong to call time. Now all I had to do was to get home.

A Rampage Of Chocolate

En route to the student halls, I realised that I was hungry and in need of some chips to sober me up. It was a 10 minute walk downhill to the chip shop (20 if you were staggering as I was) and I had exactly £1 left in my purse, just enough to buy a paper cone of chips. So I set off, with just a thin coat on a bitterly cold night in search of my remedy. By the time I got to the shop, my fingers and hands were frozen, my cheeks (which had been freed from their fixed grin) were blue and my nose had the statutory winter drip at the end. The man looked at me and smiled,
"Chips?" he asked in a heavy Greek accent. I nodded (the power of speech had not yet returned). With one scoop of his hand he delivered a portion of chips into the paper cone. I handed over my last £1 and dressed them with salt and vinegar. I inhaled their eye-watering perfume, my stomach leaping with expectation, and stepped out of the door.

As I stood on the doorstep, half frozen, holding on to my chips, I leant over and put my empty purse back in my bag. Just as I did, I felt a wetness hit my face. I looked up to see a row of pigeon bottoms overhanging the door. I wiped my face and looked at the white smear on my hand.
"Great! Just what I needed!" Then I looked at my chips. It appeared that I was not the pigeon's target. The whole top layer of my chips was covered in pigeon mayo!

I wanted to cry, but instead I put the cone in the bin and started the long, uphill walk home. I was freezing cold, totally penniless and my head was beginning to throb. Surely there was more to university life than this?

Chapter 17

Choc Soc Strikes

three weeks into university, there was a bubble of excitement brewing on the campus. Expectations were rising, particularly among the female students. The Choc Soc was holding its opening event - a *Chocolate Fondue and Fountain Extravaganza*. It sounded like the first bit of decent fun. I couldn't wait. As far as I could work out, everyone was going.

I spent time choosing the right clothes to wear, opting for the cowboy-style apparel that I had worn on my first expedition to the pub (all memories of last night's knickers and other such embarrassing events had long since been consigned to the archives). Light make-up and slightly tousled hair finished the ensemble. I looked in the mirror and smiled. Tonight was going to be a good night, a night to relax and enjoy myself. Combining friendship, fun and chocolate. It sounded like heaven to me.

Choc Soc Strikes

I went and knocked on Reeta's door.
"Hang on a minute. I'm almost ready."
"Okay. You've got 5 minutes then I'm off with or without you. I feel the pull of the chocolate already!" I heard Reeta laugh from inside. Whilst I was waiting outside her door, several others walked past. I figured that they were heading in the same direction. I knocked again.
"Alright! Alright!" Reeta opened her door, still putting on her final shoe. "I know that you love chocolate, but control yourself!" I grinned and we set off at a good pace, determined to get a good spot at the event.

We arrived at the venue with 5 minutes to spare, but already there was a big queue outside. Clearly this was a landmark event in the annual student calendar. Finally the doors burst open and we were allowed in, all handing over our £5 entrance fee at the door. In return, someone stamped our hand with a picture of Donald duck and handed us a skewer.

I gasped at the sight that beheld my eyes. Everywhere you looked there were tables covered in white linen. On each table there was a chocolate fountain and a fondue with salvers of fruit, cake and marshmallows to dip. The smell of chocolate was intoxicating. There was even one table in the corner with a banner overhead which said 'Lover's Dip'. (I am told that the dipping skewers there had 2 prongs instead of 1 so that you could both dip at the same time and kiss while you were eating the finished article. Obviously I didn't go over there myself, so I don't know if that really was true). Dominic and Heather headed straight for it.

A Rampage Of Chocolate

Someone called Jo, wearing a giant apron with the logo 'Enjoy Chocolate Heaven', stood on the stage.
"Welcome everyone to *The Choc Soc Fondue and Fountain Extravaganza*. It's good to see you all again and to see some new faces too. We've prepared lots of lovely chocolate dips for you this time, so please feel free to try out the different tables. Chocolate comes in many guises and we want you to enjoy them all. As always we have 'Lovers Dip Corner' and for the purists amongst you there are a range of pure chocolate dips at the back. We only have a couple of rules that I would ask you to observe. The first is to keep your dipping skewer with you at all times, and the second is that I don't want to see any double dipping. If it has touched your mouth then that's where it stays. That includes you Bruce!" she said pointing at a particularly dishevelled, unshaven, greasy-looking student. He grunted in acknowledgement, although I made a mental note to steer clear of his tables. "So happy dipping ladies and gents. I don't want to see any leftovers!"

With that there was a clattering of feet as everyone rushed to their preferred tables. I on the other hand didn't know where to start.
"Where d'you think?" I asked Reeta.
"*Baileys Delight* sounds nice."
"I agree." (As did at least 10 other students). I squeezed my arm through the people and managed to prod a piece of banana onto my skewer. I plunged it into the pool of brown, velvety liquid and waited a couple of seconds until I had enough space around me to pull it out safely and lift it to my mouth. Reeta and I looked at each other as we simultaneously let out a groan of delight.
"Oh boy! Now I really do know what heaven feels like!"

"Me too!" she mumbled, with a small dribble of melted chocolate oozing out of the side of her mouth.

We stood there for several minutes enjoying our 5-a-day portion of fruit, (I'm sure it still counted, even though it was covered in chocolate) before moving on to the next table. *Rum n Raisin* an equally enticing concoction, although a little more sickly. We left after only 2 dips, heading instead for the particularly popular *Molten Mint Bath*.

The smell of the mint and chocolate combination hit me before I had even reached the table. My expectation was at a high.
"Marshmallow this time I think."
"I'm sticking with fruit. After all, I want to be healthy!"
We both laughed, loving the combination of naughty but nice. I prodded a pink marshmallow which promptly fell off my skewer onto the floor. I groaned and bent down to pick it up. Just as I did, the person next to me thrust their marshmallow into the mint chocolate fountain above me at such an angle that it sprayed all over me on my ascent. I felt the warm chocolate splatters as they hit my face and saw their results on my pink striped shirt. Reeta grimaced.
"Typical!" I groaned.
"Yes it is!" a smug voice said. I looked up to see Tim, a particularly detestable guy from our residence block, laughing at me. I groaned inside. "Still, some disasters can be wiped off and others walk around on 2 legs." With that he left, taking with him my self-esteem and my enjoyment of the evening.

Chapter 18

Pigeons! More Pigeons!

As time went on, I started to make some good friends. By now Sally had opted for a more academic set - people who could relate to her super-human brain and who knew how to debate subjects such as 'the impact of conservatism on the foundation and formation of the European Union'. We still smiled at each other every time we passed in the corridor, but the reality was that there was no common ground between us - hers was very high and mine was quite low.

Many of the original cliques and mini-nations had been transformed as relationships started to form across the borders. As with real life, love caused the cross-pollination of these mini-nations, resulting in a much more balanced student culture. Friendships were now based on shared interests and commonality. Interaction was free-flowing. I was no longer excluded, but felt part of the main body. The different factions had in reality merged into 2 very specific

Pigeons! More Pigeons!

camps - those who did drugs and those who didn't. I was in the section marked 'didn't'.

Dominic and Heather had formed an unlikely union of their own and could often be found giggling in corners, whilst unsuspecting students fell foul of their pranks. Whoopee cushions and fart machines were a familiar part of their repertoire. At other times 'love' was on their agenda and they would be found entwined in the corners of the bar - a meeting of 2 sink plungers. It was not a spectator sport!

Reeta and I had formed a solid bond and held many hopes and fears in common. We were able to support each other through those first weeks and months and often sat in a room laughing over our failures. We were each other's rock; each other's foundation. The societies we had joined had turned out to be little more than titles, with few resulting social events. Those that we had attended had proved both disastrous and chaotic; a disappointment but nonetheless a necessary induction into student life. In the end we decided to give them a wide berth and formed our own social calendar, often inviting others to join us on nights out. We spent much of our time hanging out in our block, drinking coffee and eating toast and marmite. On particularly dull evenings we competed with each other to make the most interesting toastie, out of whatever scraps we could find in the bare fridge and cupboards. I became the hall's 'Queen of Toasties' with my surprisingly delicious concoction: marshmallow, crumbled digestive and drinking chocolate powder, all melted under a grill. It was 'domestic science' on a shoe-string; hardly a racy existence but at least it felt more balanced than my previous alcoholic adventures.

I seemed to get on with everyone in our residence block

A Rampage Of Chocolate

apart from Tim. At first I hated him with his arrogant ways, and he hated me with my ridiculous drunken behaviour. His smirking face at the 'Choc Soc' event was still imprinted on my memory. If ever we found ourselves in the same room together our mutual irritation became clear to all around. It was like an unpleasant tennis match. He nicknamed me 'Phone' or 'Phony' (short for 'Phone Booth'). It was a play on my name that I did not appreciate. I, on the other hand, called him 'Timmy' because he seemed to find it suitably annoying. We couldn't avoid each other because we shared mutual friends and lived on the same corridor, so we launched ourselves whole-heartedly into the sport of annihilation.

"Oi Phony! Do you fancy coming down to the bar tonight? I fancy a good laugh! Maybe you can fall off a chair for a change." Score: Love-15.

"Not tonight Timmy, I'm washing my socks - I find their company more appealing." The rest of the people in the room laughed. Score: 15-All, but with the extra point for laughter, 30-15.

"Phone Booth, you disappoint me," he continued unfazed, "I thought we could go for some chips after; with some pigeon mayo or maybe splatter our clothes with chocolate for dessert?" 30-All! I shot Reeta a look, she had clearly told him of my pigeon misfortune. She squirmed. Chris on the other hand sniggered. 30-40.

"Not tonight Timmy. That type of food is reserved for grown-ups. Let me know when you've passed puberty!" Deuce! It was a hard point to win, but I had got there. I needed time to recover, so I headed towards the kitchen to make some drinks. I tripped on the handle of my bag as I went out. Rats! Advantage Tim! I could feel my cheeks burning as I made a drink and went to the loo. With a deep

Pigeons! More Pigeons!

breath, holding my coffee, I entered the room. Tim looked up, pointed at my feet and howled with laughter, as did everyone else. I looked down and saw the trail of white loo roll stuck to my shoe. Game over!

After a few weeks I started to enjoy this sport with Tim and we even had some sensible conversations. He was actually good company, if a little arrogant. He passed judgement on everything and everyone with no sign of empathy or compassion, as if his emotions had been extracted at birth. Other than that, I started to appreciate his dry humour and quick wit.

It is funny how relationships start off and the direction they take, usually dictated by circumstance and timing. Ours was no exception. One Friday in May I found myself receiving a telephone call from Mum. Usually this would lift my spirits, but not today. She was ringing to tell me that Uncle George had cancer. I felt my colour drain. All of the memories of Uncle P and his wasted frame came flooding back. My nose filled with the stench of death and fear gripped my heart. I placed the receiver back on the hook and turned towards my room. The corridor swayed and reality faded into the background. I tried to step forward but my legs failed. Just then a strong arm caught me. It was Tim. He looked concerned.
"Are you alright Annie? Let me give you a hand." Annie eh? Wow! That was the first time he had used my real name (most of my friends called me Annie - Anne seemed too formal - but never him).

He guided me to my room and then made me a hot drink, sitting down next to me to ensure I was alright. I shared my heart and my fears with him, all about Uncle P and Uncle

George. He in turn shared some of his experiences. I wept. He grabbed a tissue and stuck his arm around me.
"You're not half as stuck up as I thought you were," he said. I snorted.
"Neither are you." We both smiled.
With that our friendship was sealed - the names Phony and Timmy confined to the archives of history. Tennis would resume, but with a more compassionate heart: no longer the desire to annihilate the opponent but instead to have a friendly knock around and just sharpen our skills (providing I was able to hold onto my racket of course).

At the weekends many of the students went home (taking the statutory bag of washing with them) so I would often find myself at a loose end. So it was this particular Saturday in June. I was sitting in my room, staring out of the window musing on what to do, when there was a knock at the door. It was Tim.
"Stick your coat on, we're going out."
"Where are we going?"
"To see the pigeons."
"What?" I thought he was back in attack mode for a minute and screwed up my face. He laughed.
"Trafalgar Square! You said that you have never fed the pigeons; so we're off to see the pigeons." With that, he grabbed my coat and held it out to me, grinning. 5 minutes later we were seated on a London bus heading for Trafalgar Square.

It was a fabulous day. We spent it hopping on and off various buses, feeding pigeons, staring through the railings of Buckingham Palace and standing in front of the sentry

Pigeons! More Pigeons!

trying to make him laugh. Then it was off to 'China Town' for an international cultural experience and quite the rudest meal we'd ever had. The restaurant we chose had 5 floors. If you were European, you were relegated to the 5th floor, where waiters would 'tut' at you and throw the dishes down in front of you. This level of 'service' was not exclusive to us. All of the people on this floor had the same experience. However in our case, the harder they tried to offend us the more we laughed and the more we laughed the more offensive they got! The food tasted great and was really cheap, so we vowed to return (if only to irritate them some more).

Our final destination was the cinema in Leicester Square. It was expensive to get in, so we took our own snacks. We chose *Out of Africa* because everyone was raving about it. We had heard nothing but good reports and it had just won oodles of awards. Whilst it was a good film, it was probably a little mismatched with our mood. We were buoyant and upbeat; an action-adventure would have been a better choice. We felt like explorers having navigated our way through the inner depths of London and fought our way through flocks of birds. However here we sat in this quiet cinema, in the peace and quiet of Africa, with Meryl Streep's voice gently speaking in the background.

Tim opened his crisps. The foil packet made a huge rustling noise. I sniggered. He grabbed a fistful and shoved them into his mouth. All I could hear now was a very loud crunching sound. The man in front turned to us with a terse,
"Sssshhh!" We sniggered again. More rustling and crunching, another, "Sssshhh!" and the packet was empty. I had long since lost the plot of the film. Meryl was still talking. Tim quietly opened his can of cola, muffling the gas emission with his coat, thus avoiding another reprimand from the

A Rampage Of Chocolate

man in front. We sat back and watched the film. He put his arm around me and drew me close. I smiled. Equilibrium was restored.

Tim put his empty coke can on the floor and I snuggled into his arms. He kissed the top of my head. I looked up at him and realised that somewhere on this crazy journey my arch-enemy had become my closest friend and now… Well, I didn't want to presume too much, so I just snuggled, shuffling my body to get comfortable. It was then that my foot made contact with the empty can and I shuddered as I heard it roll off the ledge to the row in front. Then I listened with horror as it 'clunked' very slowly down 14 ledges until it finally came to rest at the front of the cinema.

"Shall we go?" Tim whispered.
"Erm, I think that would be a good idea." We inched our way along the row and ran out of the door, through the foyer and out into the cold night air.
We finally came to rest at the bus stop and he drew me to him.
"Annie? Will you be my girlfriend?" I smiled a reassuring smile and nodded my head.
"With pleasure!" He beamed and bent forward to kiss me. My heart exploded inside and my mind raced forward, winding on the clock, but this time I stopped it. I didn't want dreams of marriage and children. Instead I just focused on the here and now, on the certainty set before me. My future looked better; my future looked more secure, but it was still not guaranteed. I had learnt from Gordon and placed a guard around my heart. The thing that I knew was that today - Saturday - I was okay. Today someone thought enough of me to ask me out; today I was loved; today all

Pigeons! More Pigeons!

was well! Tim rustled in his pocket and then handed me a chocolate bar.

"No thanks Tim. I don't need it. I'm fine."

Chapter 19

An Unstable Anchor

Dating Tim proved to be an emotionally turbulent affair. He was hard to pin down. Whilst caring in nature his lust for humour and laughter was often at my expense.

"Here she comes! Annie, now don't go getting any high ideas, now that we're an item," he would say in the first couple of weeks. It wasn't exactly the endearing sentiment that I had hoped for in front of our friends. I had more hoped for a gentle kiss and a hug, but instead he always chose to embrace me privately and mock me publicly. I would react the same way each time - with a smile and a laugh, pretending that it didn't matter. The reality was that inside I was confused, my emotions wrestling with one another. I had tethered my hopes to this guy and he was proving to be an unstable anchor.

He mockingly started to play the role of Laird:

An Unstable Anchor

"Oi, woman! Get me some coffee!" He would laugh, wink and hug me thinking that it was good fun, but the fact is that it wasn't respectful.

"Get your own coffee lazybones!" I would tease back, trying to redeem the situation.

"Now as you know Annie, I have studied history, many centuries of history and, as far as I can tell, the women always did the kitchen stuff and the men did…" He was stuck now.

"What exactly did they do smarty-pants?" I looked at him quizzically urging him to come up with even one thing to give credibility to his cause. "Go on then! I'm waiting…"

"They provided for the household!" he said triumphantly.

"Well, given that you are on a student grant the same as me and are not providing any income for our 'household' then I suggest that we take it in turns to make the coffee. By my reckoning, it's your turn, so off you go!"

He grumbled.

"Fair point I s'pose. 2 sugars?"

Everything was the same with Tim - a battle of the wills. Sometimes I lost (or couldn't be bothered to fight) but other times I won and he sheepishly retreated back into the realms of normality. His starting point was always the same - one of suppression. I had to fight to be cherished and fight to be acknowledged, especially in public.

Of course there were other sides to Tim. He could be tender and sensitive. He wasn't always the chauvinist. When I felt down he was my hero:

"What's wrong Annie?" he would say and wrap his arms around me. "Anything I can do?"

"Just hold me. I'm having a bad day."

"That's not right. You're my princess. You're supposed to

A Rampage Of Chocolate

have good days not bad ones. Who's upset you? I'll get them for you!" With that he would pretend to draw his sword and strike them down. It always worked… It made me laugh and broke my mood.

Sometimes he was my gentle confidante:
"You okay?" I would shake my head. "Do you wanna talk? It may help. You never know." At times like that, when I opened my heart to him, he would show wisdom beyond his years. We would exchange adages and laugh and comfort each other.

As he started to confide in me, I discovered that he'd had a very troubled childhood - his dad left when he was 3, so he never had a role model (which may have explained his strange behaviour in our relationship) and his mother died when he was 10. Thereafter he was brought up by his bachelor uncle on a Norfolk farm. It was a very disjointed background leading to some very distorted perceptions about relationships.

Over the years he'd had plenty of time to consider life and its emotions. He understood loneliness. He understood abandonment. He understood fear. What he didn't understand was a woman.

I cared deeply for Tim and I also felt really sorry for him. I wanted to tend the wounds of his upbringing and nurse him to health. I believed that I could show him what a woman should be and how to love. However the fact was that his behaviour was too ingrained and his heart was held captive in a prison somewhere deep inside. I had a place in his life, a special place, and he cared for me. He just didn't know how to show it.

Chapter 20

New Frontiers

I was right to guard my heart with Tim. He was a great friend but a lousy boyfriend. Whilst fun to be with, he was too used to poking fun at me and putting me down. I needed to be cherished, to be built up. Tim didn't meet that need. He seemed incapable of connecting emotionally and those 3 little words that I craved never came. It seemed that the extraction of his emotions at birth was irreversible. So at the end of my first year, just 7 weeks after the relationship began, we went out for dinner to his favourite restaurant. I held his hands across the table and spoke softly:

"Tim, I am amazed that we have come this far. It's been a really crazy journey. You know how much you mean to me. You're so precious to me. However I think we both know that this isn't working." He nodded. "So I really hope that we can remain friends for life and even call each other over the summer holidays."

"Sure," he said. "That would be nice."

New Frontiers

Gordon had taught me well. I had learnt how to break up with people nicely. I guess you could call it a life skill (or is it a death skill?). Both Tim and I knew that we would not keep in touch. The old 'let's be friends' never actually works out. It just softens the blow.

I didn't really want to say goodbye to Tim, but I knew that I had to. He was slowly destroying what little self-belief I had. Of course his absence also left a void, for I used to rely on his strength and now it was me alone. Even worse I had to face 10 weeks of summer without any direction or purpose. I pondered this problem for days until finally an idea struck me…

I ran into Reeta's room.
"Reeta! What are you doing for the summer?" I realised that I was shouting, so made a conscious effort to lower my voice as I continued: "It's just that I was wondering whether you wanted to go travelling with me for a few weeks. We could start off in Turkey and work our way backwards. What d'you think?" Reeta looked surprised and cocked her head to one side as she considered my proposition.

"I guess that would be okay, on one condition…"
"Which is?"
"That we stop off in Venice on the way back. I've always wanted to go in one of those gondolas. Anyway, how much do you think this holiday will cost?" Now there was an interesting question… cost?... and one that I hadn't yet considered. I made a few rapid mental calculations.
"Probably around £1000." I waited for her reaction. I knew that I had received some money from Uncle P's estate so

A Rampage Of Chocolate

finances wouldn't be my barrier, but I was never really sure about Reeta's situation, so I waited with baited breath.
"Okay," she said nodding her head like a wise old sage. "Give me 24 hours and I'll let you know."

I didn't have to wait 24 hours, only 4, until the knock on the door came. Reeta stood there grinning from ear to ear, world atlas in hand.
"Let's plan a holiday!"

It turned out that her father had agreed to pay for the trip. She'd sold it to him as a cultural journey from East to West and therefore cheap at half the price. Given that she was studying geography, it was relatively easy for her to persuade him to view it as a 'necessary' field trip. With promises of visits to Turkey, Venice, Austria and Paris, her Dad soon bought into the idea, giving his blessing, but, even more importantly, his money.

As we planned the journey, we added Germany to the list - just a couple of towns, but enough to get a flavour of the culture. By the next day we were ready to book our plane and train tickets. The exact timings and locations for the trip would be decided en route. With the exception of the beginning and the end, nothing else was prebooked. All accommodation would be secured on arrival and we would go wherever we wanted for as long as we wanted.

As a first-year student I had experienced a level of freedom not previously enjoyed at home. This trip promised to take me to the next level again. After all, it was a one-way plane ticket, so there were actually no guarantees that I would even come back.

Chapter 21

Gnomes and Parachutes

We flew into Istanbul at 3 o'clock in the morning. A plane chock-full of students, all looking to spread their wings and to have the ultimate backpacking experience. I stared around. It felt surreal. This was unlike any plane journey I had ever been on - this one was full of singing students, all united with a single purpose: we all had one-way tickets; we were all on an adventure. This was where it was all happening and I was right in the middle of it.

Reeta was sound asleep, oblivious, as always, to her surroundings; so comfortable in her own skin. She never tried to please. She simply did things because she wanted to. I admired her honesty and strength.

As I sat, wiling away the time, I also started admiring the strength of one of the guys in front. He was particularly striking with his ginger hair, dark brown eyes, broad grin

Gnomes and Parachutes

and muscly frame. Still, this wasn't the time to be seeking boyfriends. Reeta and I were on an adventure and there was only room for 2!

By 4 o'clock in the morning we were all sat in a park in the middle of Istanbul. A group of students huddled together for warmth, waiting for Istanbul to wake up so that we could find accommodation and embark on our separate adventures. Each of us had big plans and those plans had been thwarted by time - Istanbul was asleep even though we were raring to go! I huddled between Reeta and Gary (for that turned out to be his name). Things were looking up already!

The reality of the trip was that Reeta's dad would have approved. We took in all the sights of Istanbul from the mosque to the palace and from the old souk to the harbour, where the fishermen came in and cooked sardines on the harbour wall. The army presence, whilst somewhat intimidating, was also very reassuring. We felt safe. Our accommodation was not quite what we had envisaged, but it was all that we could afford (and all that was available) - a mattress on the roof of a hotel overlooking the mosque. It turned out that half of the other students from the plane had the same budget, since they were sharing the rooftop with us. As darkness fell on the first night, I watched as someone with bright ginger hair came up the stairs, carrying a mattress. It was Gary. I waved at him. He nodded back and headed towards us, plonking his mattress down beside me and Reeta. We had flown so far and yet it already felt like such a small world.

The rest of our holiday went without any such meetings. It seemed that everyone left in separate directions from

A Rampage Of Chocolate

Istanbul. We were heading for Venice and our first train ride was due to take 16 hours. It was a particularly packed train and clearly very popular. We were herded into a carriage and it was only when the train started going that Reeta and I had a chance to take in our travelling companions. It seemed we had joined a particularly rustic Turkish family. The man in the seat facing me sat down and promptly took his shoes and socks off, sharing the full extent of his bodily odours and flaky skin. I reeled in horror as he placed his feet on the part of the seat between me and Reeta, but in true British fashion, I said nothing. He was a particularly grotesque looking man - rather gnomish in his appearance, with his bare feet, white beard and ridiculously bulbous nose. By the end of the journey I felt familiar with all of his bodily smells and functions, for he shared them so liberally en route! I had expected to see many sights on this holiday, but a flatulent, Turkish gnome was not one of them!

Part way through the journey he got a camping stove out and proceeded to cook a 2 course meal for his family, the remnants of which were left for all to see on the floor. Every time we left the carriage to go to the toilet, it was like walking on a bed of rice. We still had 14 hours left of this journey, so I felt the best way to tackle this situation was to sleep (for as long as possible).

By 6am I could sleep no more. The jolting of the train, the smell of the carriage and the noise of the occupants was not conducive to sleep. I was surrounded by 5 snoring bodies. Even Reeta it seemed had felt to join in the soporific chorus with the gnome, his wife and his 2 sons. I decided to face the rest of the morning awake. My plan was to freshen up and then immerse myself in a good book - at least until Reeta woke up. With that in mind I trotted off to the toilet cubicle with my toothbrush.

I should have realised from the smell that this wasn't going to be a good experience, however nothing could have prepared me for the extent of the challenge ahead. It appeared that the toilet flap (the flap that released the waste onto the track) had jammed sometime in the early evening. About 40 people in the carriage had used the toilet since then, so it was full. Literally. Every time the train juddered, the contents slopped over the edge. There was no way to get to the other carriages because the connecting doorways were all blocked with luggage (health and safety was not exactly a priority on this train). It was a case of face the challenge or explode!

I assessed the situation for a minute or two and felt that there were 3 main strategies: The first was just to sit, although admittedly this was never really a serious option since the thought of the contents washing against my naked bottom was just too much to bear. The second was to straddle the entire toilet - a risky strategy since it would place my lower legs close to the offending article and it would only take one large jolt for a tsunami to engulf my legs and feet. So that left the third and only viable option: to stand on the seat and aim from above. With the floor and seat already awash this appeared to be the only safe way. So very carefully, I tiptoed across all the clean areas of floor and climbed up on to the seat, a foot on either side. I reassured myself that this was no different to using it as an 'Asian toilet' and therefore was perfectly acceptable on a Turkish train.

The trouble with plans is that there are always shortcomings if you don't consider all the pitfalls. There were 2 things that I had forgotten to consider: my height and my balance. The

A Rampage Of Chocolate

first pitfall became obvious as I climbed up and ran out of room, thus forcing me to hunch over whilst my arms pressed against the walls for stability. The second pitfall was not an issue until the train screeched to an unexpected halt, at which point I was catapulted forward (along with part of the contents of the toilet).

The end result was that I squelched my way back to the carriage and removed my shoes. If you can't beat 'em, join 'em!

So at 3pm, very tired and with soggy, smelly, rice-covered shoes, we arrived in Venice. The prospect of a gondola or an ice cream did not appeal; just that of a warm shower, a comfy bed and a decent meal!

Venice, Austria and Munich came and went. By now 4 weeks had gone by and I was starting to miss the madness of home. The freedom I had sought didn't really exist because actually we were bound by money and train times. We had tasted Turkey with all its' eastern promise; had enjoyed Venice (although it brought back memories of punting on the Cam); and had spent a week in Austria sampling the delicacies of strudel, goulash soup and hot chocolate. We had walked up mountains and enjoyed the views; sat under blankets in horse-drawn carriages; and had been tobogganing down salt mines. In Germany we laughed our way around the Munich museum of modern art (often tilting our heads upside down to try and work out what the artist had painted) and then cried our way around Dachau, the old concentration camp. Now we were on our way to Freiberg and were ready for a rest.

Gnomes and Parachutes

We arrived at 1.30pm on Saturday afternoon to find that everything had shut for the weekend. It was a beautiful day, so I looked at Reeta and suggested, "Let's top up our tans."
"But where?"
"I don't know. Somewhere hidden, that way we can get rid of all our strap marks."
"Let's try over there." Reeta pointed to a cornfield with a path beside it.
"Okay. Let's see where it goes."
We followed the path for what seemed like forever and waded through corn fields until we came to a grassy field a long way out of town. We looked around, but could see nothing but crops and grass.
"Perfect!"

Our bikinis were at the hostel, so we stripped down to our knickers.
"Wake me up when it's dinner time," I said.
"Can't guarantee it, but I'll try," Reeta replied yawning.
We lay back, enjoying the solitude and the warmth of the sun on our bodies. I soon fell asleep, dreaming of the chaos of home... Mum's unique fashion sense, her ever-escalating platform shoes and her appalling choice in men. Images came and went too quickly to capture, the only consistent thing was the whirring sound of...
"ANNIE WAKE UP!" Reeta was screaming at me, pulling me from side to side. "Look up Annie! Look up!"
Initially I couldn't see anything because the sun was in my eyes. Then I saw some black blurs. I rubbed and tried to focus my eyes... 2 parachutists were descending into our field! I stared, bewildered, a mild panic setting in. A barrage of confused thoughts ran through my head: Were

A Rampage Of Chocolate

we under attack? Was this some extreme form of policing? Was toplessness really such a crime in Germany? I had heard of manna from heaven but never men from heaven. This didn't feel heaven sent. This was no chocolate box moment. Reeta jolted me out of my frozen state.

"Annie what are you doing? Get up! Let's go!"

We grabbed our clothes and ran, putting on an item with every stride. By the time we reached the roadside we were howling with laughter and relief. I looked at Reeta - her T-shirt was back to front and her shorts were inside out. I hadn't fared much better. With labels and seams showing, we ran through the fields towards town, where we headed for the nearest bar. Cocktails in hand I turned to her…

"Shall we go home tomorrow? I think I've had enough."

"But what about Paris and lunch in front of the Eiffel tower?" she asked.

"All I want is to go home and see my Mum and to have lunch with her."

"Me too," she grinned. We clinked our glasses together, giggled and said with one voice

"Home!"

We may not have made it to Paris and the holiday hadn't quite gone as we'd planned, but it was still the breath of fresh air that we had both needed; a step of independence and courage. By the time we reached home, we were looking forward to comfortable beds and clean showers, home-cooking and a big hug. My Mum had never said 'I love you', but she did the day I arrived home; not in words but in her enormous smile.

Chapter 22

All Prepared

Life, it seems, is a strange beast with twists and turns at every corner. After my holiday I spent 2 weeks at home, before returning to university to start as a second-year student. My first outing on the first night was to the student union; 4 of us went. No agenda, we just wanted to get back into the swing. I had only been there for half an hour when one person stood out from the entire crowd. A person with bright ginger hair; his name was Gary and I had met him in Turkey.

We spotted each other at the same time and he came bowling over.
"I never did ask you where you went to Uni. I guess that's here then?"
"I guess you're right."
"Mind if I join you?"
And join me he did, for the next 2 years; through the highs

All Prepared

and lows of exams and dissertations; through far-too-many hangovers. He was kind and supportive and fun to be with. He told me he loved me in our second week and that was it: my heart was transferred to his ownership. Without meaning to, I gave him unlimited rights to make or break my heart.

This time I allowed my mind to wander. Those 3 little words gave me the confidence to plan to the end. I had visions of mini-Garys and mini-mes. The mini-Garys all had mops of ginger hair and were sitting in muddy puddles, making mud and worm pies. The mini-mes were princesses regaled in pink finery, sitting eating boxes of chocolates. I saw us into old age, caked with wrinkles, but still in love and smiling, grandchildren knocking around our feet. It was a dream I know, but to me it blurred into reality.

It was all going so well, or so it seemed, until the final term of my final year. He went off to Glastonbury to run a beer tent. I waved off a loving boyfriend, the man I wanted to spend my hopes and dreams with, and 5 days later I received back someone so distant that I hardly recognised him as the same man.

Whilst I had been back at the halls, missing him so dreadfully, he had been… Well… You can guess. The temptation was there: so much alcohol; so much attention from so many women. I didn't see it coming.

Soon after he returned, he took me out for dinner. He held my hands across the table and asked me to be his friend for life. The demotion was completed. I had been relegated. The pieces of my heart and my hopes and dreams lay shattered on the floor.

2 weeks later I left university alone. Completely alone.

During my final term I secured a highly-paid graduate job in ABTEX, the oil company, even though I had no understanding of this cut-throat industry. I was released into the big wide world, officially stamped by the university system as 'qualified' and 'suitable for senior positions'. I had survived the process and had come out on the other side. Now I was supposed to be destined for the top.

The truth was very different: I was a completely naïve, broken-hearted, 21 year-old woman, with experience in waitressing and catastrophes. I had no foundation and no self-worth. My achievements were academic and my list of failures was long. In a desperate bid for acceptance and validation I had tied myself to many anchors, but all of them had come loose. I was adrift. The familiar words from my childhood came to mind:

"READY OR NOT, HERE I COME!"

The TRANSITION TO WOMANHOOD...

Chapter 23

A Fresh Start

I sat in the car park, my heart pounding. This was it - my first day at ABTEX. This was my hope, my future. This was the new start that I had longed for. I had a chance to reinvent myself; a chance to achieve; a chance to put my hurts behind me and start afresh. No-one here knew my past mistakes. All they knew was my potential. They believed that I was capable of good things.

"I can do this!" I kept repeating to myself. "I can do this! They chose me for a reason. They saw something special in me and I am going to prove to them that this was the best choice they ever made!" Over and over I repeated this mantra. "Right! Here goes…" I got out of my car and started the long ascent from the basement car park to the reception.

"Breathe… Breathe… Breathe…" I was concentrating really hard, trying to lower my heart rate. If someone were to take

A Fresh Start

my blood pressure now, I was sure that the pump would explode. I was so distracted that I didn't notice the small metal kerb at the door. I went over on my ankle. "Aagh!" I suppressed a scream and limped through the archway into the reception, trying to feign a smile.

"Can I help you dear?" a small lady with pinched features enquired from behind a large, circular marble desk.
"Yes. My name is Anne Booth. I'm here to see Seymour Sharp. It's my first day." She looked me up and down (perhaps admiring my new suit?). I had hoped for some warmth, something to put me at ease, but I guess all her efforts were tied up with negotiating her way around her ginormous desk.
"Go and sit over there with the others. Mr Sharp will be with you shortly." With that, her hand appeared above the counter, pointing over to my left. At least, I assume it was her hand, but I couldn't be completely sure because it only just peeked over the counter, as did her head. Since I couldn't actually see any connecting arms or body, it was impossible to know whether the head and hands really belonged to the same person. It was somewhat like a magical illusion, where the different parts of the body become separated and float over a black curtain. I wondered whether there really was a whole lady behind this desk or actually a puppeteer with a head and a hand on sticks. I lingered for a moment, waiting for proof either way, half expecting a man to appear at any moment. He didn't. Still, amused by that thought I made my way over to the area that she'd indicated.

There were 3 black, leather sofas, each one supporting a rather nervous-looking person. None of them were talking. They were all just examining their fingernails and shoes.
"Are you here for Seymour Sharp too?" I asked in my most

A Rampage Of Chocolate

upbeat voice. They all nodded. No sound. Just nodding. "Right!" I said quietly. Another approach was clearly required. I held out my hand to body number 1. "I'm Anne Booth, although most people call me Annie." No answer, just a nod. Clearly I needed to force the issue. "And you are?"
"Jonathan Saunders. People call me Sandy."
"Not Sandra then!" I guffawed and then noticed the horrified expression on his face. Right, moving swiftly on (and feeling my cheeks going a little red)...
"Matthew Pratt. Matt for short." I shook his hand making a very specific effort not to comment this time!
"Simon Fisher." He beamed at me, clearly relieved for the interaction (and possibly amused at my faux pas with Sandy. I decided to plonk myself down next to him; it was after all the friendliest sofa. Unfortunately that placed me opposite a still-rather-huffy Sandy.

There was an awkward silence... I fell in with the group behaviour and studied my fingernails until there was nothing more to study. Then I moved on to my feet. I gasped in horror. I had been so nervous when getting ready that I had put on odd shoes. What was even worse was that one shoe was smooth, dark blue, with a 2 inch heel and the other was textured, black, with a low heel. No wonder I had fallen over! I crossed my feet and tucked them as far under the chair as I could. Anyway that's the way that ladies are supposed to sit. (At last my St E's training had found a use!)

To take my mind off my predicament and to raise people's gazes away from the floor (and therefore my shoes), I broke the silence again. I asked the 3 guys about their universities, their degree courses and their families. (I wasn't really interested, but it was a start point). After 5 minutes hard labour the conversation was flowing freely. Sandy, it appeared, had forgiven me and no-one was looking at their feet anymore. As a result of this shift of focus my terrible shoe error went unnoticed. 3 more people joined the group: Ellie, Doug and Toby. Doug and Toby seemed relaxed and easily joined in, but Ellie was different. With her sharp suit and harsh tongue it was quite clear that she considered herself the best and was out to win. I got the impression that she didn't like other women in the workplace; they were competition.

"So where did you say that you went to University?" she asked me.

"London."

"Which one?"

"University of East London."

"Oh!" she said in a disappointed tone. "That used to be a polytechnic didn't it?"

"Yes. Yes it did. Why is that relevant?"

"No reason..." she lied. "I'm sure it was a very different experience to mine. I attended Cambridge and particularly loved all the history and culture associated with it." Point made! She was academically taking the higher ground, setting her stall out as the supreme authority. I could see that I was going to have to watch my back.

Just then, from my position of defeat, I heard an all-too-familiar voice behind me.

"Annie! How on earth did you get here? They must have been desperate!" I froze in horror. What timing! Ellie was smiling a very big smile, clearly enjoying my further demise. "Just goes to show that they'll take anyone on nowadays!" This was one public game of tennis that I didn't want to play. I turned around.

"Hello Tim! I guess they must. After all they let you in!" Tim roared with laughter and gave me a big hug.

A Rampage Of Chocolate

"So tell me… Have you missed me?" He grinned. I just smiled and tried to divert the conversation.

"So what are you doing here then? I thought you were going off to join the MOD?" I asked him, still reeling from the shock.

"It turned out that they couldn't handle someone with my qualities."

"So you didn't get the job?"

"Erm, No. Still, I would have missed out on the highs and lows of the big bad oil world. Been working for a chap called Seymour all summer. Last week he offered to take me on permanently. Offered me the position of Area Manager; looking after petrol stations and negotiating contracts. Sounded too good an opportunity to pass up. What about you?" My heart sank.

"Exactly the same!" Looks like one of my mistakes had followed me into the workplace.

Chapter 24

Round 2 to Me!

A Rotund, balding man appeared from around the corner of the atrium.
"Morning everybody!" It was Seymour Sharp. I recognised him from my interview. "I trust you all had a good trip down last night and that you're enjoying the delights of 'The Rochester'. I hear they do a really good breakfast. Anyway, let's head on upstairs and get the formalities over with, then we can crack on with the meaty stuff!" Like a flock of sheep we all dutifully stood up and followed him around the corner and into the lift.

He led us through the open-plan office, gesticulating to various people along the way, and then ushered us into a meeting room. We each took a seat around the rectangular table. I sat between Matt and Simon. Opposite were Ellie and Sandy.

Round 2 to Me!

"I recognise that most of you have no experience of the oil industry or indeed of the position that you've been hired for. However that does not matter because we can teach you everything that you need to know. What is more important to ABTEX is that we recruit the highest calibre people, so that we can succeed in becoming the number 1 oil company in the next 3 years."

I watched Ellie shuffle in her seat and sit a little prouder. Clearly the concept of being recognised as someone of the 'highest calibre' sat well with her.

"With that in mind, we are going to put you through an intensive 6-week training program, at the end of which, we wish you each to make a 10-minute presentation to the board of directors. This is an opportunity that most people don't ever get in their careers, so consider yourselves VERY fortunate. If you make a good impression with the board then the world will be your oyster. Any questions?" Everyone shook their head, so he carried on and outlined for us the 6-week training program. It appeared daunting, but fun. It covered serious issues such as tenant law and anti-cartel practices, whilst also incorporating more practical elements, such as working behind the console on a petrol station and selling oil on the forecourt.

By 4pm we were free to go and returned to *The Rochester* ready to prepare for a formal meal with senior management. With instructions to meet in the bar at 7pm for 'pre-dinner cocktails', I retreated to my room to relax in the bath.

I rang Mum.

"Guess where I am?"

"The Ritz?" she said sarcastically.

"No! I'm lying in a bath full of bubbles. This hotel is so posh

A Rampage Of Chocolate

that they even have phones and TV screens in the bathroom! I'm just taking some time out to get ready and then I'm off to dinner with all the Senior Management of ABTEX! My room here is awesome. They've even put a chocolate on my bed! And when I was out, someone came in and folded my sheet back! How amazing is that?"
"Oh, Annie! I'm so proud of you! How did your first day go?" My head filled with visions of Ellie and Tim, but I didn't want to concern her, so I just said,
"Great! It was great."

It took a while to pick my outfit. I discarded the idea of my white skirt (too short); discounted my blue trousers (too casual); briefly considered my long red dress (too formal); and so settled for a mid-length black number with a dusting of sequins.

Now for the hair... Up or down? Up looked nice but formal, great for work (but this was work and therein lay the dilemma) and down looked great, if a little casual. I couldn't decide, so I opted for a mixture of both - a small chignon with the rest of my hair loose.

Make-up. Mmmmm. Understated or dramatic? I looked at my watch... I had 5 minutes left. Understated would have to do! I finished off with a squirt of perfume, grabbed my bag and got into the lift. Sandy got in on the floor below, so we entered the bar together. I spotted Seymour sitting at a table and went over to join him.

"What would you like?" he said, handing me the cocktail menu. I read the names in horror. I could hardly ask my new boss for *Sex on the beach* (or worse). So I scanned down and opted for the first sensible name I came to.

Round 2 to Me!

"A *pina colada* please."

"Me too!" Sandy requested with relief. Clearly he had suffered from the same dilemma.

Pina colada seemed to be the favoured option as each person arrived, with the exception of Ellie who turned up last. She had clearly chosen the dramatic option on all fronts. Her black cocktail dress was figure hugging, her eye make-up was heavy but seductive and her bright red lipstick reminded me of Mum.

"I'd like a *Slippery Nipple,* if that's Okay". She smiled coquettishly. Seymour blushed.

"Certainly." He hurried off to the bar.

Other members of the Senior Management Team started to arrive. Ellie made a beeline for the most influential one and started to hold court. Whilst I couldn't hear the whole conversation, I just heard snippets like:

"Of course at Cambridge University I…" and, "There are always lots of choices when you get a first as I did. Second degrees are so common…"

I looked at their faces (clearly something that she had failed to do) and realised that they were unimpressed. I imagine that they had seen it all before. However, in good British tradition, they smiled politely and allowed her to continue.

The Maître D appeared and ushered us into a private function room - the *Walsingham Suite*. A large table was set out, dressed in a white, linen cloth and decked with purple flowers. There were no place cards so I just sat down. Doug was to my left but the seat to my right was empty. I looked at my place setting and there was no bread roll on my side plate. I turned to Doug and whispered,

A Rampage Of Chocolate

"D'you reckon it'd be okay if I took this roll? No-one's sitting there."
"Yeah. Go for it," he consented. So I did. I reached over to my right and took the spare roll, just as Peter Hughes, The Personnel Director, entered the room and headed for the empty seat. I was caught red-handed.
"I-I-I…" I stuttered,
"Don't worry. Help yourself. I never eat the roll anyway. Trying to watch the old weight!" he laughed, patting his tummy. I smiled both in gratitude and as a way of apology. "Anyway, I always knew that you'd be trouble! That's why we hired you. You had a spark inside of you and we figured we needed some fires lit!" Wow! Praise indeed (I think).

The rest of the meal went reasonably smoothly, the only incident being when I knocked over the wine (thankfully it went over Doug not Peter). Ellie grimaced, shrugged her shoulders and then carried on - a clear reference to the fact that she thought I had let myself down. It annoyed me that I had given her the satisfaction.

I don't count the 'green bean situation' as an incident. It could have happened to anyone! I was talking to Peter about my aspirations in life and listening to his, when I paused to prepare my next mouthful. I used all of my St E's training, ensuring that I applied my best table manners. Sadly, what they hadn't prepared me for was the independent will of the green bean. I delicately loaded my fork with some lamb and potato, and then spent a lot of effort bending a green bean in two so that it would fit onto the prongs. As I lifted the fork into my mouth, the green bean decided it preferred to be straight. It uncurled from the fork just as I placed it into my mouth causing it to suddenly reappear, and hence leaving me facing The Personnel Director with a green 'tongue'

Round 2 to Me!

hanging out. He pretended not to notice and I pretended to cough so that I could pop it back in with my hand. I caught sight of Ellie smirking out of the corner of my eye.

I stood up at the end of the meal, very full and a little tipsy. Many people returned to the bar, but I was tired, so I retreated to my room for the night. Another relaxing bath, a chocolate and TV in bed. Then I settled down to sleep. Just before I did, I found myself praying, unloading the trouble of my day:
"Dear God, please help me! I'm always such a disaster. Ellie hates me already and is making me feel like a failure. I'm already struggling to feel good enough and this is only day 1. I really want to do well here. Please help me. That's all. Amen." With that I fell fast asleep…

Bang! Bang! Bang! went the door at 2 in the morning. I woke sleepily. Bang! Bang! Bang!
"Huh? What? Who? What time is it? 2 o'clock!" Even I knew that you don't go opening your hotel bedroom door at 2 in the morning just because someone is knocking.
"GO AWAY!" I shouted and pulled the duvet over my head. Bang! Bang! Bang! Okay, now I was curious, if a little cross. I got out of bed and went over to the door. I looked through the spy-hole. There was no-one there. Bang! Bang! Bang! At this point my curiosity got the better of me. I opened the door…

A very naked Ellie was crouching on the ground. As I opened the door she marched in and plonked herself down on my bed. I threw her a towel.
"I can't believe it! I only got up to go for a wee and I went out of the wrong door. I only realised when the door shut behind me and then I was trapped! My only option was to

A Rampage Of Chocolate

inch my way along the corridor, get in the lift and come up to your room. Thankfully no-one else saw me or got in the lift!" I stifled a laugh, but clearly not well enough. "IT'S NOT FUNNY!"

"But why my room?" I asked.

"Because you're the only woman here! I can hardly go knocking on the doors of one of the guys, now can I? I just wish that you hadn't been 2 floors up!" Even in her vulnerable state she was still patronising.

"I guess not. Do you want me to ring down to reception and ask them to let you into your room?"

"Please!" So I did and off she went, clad only in a towel, with not a 'Thank you!' in sight.

I got back into bed and smiled. "Maybe life isn't so bad after all!"

Chapter 25

The Presentation

I woke up with the tune *Naked* swirling around my head. I smiled as the memories of the previous night's events came flooding back. I knew that I could go to work today with no fear of Ellie. All I needed to do was to hum that tune and she would be putty in my hands. So I put on my new suit and went to work.

Ellie was subdued and less arrogant that morning, so I made a point of being particularly nice to her. She kept viewing me with suspicious eyes, clearly waiting for me to publicly reveal last night's embarrassing mistake. I didn't. So when it was coffee-break and we found ourselves alone standing by the sinks in the toilets, I approached the subject.
"Ellie? About last night…" Her hackles immediately went up.
"What about it?" she snapped. I continued gently, ignoring her tones.

The Presentation

"I want you to know that it will just be between us. I have no intention of telling the others."

"Oh! Thank you. I appreciate that," she said, clearly relieved; her whole demeanour relaxing and softening. I continued, "I think we got off on the wrong foot yesterday and I would like us to start over again." By now she was smiling and warmth was beginning to flow towards me.

"I'd like that too."

"Great!" We shook hands; the deal was done. Arch-enemy number 1 had been neutralised.

After that I was able to throw myself fully into the 6 week program knowing that all I needed to worry about was Tim. He clearly still harboured a torch for me, but didn't know how to shine it appropriately. Instead he manifested it in the only way that he knew how - with put downs. Whenever the opportunity presented itself he would jump in and tease me, mercilessly and in public. He didn't seem to treat anyone else that way, just me. That's how I knew he liked me.

The most humiliating instance was in the classroom. We were all sitting at our tables whilst Ian, the trainer, provided us with an overview of ABTEX's international portfolio. He kept referring to *Benelux*. I turned to Tim, who was sitting to my left, and asked,

"Where is Benelux?" He smiled.

"I don't know. Why don't you ask him?" So I did; out loud for all to hear.

"Excuse me please. Where exactly is *Benelux*, only I have never heard of it?" Ian looked surprised but the rest of the class (lead by Tim) roared with laughter at my ignorance.

"That would be Belgium, Netherlands and Luxembourg," Ian replied, stifling a giggle. It took the class 5 minutes to recover their poise; it took me longer to recover my reputation.

Thankfully I made very few mistakes in the first few weeks so Tim's opportunities were scarce. I purposely sat as far away from him as possible, but whenever I looked up I would always find him staring at me. It was so hard to know what to do.

Finally, at the end of 6 weeks, the opportunity came to present to the Board of Directors. We had each been given a topic; mine was: 'ways to improve petrol sales though the forecourt'. I was given the directive that it could be as radical as I liked. It was my opportunity to shine, but equally it was my reputation that was at stake. I had found it hard to conceptualise new ideas that would transform what was actually a very dirty, smelly process, but I took what I had and entered the boardroom clutching my acetates in my hand.

We all sat at the horseshoe-style table whilst we each took it in turn to present. Sandy went first. He was very nervous; I could see the beads of sweat running down his forehead as he presented his new concepts for staff uniforms. His choice of colours - pink and black- reflected the corporate tones. Although his design concept left something to be desired - bright pink T-shirts with 'ABTEX' written across the chest. I couldn't help making the comparison with *Highpoints* and the ridiculous uniform that I had been made to wear. After 5 minutes, the directors started to shuffle in their seats, clearly unimpressed. The sweat ran faster down his face, closely followed by his colour. He rocked backwards and forwards, before fainting in a heap on the floor, along with his career. The pressure of the event had clearly proved too much.

The Presentation

I watched Doug's presentation on his master plan for oil sales. I thought he had been innovative and his acetates were stunning (it helps when your degree was in graphic design). When he opened up the floor for questions Derek Bootle smiled, leant forward and then tore his ideas to shreds. Clearly this was a tougher audience than I had anticipated.

Ellie was confidant and succinctly presented her ideas to incentivise staff. The central concept of her plan involved a revised set of disciplinary procedures to address failure and a Secret Squirrel approach using a team of mystery motorists. At the end of it Peter Hughes offered his opinion:
"You've clearly researched your subject well, and prepared a thorough presentation." Ellie started to look smug. Then Peter continued… "However, I still can't help wondering if you've misread the brief?" Ellie deflated, looking puzzled.
"In what way?"
"Your brief clearly states that we were looking for incentives not punishments. I accept that in the way you've presented you may achieve the same end result," Ellie started to smile nervously with relief, thinking that she had at least attained the right outcome, "however staff turnover would probably go through the roof if we implemented your suggested plan and that would drive up our costs." Her relief turned to disappointment as she acknowledged defeat.

I was up next. Suddenly my flaky propositions didn't seem quite so appealing. This was going to be a long 10 minutes and a very short career! Still, I stood up and walked towards the hangman's noose (tripping over the projector cable as I made my approach). I stood behind the projector, placed my first acetate on the glass, switched the machine on and smiled - as did all my audience.

"M-my r-remit was to find ways to improve p-petrol sales through the forecourt." My voice was trembling. "I felt that this was an almost impossible task, unless we revisit the whole forecourt experience. So that is exactly what I've tried to do." I looked at their faces. They were riveted and smiling. It gave me the strength and confidence to carry on, all trembling gone. This was going far better than I had hoped.

"Most people don't like filling up their cars with fuel. Why? Because forecourts are dirty and smelly. Petrol is expensive and you can't even see it going into your car. You just have to trust that it's happened. Then to add insult to injury you have to stand out in the cold with nothing to look at. Children don't like it either because it is a time of waiting. Children and boredom do not mix. We cannot just market petrol on price; we need to find a way to be different - A unique selling point." They were still mesmerised as I changed to the next acetate. That is all except Tim. He was gesticulating wildly to me with his hands. Now I was really annoyed with him. Was his need for my attention so great that he was even willing to sabotage this chance for me to shine? I ignored him, and continued. "Okay. So if that is the problem, what is the solution?"

I placed my picture of the future on the glass, puffing my chest out in a triumphant stance. Doug and Sandy hid their heads in their hands. Tim grimaced. The rest of the table were transfixed. "Let's make it interactive! Let's show the customer and children what is really going on! You can see here," I said pointing to my picture, "that I have replaced the white side panels of the pump with glass so that everyone can see what is happening. The hoses are clear too, and I have

The Presentation

dyed the unleaded fuel green and the diesel purple to make it more colourful." I surveyed my audience. There was nothing but smiles, so I carried on. Radical was obviously good. "We can make this as interactive or extreme as cost will allow by adding strawberry or mint scent and even sparkles. I have introduced television screens on the forecourt to entertain the person refuelling. This will enable us to sell to them whilst they are standing there. It will also provide us with an additional income stream from advertising. I recognise that this may all appear very radical, but I've tried to find a new way of presenting our main product. I believe that this revolutionary approach will ensure that ABTEX forecourts are the forecourts of choice!

Now at this point I would like to take any questions." There was a stunned silence. Peter Hughes eventually broke the ice.

"I think I can speak for the whole board, when I say that you have given us a truly stunning presentation, and one which we won't readily forget! It was also a totally unique and original approach to retailing petrol. Thank you." There was a ripple of laughter around the table. No questions? Wow! That was unheard of. I returned to my seat, secure in the knowledge that my ideas had been well received. I had outperformed my colleagues and my fast-track career was assured.

We all stopped for a coffee break. As we left the room Matt, the tall, dark-haired assistant to the Chairman, whispered in my ear,

"Of course standing behind the projector is never a good idea." I looked perplexed. Simon tried to elaborate by making the image of bosoms with his hands. Still bemused, but starting to feel quite uneasy, I turned to Tim. He couldn't even look me in the eye.

"It was a great presentation Annie. It was just... Just that..."

"Go on... Spit it out!"

"Well you stood behind the projector!" Now his eyes were imploring me to understand, but I didn't.

"So?"

"So, they didn't listen to your presentation Annie. They weren't smiling at your ideas; they were smiling at your boobs. The huge image of your boobs that was on the screen! And when you put the final acetate up and stood up really straight... Well... The image was REALLY impressive."

"Oh!" It was all I could say; it was all that could be said. I knew that my credibility was on the floor. My legs felt weak. Tim held me in a reassuring hug. Suddenly I didn't feel like an adult anymore. I rested my head on his shoulder.

"It's okay," he whispered. "Everything's going to be okay." I wanted to believe him. I looked up into his eyes and I saw strength - a force that I needed to uphold me right at this very moment and maybe longer.

Chapter 26

Launched

The next day I dreaded going into the office. However I shouldn't have worried because there was no real aftermath from my presentation; just a few titters and nudges as I walked past people. The ridicule was soon forgotten because we were all awaiting the news of our assigned territories and that was our main focus. In the next few minutes we would find out our end destination - the place where ABTEX had decided to send us. We were going to have to lay down roots in a new place and today we would find out its locality. Truro or Aberdeen? London or Manchester? So many options! All places have different characters and offer completely different lifestyles. This destination would mould my life for the next few years and the scariest thing about it all was that I had no control over that decision. My fate was completely in Seymour Sharp's hands.

Seymour ushered us into the meeting room where our

Launched

training program had first begun. We sat ourselves around the table and automatically assumed the same seats. Such creatures of habit! Seymour pulled a piece of paper out of his briefcase and beamed.

"Right ladies and gentlemen! This is the moment that you've all been waiting for; the great reveal! I will tell each of you which territory you are going to subdue for the next couple of years. Then, when we are finished here, you need to go straight to Emily Worthington, who will give you the details of the hotel that you will be staying in for the next month. Thereafter it is for you to make your own arrangements for somewhere to live. Today, you will also receive the keys to your company car, which should be parked in the basement car park. On Tuesday next week, each of you will meet your Regional Manager who will take you through the specifics of your own territory. He will be responsible for getting you set up and started. Hopefully within the fortnight you will also get to know the other Area Managers in your region so that you feel part of a team again, not too isolated. So exciting times! Are you ready?" We all nodded and sat with baited breath.

"Ladies first I think… Ellie! You have 'The Fenlands'; not quite Cambridge as you requested, but it was the closest we could do. I hear it's not too marshy anymore!" He smiled at her, however it was not reciprocated. The Fenlands was clearly not the cultured city area that she had hoped for. Seymour ignored her reaction and continued. "Your Regional Manager is Mark Parry."

"Anne! You'll be pleased to hear that you have got exactly what you asked for. You requested 'North', so we have assigned you Newcastle." I gulped. That was definitely NOT

A Rampage Of Chocolate

what I had asked for. Now Seymour was looking to me for a response.

"That's erm… That's slightly further north than I was expecting." Seymour looked quizzical. "You see, when I said 'North' I meant 'north of the M25'. Milton Keynes or somewhere like that." There was a ripple of laughter around the table. Seymour laughed it off with a,

"I guess you'll be more specific in future! Anyway, you'll love it up there. Newcastle is great. Your Regional Manager is Mark Pricklethwaite."

He then continued around the table: Matt got North London, which was where he already lived, so he was thrilled; Simon got South London (including Twickenham, the home of Rugby) so he beamed; Toby was dispatched to Devon and Doug to Nottingham. Then it was Tim's turn. I wasn't really sure what I wanted this outcome to be. Did I want him near me or did I want him on the other side of the planet? Seymour decided for me.

"Tim, how could I refuse your request? You've got Teesside and Darlington." Tim grinned and looked at me. (My geography wasn't good so I was none the wiser. Seymour helped me out). "So you'll be in the same region as Anne." I gasped. Tim was going to be on the adjacent area to me! We were going to be on the same team. But that wasn't fair; I hadn't yet sorted out how I felt about him. One minute I found him totally infuriating, hating the way he belittled me and other times I just melted in his strength. I felt a connection to him, but was it a good one? Everyone knows that if you touch the wrong wire you make a connection, but you still get electrocuted.

My train of thought was broken by the next sentence from Seymour.

Launched

"Sandy. Your area is not yet vacant, so we are putting you on a special project until it is. You will be working with me here in Head Office." Sandy's face fell. We all knew what that meant. He had failed the test and had been stamped 'Reject'. To be disposed of safely, with minimal fuss. He tried to smile bravely.

"Right! Off you go. Emily will be waiting to see you. Good luck everybody. I expect to hear great things!"

I pushed my chair back and walked around the table towards the door, hugging Sandy on my way out. I knew that I was unlikely to see him again.

Newcastle, it appeared, was a long way past Milton Keynes. 3½ hours past to be precise! I remember looking at the sign on the motorway, wishing that I had been more specific in my request to ABTEX. I saw the sign marked *Watford Gap* and remembered that it was a division between the North and South. Today was the day that I was going to move north of the Watford Gap. That felt like a big move. It felt more of a canyon than a gap, and I wasn't ready to cross it just yet; so I stopped for lunch.

I grabbed a tray and slid my way along the selection of food. Hot or cold? Definitely hot! I needed comfort food. Bacon and eggs? Not quite the right time; too late on in the day. Roast chicken? I looked at it. It was very dry and the roast potatoes were too rubbery. Shepherd's Pie? Maybe… Spaghetti Bolognese? Definitely! I grabbed a bottle of diet coke and a big slice of carrot cake to finish off; paid and then made my way over to a table.

A Rampage Of Chocolate

It is a funny experience eating on your own in a public place. It feels uncomfortable and unnatural. Tables always have 2 seats, so it always looks like someone is missing. You feel scrutinised because there is no one to shield you. I craved a long, leisurely lunch, a time to enjoy my meal and to reflect on things left behind. However when I actually sat there I felt too much of a spectacle, too vulnerable, so I decided to eat up as fast as I could and then get on with my journey. The spaghetti was overcooked, so slipped down nicely. I went for speed-sucking rather than refined twirling. No-one could really see me because I had sat on the seat facing the window.

When I had finished I got up, put my tray on the rack (years of waitressing had trained me well) and walked through the restaurant towards the door. The lorry drivers stared at me as I went; in fact I turned quite a few heads in the restaurant that day. I had dressed up nicely for my journey, choosing to wear my smartest business suit. It was a strange choice for travelling in I know, but to me it was significant - it reflected my transition from student to businesswoman. I knew that when I crossed over this North/South border, I was going to enter a new phase of my life. There were no more courses to enjoy, no more safety in numbers. I was going to be on my own, and even more importantly, I was going to be accountable.

The admiring glances gave me a rush of confidence in my new status. I held my head up high, striding with authority towards my car. I breathed in the air - the last southern snort for a while - and opened my door. I switched the radio on. They were playing *Naked*. I remembered the transformation of events with Ellie and smiled. This song was a reminder

Launched

to me that things were certainly improving. I was finding my feet in this new world and this was the next leg of my journey. One final adjustment to my appearance and then I would be ready to embrace it. I rummaged in the glove compartment for my lipstick and pulled my mirror across to apply it. I stared at my reflection in disbelief, willing the orange spaghetti sauce that surrounded my mouth to disappear! I looked like some grotesque clown with a smeared orange mouth. All I needed was a few juggling meatballs and the image would have been complete!

I had assumed that the attentive glances were a sign of admiration, when actually people were simply staring. I dug deep inside myself and laughed.
"Just one last disaster for old times sake eh?" I said to myself in the mirror. Then I turned the engine on and started to drive, leaving the south behind me with all my mistakes. This was a new start and a new beginning. From now on I resolved to prove to everybody what I was worth.

Chapter 27

The Newcastle Circuit

The first two weeks were a whirl of activity. No sooner was I settled into the hotel, than Mark Pricklethwaite was there to whisk me off on a tour of my 'patch', introducing me to all of my customers. These ranged from the oil-covered tenant with a back street garage to the Managing Director of a PLC. It was a heady mix and I found it hard to get my bearings. At the end of the first week he left me alone to, as he put it,
"Get on with the job." The question was where to begin?

I decided to go around all of my petrol stations again and have an in-depth meeting with the owners and tenants of each one. The first meetings with Mark had all been very affable, but these next ones seemed to have a different flavour. Each person was trying to size me up, with questions like:
"So what exactly are you going to do for us? The last guy

did diddly-squat, so what makes you any different?" And then there was,

"No-one's been able to deal with this in the last 4 years, maybe you can? But I doubt it." and,

"I've been in this industry for 20 years. What experience do you have?"

I was flummoxed and shocked by their questioning. It appeared that I was straight in at the deep end. My answer to them all was the same:

"I'm not going to make any empty promises to you. If I say that I am going to do something, then I will do it. All I ask is the opportunity to be given a chance, so that you can judge me on my own results. If you work with me then I will work with you." That seemed to put out most of the fires (for the short term at least).

With every visit I gained an armful of unresolved paperwork. By the time the second week was at an end, I returned back to my hotel room and was overwhelmed with a sea of white paper! The planning for my third week was easy - plough through the paperwork! I sat on my bed in the hotel room making phone call after phone call. By the end of the week only half of the pile was left. Now I needed to find somewhere to live. My time was running out.

I scanned the local paper for accommodation. I wasn't ready to rent a house on my own. I needed to make friends and establish a social life, so I looked for house-share opportunities. There were 3 available.

The first was like walking into an episode of *The Young Ones*. There were beer cans everywhere and disused takeaway tins on the side. Dillon (the dreadlocked ringleader) lay with

A Rampage Of Chocolate

his feet up on the arm of the sofa, whilst asking me about my situation. He showed me my room. It contained a bed with a bedside table; that was all. The decoration was also lacking, with a brown, swirled carpet, red, flock wallpaper and a single curtain half-hanging from the rail. It was an easy decision to make. No!

The second was an interesting opportunity. It turned out to be a house owned by an elderly couple, George and Reeny Brown. They had clearly got fed up with aging and were trying to inject youthfulness into their lives by letting out 3 bedrooms to people in their twenties. I was welcomed with a cup of tea, poured from a bone china teapot, and a selection of homemade cakes. The bedroom that was on offer was equally welcoming, if a little twee. The bed was dressed with a patchwork quilt and lace doyleys covered every available surface. China figurines abounded. I knew that if I lived there I would be well looked after, totally mothered (maybe even smothered), but I was on the road to adulthood and I wanted to make it. I felt that this would be a stop-off on the way. It wouldn't be progress. So I politely declined.

The last house (and my last hope) was a house-share with 3 girls: Tina, Bronwyn and Liz. They seemed pleasant enough, although it is so hard to tell on a first introduction. Tina was standing at the stove, cooking supper, wearing headphones, singing to *Dynamo Box*. I realised that she probably did have a good singing voice, if she were to take the headphones out, however on this occasion she was singing extremely flat and very loud. Bronwyn was sitting in front of the TV watching *Eastenders*; she lifted her head to me in acknowledgment and grunted. So that left Liz to show me around.

We clicked instantly. She was vibrant and exuded an

enthusiasm for life. Even as she directed me into each room she made it sound enticing because of her sheer passion, her words tumbling out of her mouth in excitement.

"So this will be your room. It's certainly big enough and Irene (she's moving out on Saturday) really enjoyed the view of the park. I'm next door and Tina's on the other side. Bronwyn's upstairs, but then she likes it that way because she is quieter than the rest of us. I'm sure that you'll fit in really well here. So what d'you think?" I looked at her beaming face and knew that I could never turn her down. This was exactly what I had been looking for.

"I think it's perfect! When can I start to move my stuff in?"

"Anytime next week. Irene's moving in with her boyfriend this weekend, so the room will be free from then."

"Great."

"Now there are 2 other residents here that you need to meet."

"Really?" I said, somewhat dubiously, wondering where they stayed.

"Yes. They are the house cats… Skitty and Skatty. They're very funny and great company." With that she opened the bathroom door wide to reveal 2 cats curled up on top of the laundry basket. "Skitty is the black and white cat, she's the ring leader, and Skatty is the grey one. She looks like butter wouldn't melt in her mouth, but she's actually very naughty."

When I left the house I was more relaxed, content in the knowledge that my accommodation was assured and it looked like I would have a ready made circle of friends. I was getting used to the musical Newcastle accent, with its undulating rhythm and was starting to enjoy the candid nature of the people. It seemed that up here people were more honest and quick to tell you what was right and what was wrong. It was refreshing.

By the time moving-in day came, I was pleased to leave the hotel behind. I felt confined and trapped in the one room. I had become stir crazy. I was looking forward to homemade food. The rich hotel food was nice for a while but it became monotonous. I craved simple foods like bangers and mash, even fish fingers and oven chips. For a whole month I had dined alone in a public restaurant with all the uncomfortable feelings which that entailed. I was looking forward to companionship. I was definitely ready to move on.

My housemates decided to celebrate my arrival with a welcome dinner of spaghetti bolognaise. I chuckled at the thought of my previous experience, but this time I was not in a hurry, so I would be able to take my time and twirl. Humiliation would not come knocking on my door twice!

After dinner, with not an orange mouth in sight, we hit the town. We all got dressed in our fancy clothing. Liz wore a red, satin shirt, short, black skirt and stiletto heels. Bronwyn was more reserved, wearing black trousers and an orange and white striped shirt. Tina, on the other hand, held nothing back, putting on an extremely short, figure-hugging, floral dress with plunge neckline front and back. Her shoes were equally daring, making my mother's choices look positively dull!

Being mid-December the temperature outside was only 1°, so I reached for my coat and scarf.

"What'ya doin' hinny?" asked Tina in her lyrical accent.
"I'm just getting ready to go out. It's cold." The others laughed and Tina wrapped an arm around my waist.
"Ah, ya southern softie! You're in Newcastle now. No-one wears coats in the Toon! Anyways, we'll not be outside for long." So I reluctantly took my coat off and braced myself for the bitter night air. It took about 10 minutes before the cold started to show - the purple, mottled effect appearing on our legs - and I began to envy Bronwyn and her choice of trousers. However we were not alone; the only people wearing coats that night were the pensioners and tourists out for a stroll. Everyone bore the same hallmarks of the cold and nobody seemed to care. As the alcohol took effect neither did I.

From bar to bar and then on to a floating nightclub, I was fully immersed into the Newcastle nightlife. It was fun and happening - a tidal wave of excitement. People were drawn to me because of my accent. They took the time to notice me. It felt nice. They never stayed to talk for very long, but I didn't care. I felt like I was making progress; like I was in the crowd, no longer on the outside.

The trouble with a tidal wave is that it always leaves debris on the beach. My debris came in the form of a hangover and a cold. Clearly I was a 'southern softie' after all and a coat was a necessary piece of clothing for me! So I lay on the sofa in my pyjamas, paracetamol beside me, tissue box in hand, enjoying the delights of my second day in my new household. I had joined the Newcastle circuit and this was the small price that I must pay.

Chapter 28

Dinner Party Delights

The first year in the house worked really well for me. On the whole we got on famously. There were of course those monthly hormonal moments when headphones proved a virtue, but otherwise our personalities gelled.

Bronie (as we like to call her) was the stabilising influence in the house. She was the one with common sense and a level-head. She organised all the cleaning and cooking rotas and looked after all the bills. She preferred her own company, so you had to pick your moments if you wanted to engage her in conversation. She would always scrutinise you first to ensure that you weren't about to waste her time, then, if suitably satisfied by her assessment, she would happily engage in any subject on a completely honest and frank level. She was quite a thinker and turned out to be the oracle of the house. If any of us needed knowledge she was always the first port of call. Her idea of a great night would be to stay

Dinner Party Delights

in with a bottle of wine and a game of Trivial Pursuits. Her boyfriend, Graham, was an infrequent visitor to the house - about once a fortnight. When he came they would spend hours playing chess. I never saw any tenderness between them, but then I was never sure if Bronie was capable of such feelings. She often reminded me of Velma in Scooby Doo; a likeable but lonely soul.

Tina was even dippier than me. She floated through life on her own little cloud. Troubles never reached her (or if they did then she didn't notice) and her sole ambition in life was to reach the weekend when she would morph into a party animal. Her current boyfriend, Greg, left a lot to be desired on the hygiene front; however he had a sweet nature like Tina and seemed to hover on his own personal cloud too. (Unfortunately that cloud always seemed to float on by the bathroom)! I often visualised them sailing down the aisle in their wedding apparel, side by side on their clouds, holding hands and waving at the world as they floated on by. I enjoyed Tina's company very much. She was always so refreshingly light. There was no danger of ever getting sucked into any depth of conversation with her; she made me feel profound!

Liz was a hybrid of Bronie and Tina, level-headed but full of fun. Her brown wavy hair kind of summed her up: she was curvy to look at and her mood swings went up and down, although they never spiralled out of control. She was always up for the next challenge; always looking for something new. First it was parachuting then bungee jumping and finally scuba-diving (although I feel her interest there was more fuelled by the instructor than the sport).

For me, being in the house was a natural fit. These were the sort of friends that I would have chosen for myself and they proved a welcome distraction from work (which was not so natural). Most weekends we went out together, under the understanding that I needed my coat. The hangovers were less now because my tolerance for alcohol had improved. (Not sure that was a good thing). I was accepted on the circuit and most people knew me by sight or by name, however I had failed to make any connection on the romance front. Somehow there was always something about me that the guys didn't quite gel with. I tried various tactics to make myself more appealing (different types of clothing, new types of conversation, smoking, not smoking, heavy make-up, light make-up etc). I even studied football for a time in the hopes that it would help me to make a connection, but all I discovered was that I REALLY don't like the game. I used to look around the bars and clubs at all of the other women and wonder what they had that I didn't. Why was I so different?

One December afternoon Liz burst into my bedroom.
"I'm organizing a Christmas dinner party and I'm inviting a man that I think would be ABSOLUTELY PERFECT for you!"
"Really? When? Who?"
"I was thinking of next weekend. I'm hoping that Sandra and Dean can come too. I wonder if they're working that weekend...?" She disappeared off into a thought train all of her own, so I interrupted her.
"The man?"
"Ah yes. Well, I met him yesterday. He's SO GORGEOUS; about 6 foot tall, black hair and amazing brown eyes. He's just joined our office and I immediately thought of you. I don't know much more about him than that, but I do know that you two would look perfect together."

Dinner Party Delights

"His name?"

"Devon."

"Okay. I'll give it a go. I've got nothing to lose. Did you tell him you were setting him up?" At this Liz looked sheepish.

"Not exactly, no. I just told him that a group of us were getting together over dinner and wondered if he'd like to join us. I reckon that as soon as he meets you he'll fall for you, after all you are totally irresistible!" I shrugged my shoulders. It didn't sound like the perfect situation to me, but I had no success any other way, so why not?

By the time Saturday came I was actually really nervous. I had obviously put a lot more expectation on this evening than I had realised. I wore a new, red, v-neck dress for the occasion and a fun pair of flashing Santa earrings (it was Christmas). Even Bronie dressed up for the event, forcing herself into a purple velvet dress (that was a bit too tight around the waist). It was the first time that I had seen her legs. I imagine it was also the first time that they had seen a razor for a long time, judging by the cuts all over her shins! Tina opted for flamboyant pink with lots of frills, her white blonde hair a cascade of tousled curls. Liz went for the classic little black number. For the men there were no such choices to be made; 'black tie' means exactly that.

The doorbell went. Liz answered it. It was Sandra and Dean. They were a fun couple that Liz knew from years back; it was good to see them again. They bounded into the living room. Dean clapped his hands and declared,

"Let the party begin!" We all laughed. Liz left the room to

A Rampage Of Chocolate

check the contents of the oven. Just then the doorbell went again.

"Can you get it Annie, I'm just a little caught up at the moment?" Liz shouted.

"Sure thing!" I ran to the door, opened it and was left completely speechless. There before me stood my dream man. Devon was just as Liz had described him, only better. His face was very slightly weathered so that his eyes and hair had a softness to them. It made him appear striking, but approachable. I melted in his very presence.

"Can I come in?"

"Oh! Yeah! Sorry!" I realised that I had been standing in the doorway staring. "Go ahead, into theeeeeee…" The word 'lounge' escaped me in the heat of the moment. Devon cocked his head in expectation of the end of the sentence, so I gesticulated wildly instead and he got the hint. I collapsed against the wall and breathed deeply until I regained my composure. This really was going to be a big night!

The doorbell went again. It was Ben, Liz's oldest school friend (and for a short time, boyfriend). He often came around to the house, particularly when we were having film nights. I was relieved to see his familiar face; it helped to relax me.

"Hiya Annie," he said warmly. "You're looking flushed. Are you okay?"

"Yeah. Fine." I ushered him through, my heart now beating slower.

With one more breath I walked through the doorway into the lounge, tripping over Sandra's handbag handle as I went.

"Oh sorry love. Good trip?" she laughed.

Dinner Party Delights

I smiled sweetly at her; that was my big entrance blown. I was saved by the bell (or rather Liz's not-so-dulcet tones). "Dinner!"

We headed towards the table and sat where Liz had positioned us (using a system of named beer mats).
"Classy!" teased Graham holding up one of the beer mats.
"I aim to please!" retorted Liz. "The menu for tonight is tomato and basil soup followed by duck à l'orange, with a trio of chocolate puds for afters."
"Yum!" trilled Tina.
"Sounds gorgeous. Well done you!" acknowledged Dean.
The rest of us just nodded approvingly and started to salivate.

Liz went around the table placing soup dishes in front of each person, starting with Ben (probably because he was the tallest). I sat staring at the orange mixture wondering how to eat it without slurping, ever conscious of Devon to my right. Ben smiled at me from across the table. Maybe he'd read my thoughts. He too seemed hesitant.
"Tuck in everyone. I don't want it to go cold."
I waited for the conversation to kick in before I started, that way any minor slurps would be drowned out. I needn't have worried though because Dean made enough noise for all of us!

"So what do you do?" Devon asked me, just as I had taken a mouthful of soup. I swung round a little too quickly to face him and the tidal wave of orange liquid inside my mouth leaked out of the side. I dabbed it carefully with the napkin and he pretended not to notice.
"Oh you know." For some reason I had been hit with an attack of embarrassment and had nothing to say.

"No I don't, tell me."
"Um, well. I, erm. I work in the oil industry." It was the best I could do under the circumstances. My mouth was not functioning properly and neither was my brain. I made my excuses and left the room for a while. I shot into the bathroom, locked the door and faced myself in the mirror for a heart-to-heart.
"Annie you're being silly. Devon doesn't even know you or like you and you know nothing about him. For all you know he could be a secret murderer." I mused on that thought for a minute. Suddenly Devon didn't seem quite so appealing and I felt that I could face him again without being so flustered.

I returned to the table and waited for the main course. The duck looked amazing - all brown and crisp - with an array of vegetables and mashed potatoes. I took the first mouthful and without finishing muttered,
"Oh Liz! That's beautiful. I think I've died and gone to heaven. It melts in your mouth."
"That's coz you're such hot stuff Annie!" Liz responded. I felt my cheeks burn red and didn't dare look at Devon. I flicked a pea at Liz; my way of telling her she'd gone too far. The pea missed and hit Ben, who had not been paying any attention to our banter.
"Like that is it!" he replied, playfully flicking some potato off his knife. The mash sailed through the air landing directly on Dean's neck. Ben squirmed in horror.
"Okay. That's war!" Dean exclaimed, hurling a missile of creamed leeks. Greg and Ben rose to their feet.
"You're on!" And so it began, the great Newcastle food fight, all started by one innocent pea and one not-so-innocent me.

Dinner Party Delights

"STOP!" bellowed Liz so loudly that everyone froze on the spot. We all looked at her and saw the redness of her eyes as they welled up with tears. I surveyed the devastation and realised that this was my fault.

"Sorry Liz," I mumbled in shame.

"Sorry Liz," Ben echoed. There was a stony silence as we all apologised and sat down to finish what was left of the main course (discretely wiping the food off our chairs first).

"That was really lovely," Devon said when he had finished, but Liz just scowled. Her efforts had mostly been in vain and the pain of it showed.

"Here, why don't you sit down. I'll pour you a large glass of wine and I'll clear up," offered Ben.

"No! Let me do it. It was my fault. In fact, why doesn't everyone go back into the lounge and sit down and I'll call you back when the table is ready for dessert." Liz nodded and led the way through to the other room, Ben trailing behind. Devon lingered and started to help me clear (for which I was very grateful since it was no easy task; there was mashed potato everywhere).

"I really didn't mean for that to happen. I feel really bad," I admitted.

"I know. I saw what happened. It was just an unfortunate set of events. You just need to improve your shot that's all." I chuckled. "Anyway, do you intend to wear that mashed potato in your hair all night or would you like me to get it out for you?" I shuddered at the thought of a stripe of mash in my hair, but was beyond caring since I had long since given up on the idea of impressing Devon.

"That would be helpful. Thanks."

"Anyway, I was wondering whether you would like to come out to dinner with me? On the condition, of course, that you

don't flick any more peas!" I laughed at the friendly tease, glad for a moment that Devon had never seen the profiterole carnage left behind me at Highpoints. If he had I was sure that he wouldn't have made such a brave invitation. Still, who was I to warn him?
"Definitely!" I said and grinned.

As I wiped away the last of the mess on the table, I looked over at the living room. Conversation was flowing again and the box of Pictionary was coming out. Normality had returned. I breathed a sigh of relief, thankful that I hadn't spoilt the evening after all. I went into the room, followed by Devon and announced,
"Your table awaits you ladies and gentlemen." I was greeted by a sea of smiles. Clearly I had been forgiven.

"Crackers!" Liz exclaimed. "We forgot to pull the crackers!"
Devon looked at me, winked and whispered,
"I've already pulled mine."

Chapter 29

Dating Devon

The following Friday I could hardly contain my nerves. This was the moment I had waited for, the completion of what I required to make me feel whole.

I was doing well at work and Mark Pricklethwaite had given me various commendations, so I was starting to feel secure there. Unfortunately, he'd now chosen to leave ABTEX and was going to introduce me to my new boss, Martin Dower, on Monday. Mark tried to dispel my anxiety over the change by saying:
"You don't need to worry about Martin he's great and I'm sure that he'll value you as much as I do." Praise indeed and the reassurance that I needed to know that I was worthy of my position.

My friendships were equally secure. Liz, Bronie and Tina had become solid rocks in my life. They all seemed to enjoy

Dating Devon

my company as I enjoyed theirs. The only gap that remained was the love gap. The one that, when filled, declares that you are worthy of being loved. So here I stood preparing for my first date with Devon on the threshold of total fulfilment.

I looked in the mirror and smiled. 2 hours of preparation had paid off. The hair was good, the make-up flawless and my new outfit - a red shirt with a sweetheart neckline and a short black skirt - suited me perfectly. Even my new stilettos weren't too tight. I spun around one more time and declared,
"You are looking GOOD Annie Booth!" The doorbell went, my heart leapt and I ran out of the room, blowing a kiss at my reflection as I went.

I opened the door. It was Ben; a wave of disappointment flooded over me. He looked smarter than usual in his jeans, shirt and jacket and he was clutching a bunch of flowers. He reddened when he saw me.
"You look lovely Annie."
"Thanks! I'm going on a date with Devon. In fact I thought you were him."
"Oh!" He lowered his eyes. "That's nice. I hope you have a great time."
"I'm sure I will. Aren't you coming in?"
"Oh! Yes, yes I will. Thanks."
"Are the flowers for Liz?"
"Erm. Yes." Just then Liz came around the corner.
"Ben! I didn't know you were coming around. That's brilliant come on through." He held out the flowers.
"Flowers? What have I done to deserve these?" He looked a little flummoxed at the question and then seemed to fumble the reply.

"It's for the other night. Just to say thanks... and sorry... for the mess."
"Oh that's so sweet! You didn't need to."

Liz stopped dead in her tracks and viewed me up and down.
"Wow Annie! You's lookin' good!" I beamed. She continued, "Although you may want to cut that label off before Devon arrives." I looked at the back of my skirt, yelped and ran off to the kitchen to get the scissors, just as the doorbell went again. Liz let Devon in.
"She's in the kitchen, doing some finishing touches." I appeared grinning. (I didn't mean to grin, but I couldn't help it. I was so excited).
"Are you ready?" Devon asked extending me his hand.
"Yes. I just need my coat." I heard a big 'tut' from behind me as Liz aired her disapproval.
"Still a southern softie at heart!" she teased. I winked at her, allowed Devon to help me on with my coat, and we headed towards the door. As I was leaving I caught sight of Ben. He was leaning against the lounge wall looking a little out of place. It wasn't like him to be so quiet or awkward in the house; he practically lived there. I didn't like seeing him like that. For a second I was tempted to stay and speak to him. Only for a second. Devon took my hand and whispered,
"You look gorgeous. C'mon, let's go." The thrill of his words passed through me; my thought train derailed and all temptations to stay evaporated. I lost all sense of reality and was only aware of the warmth of his hand wrapped around mine. That sense of security that I had missed for so long. I floated out of the door, into the next leg of my adventure.

"I've booked a table at *Spirito d'Amore*. I hope that's okay?"
My jaw fell open.

Dating Devon

"Okay? Of course it's okay! I've heard such good things about their food, but I haven't been there yet. Normally you have to wait weeks for a table. However did you manage to get one on a Friday night so quickly." He smiled kindly, squeezed my hand and said,
"They know me well." I sighed in admiration. All of a sudden Devon had been catapulted to the heights of my esteem. If he had favour at *Spirito d'Amore* then he must be more important than I had realised.

We talked so easily over dinner and found much in common. He loved to enjoy the finer things in life: restaurants, theatre, and holidays. He talked for ages about his aspirations at work and his desire to have a family one day. I could listen to him for hours (and did). The more he spoke about himself the more perfect he seemed to me. Without a doubt I was falling for him.

I liked the restaurant; they were very attentive, always ensuring that our glasses were full. We occupied a discreet table in the corner near the pizza preparation area. It was perfect because it felt like we were alone.

The wine started to go to my head and I felt it was time to take a moment out to recover; so I disappeared off to the toilet. As I looked in the mirror beyond the basin, I noticed what appeared to be a very bad attack of dandruff on my shoulders. I peered closer and began to rub it off. I was bemused. I had never had dandruff before. Why start now? I was both baffled and embarrassed. I wanted to hide, but I couldn't just leave Devon alone; I had to face him. So I brushed my shoulders until they were clear and then shook my head to ensure that no more fell out. I then made my way back to the table to face Devon.

I was still musing over what to do or say about my newly acquired dandruff problem when I reached the table. As I did, I noticed a pile of white powder on the floor behind my seat and then I saw the chef gaily tossing flour over the pizza bases and spinning them up in the air. I started to laugh.
"What are you laughing at?" asked Devon.
"I don't have dandruff, I have flour!" Devon screwed his face up, clearly not understanding. So I explained it in full and he laughed too.
"I'll call them over and get us moved," he said authoritatively.
"Oh please don't! I don't want to make a fuss. I'll just move my chair over to the left, out of the danger zone."
"Only if you're sure?"
"I'm very sure. Look at them, they're very busy. I've been a waitress. Let's not complicate their lives any more."
"Okay then. You're very sweet," he said cupping my face in his hand. I lowered my eyes and blushed. Inside a warm liquid started to flow over my heart. I had forgotten the guard and now it was too late.

As we walked home he stopped to light a cigarette. I was surprised because I hadn't realised that he smoked. He offered me a cigarette and I didn't want to offend him. I wanted to enter Devon's world fully, so I took it. He held out the lighter and a roaring flame erupted from the outlet. I bent forward to meet the flame and in doing so experienced the mismatch of stilettos and wine. I teetered forward, the end of my nose engaging with the end of the flame.
"Ow!" I hollered. "My nose!"
Devon looked apologetic, if a little irritated.
"Maybe this will make it better." He drew me towards him and kissed me on the end of my nose, then he moved down to my mouth and we embraced for the very first time.

Chapter 30

A New Boss

On Saturday morning I looked in the mirror and groaned. There was a big scab on the end of my nose, a memento of the night before. Thankfully Devon had not seen the true extent of the damage, since he had walked me back to my house in the darkness of the night. He had chosen not to come in, but instead had kissed me in the secrecy of the doorway and then left, promising to ring and to see me next Friday.

"Not tomorrow, it's Saturday?" I had asked.

"No. I am already committed, and anyway you are my 'Girl-Friday'." He was firm but smiling and then he was gone.

The rest of the weekend passed in waves; waves of excitement and goose bumps at the thought of Devon, and waves of anxiety at the week ahead. I was dreading meeting my new boss; he came with a terrible reputation. Apparently he was a stickler for precision and formality. Although Mark

A New Boss

Pricklethwaite had reassured me about him, I felt unnerved and now Mark was no longer able to accompany Martin so I would have to meet him on my own. I didn't like change; I cherished stability and longed for it in all aspects of my life. I started to prepare for the meeting on Monday. That included tidying the house.

I had agreed with Martin that I would pick him up from the train station promptly at 9am on Monday morning, return with him to my house to cover the paperwork and then continue with a tour of my area for the rest of the day. I would then see him again 2 weeks later in Nottingham at a team meeting, where I needed to give a 10 minute presentation on my results. It all felt very serious and grown up.

I had chosen to bring him back to the house because that was my office space. However it didn't look much like an office - underwear was interlaced with paperwork and Skatty had left paw prints over my latest credit report. The least I could do was to tidy the house and to turn the dining room into a business-like workspace.

Bronie and Tina just stared at me as I ran around the house busily hoovering and dusting. They sat immobile in front of the television, lifting their feet up at the appropriate moments. As I started to clean the dining room, I noticed the cats staring at something beside the bookcase. Occasionally they stretched out a paw in a vain attempt to reach whatever was there. They had favoured this position all week, but I had only just taken notice. I came up beside them.
"What is it Skitty?" She turned her black and white face towards me and mewed.
Skatty scratched down the side of the bookcase, so I bent

A Rampage Of Chocolate

over and peered in. It was too dark to see, so I reached in with my hand and soon found something soft and mushy. I pulled it out... Duck à l'orange!

Monday came and I was up at 6am, adrenalin coursing through my body. I put on my smartest suit, picked off the cat hair and then tied my hair up in a bun. I rearranged my paperwork several times, screamed at Tina for leaving her dirty breakfast things lying around and then took 3 deep breaths. The clock struck 8am. It was only a 15 minute drive to the station, but I figured that if I went now then I could do the finishing touches to my car. I had cleaned it inside and out, but there was still a bit of rubbish removal to do.

I got in the car and set off. The drive passed quickly although the nerves were getting to me. (I had almost caused 3 accidents on the way by not concentrating). So I was relieved to see the railway station ahead. At least then I could park up and take the time to pull myself together.

As I drove through the archway to the station car park I noticed a space next to a bin, so I parked alongside it and started the process of decluttering the car. As I finished on my side, I shut the door and went to the soon-to-be-Martin's side and embarked on clearing the rubbish from his doorwell. The chocolate wrappers were a few more numerous than I would have liked to admit, so I buried them out of sight in the bin. All that remained was to dispose of the large, white toilet roll that was still in there from my cold and then I would be ready. I placed it in the bin, however the bin was quite full so the toilet roll sat there on display for all to see. I was a bit embarrassed, so I leant forward to push it down out

A New Boss

of sight. As I did so my bottom touched the passenger door, which closed shut, causing the locks to activate. I stared in horror at my keys hanging from the ignition. I was locked out of the car and my new boss was arriving in half an hour. My colour drained. I felt sick.

I started to pace around in small circles (it is a strange thing to do in a crisis I know, but for some reason we always think that it will help. It doesn't, but at least it means that you're doing something). Suddenly I had a brainwave. I could take a taxi to my house to collect the spare keys. I still had time. If I was lucky then his train would be late and he would never even know. I ran towards the taxi rank and garbled an explanation of my predicament to the driver, who looked totally bemused.
"So where exactly am I taking you to, Miss? That's all I need to know."
"25 Gosling Drive. Or is it 26? I can't quite remember! Anyway, just drive to Gosling Drive and I'll show you." He set off and I tapped my foot with impatience the whole way there. Relief only set in when I set eyes on the front door; number 26. That relief was quickly replaced by panic as I realised that my front door keys were also in the ignition!

I ran back to the taxi.
"Just wait there for me. I'll only be 2 minutes. I've just got to go around the back and break in." He raised an eyebrow, but said nothing as I ran off down the alleyway to access the backyard. I found a rock and broke the window on the back door, reached in and turned the key. I felt the pain as I caught my hand on the jagged glass, but I didn't have time to tend to my wounds, so I just grabbed my spare keys and a handful of plasters on the way out. I jumped into the taxi.

A Rampage Of Chocolate

"The station again is it?" he said coolly, as if this were an everyday occurrence.

"Yes please." I looked at my watch. I was going to be late.

When we turned up, there was a solitary man dressed in a blue, pin-striped suit waiting at the exit. I hopped out of the cab and went to greet him.

"Martin Dower? I'm Anne Booth." I extended my hand to greet him and forced a smile.

"You're late. That's not a good start," he barked, without reciprocating the handshake.

"Yes, I am. I apologise for that. I shall explain in the car. It's over here." As we walked to the car I noticed that the toilet roll had resurfaced, so all of my previous efforts had been in vain anyway.

As we journeyed to the house I explained my unfortunate set of events, exhibiting the plasters on my hand as proof. It didn't seem to make a difference. With Martin, late was late no matter what the reason. We travelled in silence for the rest of the way.

As I entered the house I felt a sigh of relief. I was on safe ground. Maybe here we would be able to get this business relationship back on an even footing. I lead the way through to the dining room, discreetly removing Tina's pink bra from the radiator before he noticed.

"Leave your case there and I'll make you a drink. What would you like?"

"Tea with Milk and 2 sugars please." The fact that he said please was progress and gave me some hope. Just then I caught sight of the pile of glass from my earlier break-in.

"While the kettle's on, I'll just clear up the glass if that's okay. I don't want anyone to hurt themselves, particularly

A New Boss

not the cats." As if on cue Skitty arrived to introduce herself to the newcomer. She rubbed herself along his shins, leaving a white trail of hair as she went. I saw Martin recoil in horror. I handed him a hair removing brush and tried to laugh it off:

"Sorry about that. Hazard of the job I guess!" He grunted. I changed the subject. "Did you say 2 sugars?"

"Yes." Clearly another man of few words.

"Righto!" I poured the water into his cup and started to stir. As I did so I heard a scraping noise and a terrible smell wafted under our noses. Skitty emerged from her enclosed litter tray. Martin shuddered in disgust.

"Ah! I hadn't thought about that. Let me put it outside." I lifted up the litter tray and started to take it out of the back door. Unfortunately I caught the edge of the tray on the wall causing the bottom to separate from the lid, depositing all of the contents onto the floor. I watched helplessly as cat poo rolled past Martin's feet. He looked down. Then he looked at me. He didn't need to say anything.

"Why don't you take your drink through to the dining room and I shall be through in a minute," I suggested. He grudgingly obliged. "Note to self," I thought, "hold all future business meetings at hotels."

The rest of the day did not improve. We were late leaving my house due to all of the unforeseen clearing up, so I put my foot down in an attempt to make up time. The local police took exception to this, so switched on their blue lights in protest and pulled me over. I sat in the police car on the hard shoulder of the A1M staring at my car as the policeman wrote out a ticket and explained what I needed to do next. All I could focus on was the outline of Martin tapping his fingers on my dashboard. The policeman looked at me with compassion.

A Rampage Of Chocolate

"Don't worry love, so long as you stick to the speed limit from now on, this day will only get better." I saw Martin look at his watch.
"Somehow I doubt it."
"Really?"
"Yes. That's my boss in the car and this is the first time he's met me. So far it hasn't exactly gone to plan and he's not taking it too well."
"That's his problem, not yours. Some people just don't know how to relax and enjoy the ride." He smiled at me. It was funny really… The only kindness I had received that day was from a police officer giving me a fine!
"Thanks!" I took the ticket out of his hand and left the safety of his car, bracing myself for the onslaught that was about to come.

"I've rung and cancelled the last 3 appointments of the day. We need to be realistic. There's no way that we're going to make them. I shall see them next time I'm up. Let's get on now and try and salvage whatever is left of this day." Any warmth in Martin's voice had now evaporated and had been replaced by ice. I obediently started the engine and started to drive. I felt my lip start to wobble, so I bit it hard. My thoughts turned to Devon and warmth started to return to my insides. It was the comfort that I needed. I started to smile. Thank God for Devon; at least one part of my life was going well.

I was relieved to see the end of that Monday. Martin was unrelenting in his hostility towards me. I was left under no illusion as to who held the authority in this working relationship (if you could call it that) and the consequences of not improving. His parting words to me were,
"Thank you for this insight into how you run your area and

A New Boss

conduct yourself. I'm sure that if we work together you will achieve the standards I expect. There is no room in my team for sloppiness." With that he smiled at me, his first smile of the day, and extended his hand. I took it and smiled back.

"Note to self," I said as I watched him leave, "the job pages come out tomorrow." I got back in the car and opened the glove compartment. I rummaged around in the empty wrappers (this was one section I hadn't cleaned out that morning) until I found a chocolate bar. "Finally! Something good to come out of this day."

Chapter 31

A Change of Season

The rest of the week did not go much better. Those people who had met Martin on the Monday needed to be pacified on the Tuesday; his abrasive manner had not been reserved just for me.

"Who the bloody hell does that man think he is?" raged Percy from the back street garage. "I may be covered in oil but I am no monkey! He treated me like I was something he just trod in." I looked at my watch. It was 8.05 on Tuesday morning and I had only just woken up.
"Welcome to my world!" I muttered under my breath. "I'm sorry to hear that you think that Percy. I really feel that there must be some misunderstanding. Martin was singing your praises as we left your site." Lies weren't my strong point, but I figured that in this case they were a necessary evil. There was silence as Percy digested my lie.
"Really?" he responded.

"Yeah."

"So what was he saying exactly?"

"Erm," I dug deep for a truthful statement that Percy could hang on to. "He was most impressed with the family feel of your service station and how you recognised all of your customers by name."

"Oh, well. I must have got it wrong. Sorry to blow up at you. Nothing personal; you know I've got the highest respect for you."

"Sure Percy. No worries."

Of course the truth about what Martin had said about Percy was a little different than I had put forward.

"This man needs to clean up his act or else."

"Or else what?"

"You'll be finding yourself a new tenant."

"How exactly do you propose that I do that then? The man has been there 26 years and has more rights than you or I." Martin had glared at me and then stated with a menacing growl,

"There are always ways and means. Anyone's life can be made uncomfortable." I remember squirming at that statement; I wasn't sure that he was just talking about Percy.

I really liked Percy and valued what he did. He ran a fantastic little site in the back of beyond and offered a service to the local community. People went there because of him. All I needed to do was to help him to remove the various cars from off the forecourt and to wipe the grease off himself before Martin came next time. I was certainly not about to employ bully-boy tactics and I was starting to seriously doubt the ethics of the person I was working for.

4 more similar calls later and I finally managed to dress.

A Rampage Of Chocolate

"Time to read the job section I feel!"

When Friday came I was so grateful to see Devon. He was my knight in shining armour, coming to rescue me from the storm. Wearing a new little black dress (and with the remaining scab on the end of my nose firmly covered with make-up), I picked up my coat, took his hand and walked through the door.

"Thanks for the roses. They were beautiful."
"I'm glad you liked them." He smiled warmly at me.
"They were the highlight of my week. Everything was going so badly and then the doorbell went and a lady stood there with this huge bunch of roses. It was such a lovely thought of yours and the timing was perfect."
"I aim to please!" He put an arm around my waist and pulled me close to him. We carried on walking.

"So where are we going tonight?" I asked.
"*The Bombay Palace*. If that's okay?"
"Definitely!" I smiled. *The Bombay Palace* was the best curry house in the whole of Newcastle and was renowned for its unique spice combinations.

We stopped off at *Profumo's Cocktail Bar* and ordered a punchbowl to share. The waitress brought us a deep blue, glass bowl with 2 straws. We both leant forward and started to drink. It was somewhat reminiscent of the spaghetti scene from *The Lady and The Tramp*. Whenever I looked up his brown eyes were fixed on me; it was hard not to melt. I had never experienced a man that was this attentive before. It made me feel valued and special.

A Change of Season

"Come on let's go!" Devon said. "Our dinner awaits." He hailed a cab and we headed for the harbour. There tucked away down a side street was a smart, white-fronted building. The owner greeted us warmly at the door.
"Good to see you again Sir."
"Do you come here a lot?" I asked.
"Quite frequently," he replied with an enigmatic smile. "The food here is beautiful."

The waiter ushered us to a corner table. It was beautifully decorated with gold and white linen tablecloths and an ornate Indian candleholder. There were no pictures of waterfalls in this restaurant. Everything was minimalistic and tasteful - planned and executed with the precision required to cater for an upmarket clientele.

"If you haven't eaten here before, then I suggest the 9-course menu. It's fabulous."
"9 courses!" Devon obviously saw the horror on my face and laughed.
"Not 9 full courses, just a taste of lots of different flavours. Trust me, it will be alright."
"I do trust you Devon. I really do." So with that statement, we embarked on a 9-course extravaganza. A true feast both to the eyes and to the tongue. He gently fed me my onion bhaji and as he did so I felt tingles run all the way through my body. I still couldn't believe that someone like Devon would be interested in someone like me, but he was. The proof was that we were here, in a beautiful restaurant in Newcastle and his eyes were fixed on me.

"So, my Girl-Friday," he said as we approached course 8. "What are you doing next weekend?"

A Rampage Of Chocolate

"Nothing planned. Why?" I said optimistically.
"I just thought you might like to come to Paris with me. I've got an apartment there and would love to show you around."
"Wow!" was all I could say. I was so overwhelmed. My fairytale had just got even better. "Um. Yes!" I wanted to jump up from the table and throw my arms around him there and then, but I restrained myself and choked on my wine instead.

All my troubles at work faded into the background. My future looked bright. My future was Devon. Paris beckoned along with promises of romance, gentleness, kindness and love. Now I had nothing to fear. My ship was stable again.

The rest of the meal passed without event. Devon asked me lots of questions about myself and showed total interest. I shared hopes, dreams and aspirations. He smiled gently throughout. When the time came to pay, I reached for my bag but he waved one hand at me.
"No. Let me. This is my treat."
"Okay. Thanks. At least let me pay for the cab home." He nodded his agreement.

When the cab pulled up at my house, Devon got out and escorted me to the door, indicating to the driver to wait. As we stood in the darkness of my doorway, he pulled me close to kiss me, pressing slightly too hard on the scab on the end of my nose.
"Ow!" I whimpered. He laughed.
"I'll pick you up at 6pm on Friday. Make sure you bring your passport."
"Of course!" I smiled at him and waved goodbye, watching as the car sped off down the road.

A Change of Season

I lingered in the doorway for a moment, dreaming of the future; dreaming of Paris. I floated into the house, inhaling the atmosphere of peace and security. My life felt good; on a firm foundation.

Liz was the first to spot me.
"What on earth are you smiling at? You look like the cat that got the cream."
"Not cream exactly, just Paris." I sat down and told them about Devon's invitation. Bronie was unusually animated about the concept.
"Wow, Annie. That's big! He must really care about you."
"That's what I reckon." I agreed. Liz, on the other hand, was slightly more sceptical.
"Are you sure about this Annie? I mean, you don't want to go diving in the deep end do you? Not until you really know him. After all, that will only be date number 3." I was surprised by her reaction but studied her eyes. There was no sign of jealousy, just loving concern.
"Of course I'm sure Liz. Who wouldn't be sure about Paris? Devon is such an amazing gentleman; he really knows how to treat me. I'm enjoying every minute of this. I just love being around him." Liz opened her mouth to speak, but changed her mind, instead she went into the kitchen to put the kettle on.

The doorbell went. It was Ben.
"It's a bit late for you to pop by isn't it?" I enquired.
"Yeah, I guess it is. I was just passing, saw the lights on and thought I would come in for a hot chocolate." With that he produced a carrier bag containing a jar of hot chocolate powder and a packet of chocolate biscuits.

A Rampage Of Chocolate

"You are such a mind-reader!" I gushed and gave him a big hug. He blushed. With that Liz shouted,
"I declare the late night movie theatre open!" So Bronie grabbed the blankets and a video and we all snuggled up on the sofa to watch *Chitty Chitty Bang Bang*. It was the perfect way to end a perfect night - bouncing along on the settee, singing the songs at full volume with my best friends. We laughed and smiled so much that my cheeks ached. My heart was so light and airy that I felt there wasn't a weight in the world heavy enough to hold it down.

The next morning (well actually it was more like lunchtime) we were awoken with even more good news. Tina came bounding into the kitchen following her outstretched hand.
"Come and have a look at this girls!" She waggled her left hand around, showing off her newly acquired engagement ring.
"Is that for real?" I asked. "I mean, are you and Greg getting married?" She nodded as the realisation dawned on us.
"Shut your mouth Bronie, you're going to dribble!" laughed Liz. None of us knew how to react, what to say or what to do.
"You're gonna have to share every detail. How did he propose? What did he say? You know... We want to know everything!" I was bursting with excitement for her. This was the first of my friends to get engaged and I wanted to know what it felt like. We all did, even Ben, who was still there from the previous night.

Tina sat on the sofa, hand still outstretched. We crowded around her, like children around their teacher's feet, hanging onto her every word.
"So, last night Greg said that he wanted to take me somewhere

A Change of Season

special." She paused for dramatic effect, surveyed our faces and then continued. "He turned up as usual to pick me up in Bertha," (Bertha was his purple camper van. It was the second love of his life because he had lovingly restored it from a rusty heap of scrap). "When I got inside he had scattered flower petals over the seat cover. Then he produced a giant pink flower for my hair. Look." She bowed her head to show us a stunning amaryllis, although a couple of the giant pink petals had by now fallen off. "Then he drove me to the restaurant at Ramekin Rock where we had a fish supper with champagne. After that he took me out onto the rock edge and asked me to marry him."
"So what did he say exactly?" Tina started to laugh.
"He said. "Tina you are the breath of fresh air in my life that makes breathing so enjoyable. I want to be with you forever. Will you marry me?" Then he produced a ring box and opened it."

We all sat there open-mouthed, imagining the whole event. Then Bronie brought us all down to earth by uttering the words that all of the rest of us were thinking.
"What? Greg did all of that?" Tina fell back against the sofa with laughter.
"Yes he did! But apparently his sister helped him to plan it. She was the brains behind it, not him. The only parts he planned were the restaurant and the petals on the seat. Still, I think he did really well and I'm really proud of him."

Suddenly Ben jumped up.
"I think it's absolutely brilliant and a celebration is required! Let's all go out for dinner tonight." We all agreed and then pounced on Tina again to marvel at her ring.

Chapter 32

Battle Scars

Saturday evening came and our whole house was still bubbling over with the excitement of Tina's engagement. With that and Paris looming fast, I found myself humming *Love is in the Air* very loudly as I got ready to go out. All it needed now was for Liz to find herself a man and our household would be complete.

"Come on guys. I'm ready! What's keeping you?" I bellowed cheerfully. A muffled voice came out of Liz's room.
"I could do with a hand here... I'm a little stuck!" I shot upstairs and into her room, only to find her walking around firmly wedged in a dress. Her arms were pinned up in the air with the dress half way down, unable to go over her hips and unable to go back up.
"I don't understand it. I only wore this dress last week. It's not like I've put on loads of weight or anything."
"Would you like me to undo the zip?" I asked, chuckling.

Battle Scars

"Oh!" Liz exclaimed. I released the zip (which Liz had completely forgotten about) and the dress then eased nicely over Liz's figure.
"Thank God for that! I thought you were going to have to cut me out." We laughed.

When we got downstairs the others, including Ben, were all ready.
"Forget dinner. Let's celebrate!" Ben yelled. We all bundled for the door, popping through the other side like peas from a pod. The mood was upbeat and we were friends on a mission.

We entered the first pub we came to - *The Rat and Cabbage* - and ordered a drink each. We sat down at a table, glasses in hand.
"To love and marriage! Both are underrated and definitely worth waiting for," toasted Ben.
"To love and marriage!" we all agreed. I choked on my drink and got it all over my face. I wiped it off with a tissue, along with half of my make-up.

"So Liz, you're the only single person here now; we need to find you a man. Isn't there anyone on the horizon for you?" I asked. Liz blushed.
"Don't forget me! I'm single too. Or don't I count?" protested Ben staring at me like a dog that's had his bone removed. I looked at him and saw the hurt in his eyes. I was quite shocked at his seriousness. It was only a small oversight after all. Anyway, I had never really considered the fact that Ben was single before. He was just Ben - a person who never talked about girlfriends and was always round at our house - a safe male figure. He was a shoulder to lean on

A Rampage Of Chocolate

when you needed one; a solid, dependable, friend; part of the comfortable furniture of life.

"Yes Ben. You do count. I just guess I've never pictured you with anyone, that's all." I kept looking at him, repackaging him in my mind. I had placed him in a box marked 'male best friend', and the trouble with that is that male best friends are supposed to stay single. I relabelled his box to read: 'single, male best friend'. "Actually Ben, you would make someone an amazing boyfriend. They would have to be very special to go out with you…"

"And they'd have to be approved by us first!" Bronie chipped in. "After all, they'd automatically become part of our household." Ben blushed and lowered his eyes.

"Let's change the subject. You're all embarrassing me."

"Yes let's!" agreed Liz.

We finished our drinks, left the glasses on the table and headed for the door. As we got outside I had an idea.

"I've just realised where we are. *Profumo's Cocktail Bar* is near here. Let's go and celebrate in style with a punchbowl. It's quite tucked away, so you have to know it's there, but it's great."

"Definitely!" they all agreed.

We opened the door to Profumo's and entered the blue lit room. Everything was purposely dim and misty. They had gone to great lengths to recreate an atmosphere of intimacy and discretion.

"Blimey!" said Ben. "This is something else!"

"And so are the prices!" whispered Bronie, gazing at the cocktail list.

"Oh don't be such a killjoy! Just one punchbowl and we're out of here!" We sat down and a waitress came and took our order, exchanging it for a tray of nibbles. We all stared politely at the tray of Japanese crackers and coated nuts, but as soon as she'd gone we dived in. Soon the punch bowl appeared along with 5 straws. The bowl was made of red and green frosted glass and it contained a light blue liquid. As I leant over to take my first sip, I caught sight of my reflection in the mirror on the wall. Or rather, I caught sight of my scab. Clearly the make-up that I had wiped off earlier had been the critical make-up that I had spent hours applying. Typical!

We all leant forward and sucked with all our might, having a battle with our straws at the end.
"It's mine!" challenged Ben, trying to flick our straws out of the way to get the last few drops.
"No chance!" declared Liz, her competitive edge kicking in. She flicked his straw out of the way, inhaled the remains and punched her arm triumphantly in the air.

Just then the door opened. It was Devon! My heart leapt. I pushed back my chair so that I could go to greet him, but stopped as I saw him extend his arm to usher in a tall, slim brunette. I watched in slow motion as he placed his arm around her waist and led her to the very table that we had occupied only 24 hours earlier. He smiled at her and held her hand across the table. I was frozen to the spot.

Liz stretched out her hand and squeezed mine.
"I wanted to tell you," she whispered lamely, "but you were so happy. I just couldn't do it. I'm really sorry." For a moment I took my eyes off the scene in front of me and turned to look at Liz. She was welling up. "I just didn't know that he was like that, otherwise I wouldn't have introduced you."
"But who is she?" I asked.
"Natalie. She's our secretary."

A Rampage Of Chocolate

Ben shut his eyes and shook his head, then sat staring downwards. I could see his anger burning on my behalf, the protective instinct of a friend. Everyone else was silent as they looked to me for the next move. They were looking to the wrong person, for all I felt was numb and incapacitated.
"I think I'd like to go now," I mumbled. At least I think the words came out; I know that I thought them.

As we pushed our chairs back to leave, mine scraped on the floor. Devon turned his face towards the noise and saw me. He winced and then looked away. Natalie turned to look at me too. She'd obviously spotted the reaction in Devon. I found myself staring into her beautiful, olive-skinned face whilst rubbing the scab on the end of my nose. There was no comparison. I was his Girl-Friday and this was his Girl-Saturday. It wasn't even a fair fight - Saturday won hands down.
"Goodbye Devon," I mouthed as I left.

As I walked out of the bar I left my heart lying wounded on the battlefield. I felt that it was ready to die, but it kept on beating and I kept on breathing. Big deep breaths. All the way outside.

Ben put a protective arm around me.
"Don't let that swine ruin your evening. He's the one with the problem, not you. He's missed out on an amazing person."
"Ben's right you know," agreed Liz. I felt the tears trickling down my cheeks. I dug deep for strength, but found only hollow words.
"Yeah you're right. I am worth it. Let's show him what fun

really is. Tina, this is your evening and we're going to enjoy it."

"We'll make a Northerner out of you yet!" sang Tina proudly. I smiled and stepped bravely on, automatic pilot now in operation.

We went from bar to bar, celebrating Tina's good fortune. I was grateful for the alcohol and for the occasional toilet in which to shed a private tear. I was too drunk to speak, although I could still manage to walk, albeit in a zigzag fashion. Occasionally an optimistic suitor would try to engage me in conversation, but then they would look into my face and think better of it. I'm not sure if it was the scab, the mascara streaks or the emptiness that put them off, but whatever it was, it suited me. Right now I was off the market.

Liz and Ben took me in hand.
"Come on you. I think we need to get you something to eat." I wasn't hungry, but I was compliant, so I nodded my head and went with them, Tina and Bronie following on behind.
"Kentucky?" The others nodded their agreement.
"Okay. It's down here." Liz led the way and we all followed like obedient children. She was the matriarch of our house and we were happy with it that way.

By the time we reached the KFC we were freezing. The temperature had dropped substantially whilst we'd been out. Unlike the others I was wearing a coat, but the alcohol had thinned my blood too much and even my extremities were blue.
"A bit chilly out there?" the girl behind the counter asked with a huge smile. "What'll it be?"

"A giant chicken bucket please," ordered Liz. 5 minutes later we were holding a warm bucket of sweet smelling chicken. We started the walk home.
"It's no good," moaned Ben. "I'm not going to make it. We have to stop and eat now."
"I agree. I'm famished," said Liz.
"Me too!" trilled Tina. I just shrugged. In the scheme of things I really didn't care. I was back to basics - living or dying.
"That's all very well, but it's too cold to just stop and eat outside. So where exactly do you suggest we go?" pointed out Bronie, ever the practical one. We all looked around.
"What about in there?" asked Ben pointing at a telephone box. We all looked at him as if the suggestion of 5 of us squeezing into a telephone box to eat chicken was an impossible idea. Ben's faced seemed to illuminate at this challenge.
"Look. It can work. We can all squeeze in there, put the bucket on the floor and every time we want another piece of chicken then Bronie can pass it to us."
"Why me?" protested Bronie.
"Because you're the shortest." She looked hurt. "Sorry Bronie, but you are!" She shrugged her shoulders in submission and we all headed for the telephone box.

It was more of a squeeze than we had anticipated, so Liz held the door closed with her hand, whilst Bronie passed up the chicken. The warm meat slipped down beautifully and with every bite I felt my senses returning and warmth flowing to my limbs. For a short moment I enjoyed the meal, allowing the pressing of bodies to push my worries outside of the door.
"What do we do with the bones?" asked Tina. "We can't put them on top of the new chicken."

"Throw them outside," I yelled. My drunken idea was met with silence.

"Okay. Let's!" agreed Ben, "We'll throw them outside and then pick them up as we leave." So with that we had a system of 2 commands. Whenever we shouted, "Chicken!" Bronie would pass up a new morsel for us to eat and whenever we shouted, "Door!" Liz would open the door, we would all duck and a bone would go flying out. It was an ill-conceived system, born out of a drunken stupor, but amazingly it worked.

Finally the bucket was empty and we were prepared for the final leg of the walk home. Ben went over to the pile of bones, ready to pick them up. As he stood there, a cheeky grin crept across his face. He turned to us and pointed at the bones.

"Poor Devon. He never knew what hit him!" We roared with laughter and headed off home.

Chapter 33

Team Meeting

By the time Monday morning came the devastation over Devon had really kicked in. I looked in the mirror and groaned at the black circles under my eyes and the puffy red pockets at the top of my cheeks (a legacy from my river of tears). I grimaced at the thought of facing Martin in this condition. The only good thing was that my scab appeared to have been swept away in the course of all my nose-blowing.

As I dressed, I considered the meeting that lay ahead. My presentation was prepared and I knew all of my figures, so all I had to do was to sit through the rest of the meeting without crying. It was a question of being a British bulldog - gritting my teeth and getting on with it. I growled at myself in the mirror in a vain attempt at a bulldog impression, even managing a smile at the ridicularity of it.
"Oh well! Here goes." I picked up my briefcase and headed for the door.

Team Meeting

The 2 hour journey passed easily because the whole way I sang along to *Dynamo Box* at the top of my voice. I shook my shoulders and arms in an attempt at dancing whilst driving. At one stage a police car sped by and then slowed down to come alongside again. Clearly they wanted to take another look at me shaking my stuff. The policeman in the passenger seat lowered his dark glasses and peered over. I smiled, waved and then carried on. He sped off, no doubt bemused by the sight.

I pulled up in the hotel car park, grabbed my case and started to get out.
"Annie!" bellowed a big voice. It was Tim. He marched over and enveloped me in a huge hug. It was exactly what I needed.
"How are you doing? Long time no see." He was beaming at me.
"I'm doing well," I lied. "How about you?"
"You know. So-so. Dodgy dealers, tricky tenants and way too much paperwork, but otherwise I'm fine. Bought myself a house. You should come over."
"Seriously? A house? That's a bit grown up isn't it?" Tim smiled in response. He popped his briefcase down, adjusted his tie and cleared his throat, attempting a smug adult impression. I crossed my arms, unimpressed, and pushed his briefcase over with my toe, sending him scrambling. The familiar exchange lifted the weight of the cloud around me for a minute. It felt nice to have him near. Once again his presence and strength had made a reassuring appearance in a time of despair.
"Come on," he winked. "We don't want to be late. Old Dower will be dour if we do!"

A Rampage Of Chocolate

We walked into the meeting room together, gathered a coffee and sat down. I was planning to sit next to Tim, but Martin had put name tags out and I was allocated the seat next to him. I guessed it was the equivalent of the naughty step. My saving grace was that Tim sat opposite, so at least there was one friendly face.

Adrian, Terry and Ian arrived soon after and took their seats, so the team was complete. Martin started the meeting by looking at his watch.
"Excellent. Everyone is here on time. That's what I like to see. So welcome everyone to our first team meeting together. I'm not one to mess around with the social niceties, so let's crack on…" And crack on he did. He droned on and on and on, covering every procedure and company policy that affected us. He called it 'laying the foundations'. I called it 'boring us into submission'. I occasionally amused myself by looking over at Tim, who would wrinkle his nose to make me laugh. At one stage I noticed him doodling so I craned my neck to try and see what he had drawn. Tim held it up discreetly for me to see… It was a pigeon bottom and a cone of chips. I sniggered and glowered simultaneously. Martin glared at me, so I proceeded to pretend to turn it into a cough and sipped some water, staring back at him with innocent eyes.

"Okay. So now that we are all clear on our expectations of each other, I should like to move on to point number 2 on our agenda - Area Results. Anne I should like you to go first." My heart started racing, but I ignored it, stood up and proceeded towards the projector.
"Just be careful where you stand," quipped Tim. I glared at him. Adrian sniggered (clearly word had spread about my previous presentation phenomenon).

Team Meeting

I carefully placed the acetate on the glass, pointedly stepped to one side and then started to speak.

"This quarter I have achieved all of my targets." What a relief it was to be able to say that. Even if Martin didn't like me, at least he wouldn't be able to criticise my results. I looked to him for approval, but instead I received,

"Would you please put your figures the right way up? They're upside down." My insides sank. How did I manage to fail, even in success?

"Oh!" I replied weakly. I attempted to turn the acetate around but my hand was shaking so much that I couldn't square it up again. By now my stress was showing and I was aware that I had broken into a sweat. I felt a trickle running past my temples and even my fingers were damp. So when I removed my hand from the acetate the plastic stuck to my fingertips and it wafted across the floor. Martin rolled his eyes.

I recovered my acetate, but I never recovered my professionalism or my poise. I fumbled my way through the rest of the presentation and was totally grateful for the opportunity to sit back down. Martin rubbed salt into my wounds.

"Adrian. Up you come. You show us how it's done." And he did. Adrian sailed through his presentation with confidence. His acetate changeovers were seamless and there was no evidence of any shaking in his voice or limbs.

"Well done Adrian. You'll be a tough act to follow."

Tim was next followed by Terry and then Ian. They all did well and all received praise. I had the best results out of the whole team and yet I was the failure. I sat there feeling completely isolated.

"Well done gents. Good presentations and good results too." It was subtle but it was there. I had been written out of his acknowledgment. Mentally I suspect he had already crossed my name off the team list. "Let's break for coffee. Back in 10 minutes." With that Martin left the room.

Tim came over to me and gave me a hug.
"You didn't really deserve that Annie. It was a crap presentation but your results were good."
"Thanks. I think!"
"Come on. Let's inject some caffeine into that system of yours. It's bound to do the trick and get you up and fighting again. He won't know what's hit him." I smirked, allowing myself to be rallied a little for round 2.

When we reconvened Martin made it painfully obvious that I was persona non grata. If ever I answered a question he would just stare at me blankly and then move on to someone else, even if the answer I gave was correct. It was as if I was boxing a shadow, only the shadow keeps moving. Every time that I thought I would recover my position with a punchy answer, it somehow failed to impact. Even my colleagues were shocked at this rough-handed treatment. When we broke for lunch they each came up in turn with a word of consolation or advice:
"I don't know what you've done to upset Martin, but it looks pretty serious. Are you okay?" It was the first time I had ever seen Adrian drop his arrogant exterior, but he was genuine in his concern. I nodded. He patted me on the shoulder and left. Terry rubbed my shoulders as he went past, a clear gesture of friendship. It was interesting to see how these colleagues could recognise a dirty fight when they saw one and were prepared to tend my wounds, yet the courage of

their convictions did not prompt them as far as making a public challenge.

"You never gave a wrong answer you know," offered Ian as he walked past. "I don't know why Martin had a problem with them. Strange!"

Of course I did know why. I remembered only too well the words that Martin had spoken to me on our day together…

"There are always ways and means. Anyone's life can be made uncomfortable."

Ian left to join the others, leaving only me and Tim. I looked into Tim's eyes and my lip quivered.

"What do I do Tim? What do I do?" He paused for a moment before answering.

"You vote with your feet, Annie. That's the only thing you can do. He's out for your blood. It's obvious. Don't let him have it." He drew me close and held me tight and safe. I could hear his heartbeat and it comforted me. It was almost as if his was beating for both of us.

"Come on Annie. We need to go. We can't be late for lunch." He kissed me on my head and released his grip. I felt a screaming inside - a voice scrambling for something secure to hold on to. That voice that says you can't cope without him; that you just can't do it alone. I tried to recall why I had finished our relationship, but in a moment of panic I received nothing.

"Tim?" He turned to face me. "I… I… Why…?" I snorted. I couldn't find the words. "Don't worry. Let's go."

Lunch was a welcome distraction. As the last to arrive, I was seated far away from Martin so I could relax. Tim and Ian were on either side and set about cheering me up. I didn't feel like responding. Numbness had set in, but the friendly banter gave me an alternative point of focus (for a while at least).

The afternoon dragged horribly, but with visiting speakers up front the pressure was at least off me and they all treated me with respect. When 4pm came, Martin wrapped up the meeting and released us to go home. I grabbed my papers, placed them in my briefcase and all but ran to my car. I leant against the door breathing in the fresh air, checking that I was still alive. I needed to clear my head before I faced the 2 hour drive home. I felt a tap on my shoulder.
"D'you fancy coming for a drink? 'One for the road' as they say." It was Tim. I smiled at the welcome offer.
"I can think of nothing better." So I placed my things in the car and then we walked to the pub on the other side of the car park.

Tim brought the cokes across to the table.
"Sorry it's not something stronger; I just thought that wouldn't be a good idea. I am right in thinking that you still have it with ice and no lemon." I smiled.
"Absolutely. I'm surprised you remember."
"I haven't forgotten you Annie. It was you who left me, remember?" I hung my head in shame.
"But that's just it, Tim. I don't remember. It's all a blur. I remember the good things, but I don't remember the detail. I don't remember why we split up."
"Something about 'it isn't working' and 'being friends for life'. After that you buggered off and I didn't see you again!" He guffawed.
"Sorry Tim," I said gently.
"Don't be. We've all grown up a bit since then." He leaned

over and took my hand. "I never even got the chance to tell you that I loved you." I looked up, shocked. His eyes were sincere. The 3 words that I had craved from him, and now here they were and yet he was no longer mine. A tidal wave of emotion caught me up and deposited me in a vulnerable place.

"Loved or love?" I was surprised at my own boldness, but the words had just slipped out. He paused for what seemed an eternity.

"Love." I squeezed his hand, both in response and for stability, a maelstrom of thoughts swirling around my head.

"I never knew."

"I never said." There was silence, neither of us knowing where to go from here. Words seemed inadequate; so he leant over the table and kissed me. I responded and our relationship was sealed.

So, there it was. In my most vulnerable hour, with my heart broken and my job prospects shattered, a knight in shining armour rode along and swept me onto the back of his charger, just as he had done so many times before. This was the gentle Tim, the strong Tim, the one that I so admired. His timing was perfect, my situation desperate and he said the 3 little words that unlock the door to any girl's heart - 'I love you'. Not once did I stop to think how I felt about him; nor did I consider the desires of my own heart. All I knew was that right now this man gave me strength and that was exactly what I needed. I didn't have enough faith in myself to go it alone. I needed to know that someone else believed in me too.

Some relationships are built on the rock of love, others on the gravel of lust, but ours was built on the quicksand of my selfish insecurities.

Chapter 34

History Repeats

Monday evening I returned to the house. Bronie was in her room and Liz and Tina were chilling out on the sofa.
"How'd it go?" enquired Liz.
"Bit of a mix really. The meeting was a write-off and I *definitely* need to find myself a new job. Having said that, I am now back with Tim."
"Tim? The one from university, who was always putting you down? That Tim?" My stomach churned over as the memories of the chocolate fondue and the cruelty of his tongue came to mind.
"Yes, that Tim. But he has grown up a lot since then. He's really changed." Liz rolled her eyes in exasperation.
"Really?"
"Yes really!" I said crossly, starting to feel uncomfortable.
"How d'you know that he's changed?" Liz pursued. I started to question myself.

"Because he said that he loves me. He never did that before." I tilted my nose upwards in triumph. Liz looked thoughtful. "And how do you feel about him, Annie? Do you love him?" For once I had no answer. Or at least, I did have an answer, but I didn't care to repeat it out loud. The truth was that I cared about Tim, but I didn't love him; I just needed him.

The doorbell went (just in time). It was Ben. "Come in," I said opening the door wide.
"No I won't. I'm not stopping. I just brought you these. I thought you might need them." With that he handed me a huge box of chocolates. "I'm sorry about Devon. He had a real treasure in you. He was a fool to lose you like that. You deserve better."
"Thanks! I don't know what to say!"
"Don't say anything. Just enjoy them." He turned and left. I looked at the box and smiled. He was right, I did need them.

I retreated to my room and scoured the jobs pages again. I had already applied for 2 positions locally, but now I needed to start seeking in earnest. An advert caught my eye:

INTERNATIONAL OIL COMPANY SEEKS

SHOP CO-ORDINATOR
North East and Scotland

Retail or Oil Industry experience required.
Salary details upon application.

To apply, send your CV to...

The closing date was Wednesday, so I spent the rest of the

A Rampage Of Chocolate

evening preparing my CV and an application letter. It was also time for a quick prayer (one of my S.O.S prayers. I only ever seemed to send Him a signal when I was in need).

"Okay God. I'm really in a fix this time. Martin's out for my blood and quite frankly I don't know how to turn it around. You and I both know that I need this Shop Co-ordinator job." I waggled the advert in the air so that God could see it. "Would you sort it out for me, please? I promise not to mess this one up. Honest! Amen." (As always, my prayer was short and to the point; I always figured that God was far too busy for the fluffy niceties of life).

By 11pm I had finished my CV and had created an award-winning application letter to accompany it. I reread it one last time and nodded approval at my own handiwork. On paper I did look really good, so I felt a renewed optimism about my chance of success. With confidence flowing, I strided to the postbox and inserted the envelope with a smile. I must have posted my confidence along with the letter because almost immediately I was engulfed with fear again. After all, why should I expect to get that job when there were so many other people out there with more experience than me? What had I been thinking? Even if they did like my application, what would I say in the interview? My heart sank, my smile left and by the time I got home I was a wreck.

I spent the next 2 weeks trying to salvage what was left of my career. I ensured that I submitted everything ahead of any deadlines and proactively went around all of my service stations to make sure that there were no outstanding issues.

History Repeats

Martin seemed to be avoiding me and I avoided him. It worked better that way.

There was one matter in particular that I knew I needed to resolve - Twyvale Service Station's lease was about to expire and I needed to complete the rental negotiations. Unfortunately we'd come to an impasse on the rent increase. John MacIntyre felt that a £2,000 increase was fair and Martin had given me a £5,000 target, so I couldn't accept anything less. Neither of us were moving from our positions. I knew that I had to resolve it somehow; so, I came up with a plan.

"I've got a proposition for you John," I said shortly after arriving.
"Lucky me!" he quipped, leaning forward on his desk, his eyes dropping to my blouse. I scowled and flicked my pen back and forth (I think it was nerves - I really didn't like negotiations).
"Not that kind of proposition!" He smiled, sat back in his chair and laughed. I fiddled with my pen even more, but the rest of me kept my poise.
"You do disappoint me, Annie! Still, go on. I'm intrigued."
"Okay, so here it is. If I am to summarise where we have got to so far," (I was quite chuffed with that wording and approach - I thought it sounded professional), "you are prepared to agree to a £2,000 increase in rental and I would like to see £5,000."
"Yep!" He crossed his arms tightly across his chest; (I had studied enough body language at University to know that wasn't good). I gripped my pen for security and continued.
"I am prepared to offer you a compromise." His arms uncrossed.
"How about we stagger the increase? £2,000 in year one,

A Rampage Of Chocolate

£4,000 in year 2 and £5,000 in year 3? That way you get what you want and we also end up with a fair rental in the final year." John rubbed his chin. Like me he was aware that his lease was about to end, so he knew that we needed to come to an agreement. We also both knew how profitable this petrol station was to him. I spun my pen around between my fingers while I waited for his reaction. The 3 minute wait seemed like an hour. By the end of it the pen was a blur because it was rotating so fast.
"Okay. But it needs to be £3,000 in year 2."
"No, £4,000." I had to be stubborn. I knew that it was unlikely Martin would accept much less.
"£3,000, or the deal is off," John said, crossing his arms again, but smiling as he did so.
"Let's split the difference?" I offered, but John was having none of it. He had gone into stubborn mode. He crossed his legs too. The barrier was up.
"Nope!"

Suddenly I had a brainwave. It was risky, but I was desperate and I knew that John was a gambling man.
"John. You and I both know that we need to agree this today, so let's toss a coin. If you win then year 2 increase is £3,000, but if I win it's £4,000." Paul beamed at the suggestion.
"Okay, you're on! Heads I win." We got a pound coin out and tossed it up in the air. I prayed my usual S.O.S style prayer quietly under my breath as I watched it spin; the rotations of my pen secretly matching every rotation of the coin. It landed. I held my breath as I looked.
"Damn!" John exclaimed, throwing himself back into his chair. It was tails. I heaved a sigh of relief. "You win Annie." He extended his hand across the desk. "£4,000 it is. Fun doing business with you though. I guess you'll be wanting another coffee out of me too?"

History Repeats

"That'd be nice. I'll just nip to the loo first."
"You know where it is."

I headed off down the corridor, so pleased to have this matter resolved. Now Martin would have nothing to complain about; I had met all his objectives. I reached the toilet door and pushed it open. As I did, I noticed a spot of blue ink on my hand.
"Bloomin' pen!" I muttered. I entered the room and found myself standing directly in front of the mirror. It took me a couple of seconds to process what I saw… My face and clothes were covered with ink blotches. Somehow, during the course of the negotiation, I had transformed myself into Mr Blobby. The success of the negotiation immediately evaporated, and was replaced by irritation. I spent the next 5 minutes scrubbing the blue off my hands and face, although nothing could be done about my shirt and jacket. I braced myself and went back in to face John.

He beamed at me as I entered his office.
"You're looking a bit whiter!" he teased. I grimaced.
"Why didn't you mention that my pen was leaking?"
"It was too funny. I wanted to know how blue you would get before you realised. Anyway, it was worth £1,000 to watch that." I growled at him playfully and then laughed.

By the time I got home I could relax again knowing that my area was secure, so I decided to treat myself to a takeaway. I picked one up on the way home and threw my clothes in a pile by the door. I would pick them up later. Right now all I wanted to do was to collapse on the sofa. Tina was already home, watching TV.

A Rampage Of Chocolate

"Tim rang for you. Said he'd call back later. Oh! And you have post. I put it by the kettle."
"Thanks Tina." I went into the kitchen, took a plate out of the cupboard for my Chinese and then picked up the letter. My heart skipped a beat when I saw the logo printed on the outside - 'AZOIL'. I ripped it open as fast as I could and pulled the letter out.

Dear Anne,

We are pleased to invite you to an interview on Wednesday 5th February at 12pm…

"Tina! Tina! I've got an interview! It's next Wednesday." I didn't wait for her reaction I was too busy waving the piece of paper in the air, dancing around the living room. Hope filled the air. My way out was at hand. This was the answer to the mess I was in; I could feel it in my bones.

Just then the phone rang. It was Tim.
"Hiya Annie. How are you?" He didn't wait for a reply, but instead continued apologetically towards his point. "Sorry I haven't rung before. I wasn't sure if you'd changed your mind." He paused.
"I haven't changed my mind Tim. I want us to have another chance." I could hear the tension leave him. His whole tone relaxed and his boldness returned.
"Fantastic! So when are you going to come and see my house then?"
"Friday?"
"Sounds good to me. Straight after work?"
"Sure."
"Okay. I'll email you my address and directions. I'll cook. You'll be impressed. See you Friday." With that he hung up.

History Repeats

There was no tenderness; it was more like a business call. He never stopped to enquire how I was or long enough to find out about my interview. Tina saw the disappointment on my face. She held out a hand to me.

"It's early days. Maybe he's not very good on the phone. Some people aren't you know. Men are a funny breed; they just don't understand women." She was right. I shouldn't read so much into things. Tina tried to change the subject. "AZOIL eh? What are you going to wear to your interview?" For a few seconds my thoughts turned to the hope ahead, and then I remembered...

"I don't know. I've got Friday to worry about first!"

Friday evening came and I felt a heady mix of nerves, excitement and dread. Tim was so sweet and I really wanted this relationship to work, but I dreaded the thought that it may not. I knew that my motives for seeing him were selfish, but I justified it to myself on the basis that I cared about him. I needed tenderness and strength - a lion and a lamb all rolled into one. I didn't feel strong enough at the moment to walk my journey alone. I needed someone beside me, someone who believed in me. I just hoped that I was right about Tim.

I pulled up outside his house. It was a modern terrace with a plain patch of grass at the front. All of the neighbours had well-tended floral selections, but not Tim - his front garden was functional. The door burst open and Tim stepped out to give me a big bear-hug. It felt so good that I went weak at the knees. I could feel the lion already.

"Welcome to my humble abode!" he said with a giant grin on his face. I stepped inside and laughed. It was so clearly a

A Rampage Of Chocolate

bachelor pad - drawings of naked ladies adorned the walls, a huge TV was the centrepiece of the room and all of the furniture was black, with not a cushion or accessory in sight.

"What's that smell?" I asked.
"Goulash! It's the only thing I can cook (apart from sausages and stuff like that)."
"It smells good."
"I'm pleased. It won't be ready for an hour, so I thought we could have a drink first and just chill for a bit." It was obvious that he was trying too hard. It all felt very formal and a little awkward. Lots of thoughts floated through my head - how do we kiss again? Should I drink because if I do that, then I have to stay the night and if I do that then where will I sleep? Panic crawled through my veins. Tim shoved a glass of wine in my hand and I took a great gulp. The panic retreated.

Tim and I stared at each other. Neither of us knew how to make the first move. Suddenly I spotted his table football.
"Can we play? I haven't done this in ages."
"Okay, but be warned - I'm an expert!"
"Don't be too confident. I used to be pretty good at this myself," I lied.

Table football was exactly the icebreaker we needed. We became totally transfixed by the game and our tension left. We laughed so much at my ridiculous attempts at kicking; it appears that this sport eluded me too - I was rubbish! The score stood at 24-5 to Tim, so at that point I admitted defeat. He came round to my side of the table and put an arm around me and pulled me gently in to kiss me; the lamb at last. His hand wandered, I replaced it around my waist. Not a lamb, but a wolf in sheep's clothing!

We had great fun that night and just hung out together. We ate, played video games and watched some TV. We laughed a lot, like the2 good friends that we always were. Our banter was rapid-fire and not too offensive. The familiar tennis matches resumed. When night came I asked to sleep in a separate room. Tim looked hurt.
"Tim, I don't want to rush into anything. I've done that before and it's never ended well. My whole life is up in the air right now, let's take this really slowly. I'm not going anywhere and neither are you." He nodded reluctantly.
"Okay, if that's what you really want."
"Thanks." With that I kissed him gently on the lips. "I'll see you in the morning."

When morning came I woke up with that 'where am I?' feeling. I looked around the bare room and remembered I was at Tim's. I smiled. I could hear some clanking sounds from the kitchen, so he was clearly up already. I threw a jumper over my pyjama top and headed downstairs. He was in the kitchen preparing breakfast. He didn't hear me come in, so I crept up behind him and gently kissed him on his neck. He turned around and grabbed me. I squealed.
"Good morning Madam. And what time do you call this then?" he teased.
"Late I hope. I was waiting for room service, but it never came. I need to complain to the management or I won't be coming back again."
"I see," he said, turning around and grabbing a handful of bubbles from the washing up bowl. He chased me around the kitchen and shoved them on my chin. "I'm afraid

A Rampage Of Chocolate

that bearded ladies aren't welcome here anyway. We have standards you know."
"You have standards, huh? So what would the standard be if you kissed a bearded lady then?" I wrinkled my face up.
"I don't think we have a policy on that." He grabbed me and I felt the bubbles popping against my skin as he pressed his face to mine.
"Seriously though, Annie, breakfast is in 2 minutes, is that okay?"
"That's great," I replied, wiping away the rest of my bubble beard.

Breakfast was perfect. A good fry-up always hits the spot. In fact the whole morning was perfect. Tim was attentive to my needs and fun to be with. It rekindled memories of Trafalgar Square and the fun that we had in London.
"I was thinking that we might hook up with a couple of my friends around lunchtime. Is that okay? I'd like you to meet them. I thought we'd go bowling."
"Sounds good to me."

We spent the rest of the morning larking about and left for bowling around 12pm. By now I felt comfortable with Tim, reassured that my decision to date him again was a good one. His university bravado had subsided; now he was just fun to be with. We hadn't talked in depth about anything. In fact I had even forgotten to mention my job interview. We'd kept our conversation to lighter matters, concentrating only on re-establishing our bond and our common ground.

By the time I was introduced to Sally and Jake I felt that I had been with Tim for years. They treated me that way too, so it was no effort to get on with them. They were easy-going and just accepted me as I was. Tim seemed pleased with my integration and so relaxed even more.

Bowling wasn't exactly my thing, but I was always willing to have a go. It was 3 years since I had last played, so my technique was a little rusty. I stood and threw the ball (I realise now that you are supposed to roll it, not throw it, but we all live and learn). The ball bounced off our runway into the neighbouring lane where it went down their gutter, causing their player to miss a go. Before I had a chance to apologise Tim leapt in.

"Sorry about that!" he yelled across the lanes. "She's always been clumsy. You should've seen her at university!" They received his apology and I received his wound. I took a sharp intake of breath and bit my lip. I rolled the ball again, this time going down my own gutter. I went and sat down.

"Don't worry about it," said Tim, pointing at the score. "You can't be good at everything." I smiled weakly, still recovering from my wound. "We can always get them to put the bumpers up if you'd like?" He winked at me and nudged me in the ribs. "Come on! Don't be so serious. You know I'm teasing." The trouble was that teasing hurts and I had just received a painful reminder that Tim's tongue was still sharp.

Sally and Jake ignored Tim's witticisms and continued with their turns, each of them scoring a strike. Tim stood up to take his.

"Now watch how the professionals do it, Annie." He grinned - as if a grin makes it alright. Sally turned to me.

"So how long have you guys known each other?"

"Since uni. We lost contact for a while and then ended up working for the same boss and here we are."

"Okay. That's pretty cool. It was obviously meant to be,"

A Rampage Of Chocolate

she said nodding. I had never considered the destiny angle of our relationship, but she did have a point. "So how come you never got together at uni then?" Sally continued.
"Well, actually we did!"
"What, you went out together at uni?" Sally looked really surprised.
"Yeah, we did. Not for long. Only 7 weeks… At the end of our first year."
"Oh!" Sally considered what I had said. "So why did you break up?" I gulped.
"Because he kept putting me down." I almost fumbled the words out of my mouth. I recognised as I said them that the situation had not changed, or at least in public it hadn't. The question was - is it enough to be loved in private?

Chapter 35

Revelation and Interrogation

When I got back to the house on the Sunday, Liz looked radiant.
"What's happened to you?" I asked.
"Nothing much," she answered coyly.
"That's a big fat lie!" yelled Tina from the kitchen. "She's got herself a man."
"Really? Who?" Liz grimaced a bit before she revealed his identity.
"Dean."
"Dean! But he's going out with Sandra!" I yelled (without meaning to).
"Sandra left him over Christmas. She ran off with her boss. Turns out they hadn't been getting on well for a while, but he still didn't see it coming."
"So how did you 2 get together?" I enquired, still trying to fit the pieces together in my brain.
"We just went out for a drink last night… and… well, we

realised that we both liked each other. In fact, he admitted that he was going to ask me out 3 years ago, just before he met Sandra, but I had just started dating Ben, so that put an end to that. Of course, I never knew, and by the time Ben and I had finished it was already too late."

"Why did you and Ben finish?" I asked cagily. I had always wanted to know, but had never found an opportunity to ask.

"We just had different interests and outlooks. I wanted someone more... I don't know... someone... unpredictable and dangerous. Ben was just too... attentive... loving... kind. Anyway, he makes a fabulous friend and, one day, I'm sure that he'll make someone an amazing husband. I was too young and silly really." I pondered on what Liz had said. It made me feel very protective of Ben. It is funny how different we all are. The qualities that Liz had rejected in him were the very qualities that I had been searching for. The ones that I had found so lacking in Tim. Liz continued, "The spark between Ben and I disappeared years ago, and nowadays he's only got his heart set on one woman." Liz looked at me, anticipating my next question.

"Oh! I didn't know that there was anyone." I felt disappointed, a surprising dulling of my senses. "Really? Who is it?" I needed to know. I was intrigued, but this was more than just curiosity. Liz stared at me as if transferring her thoughts telepathically.

"Don't you know?"

"Know what?" I asked naively.

"It's you!"

Liz waited for me to ingest what she had just said. I could feel the whirring in my brain as I tried to make sense of the situation. I had always assumed that Ben was here to see

A Rampage Of Chocolate

Liz. In fact, I had even thought that one day they would get back together. I had certainly never considered Ben for myself. Now I was dumbstruck and confused. The conflicts in my brain raged furiously - my need to be loved, to have a man now; my promise to Tim to give our relationship another chance; my fondness for Tim; his cruel tongue; my fondness for Ben; his wit, humour and kindness. I became uncomfortably aware of my motivation for dating Tim and the fact that it was fatally flawed.

Liz recognised my turmoil and thought the timing right to release another bomb.
"Annie. Let me ask you a question… Have you ever turned down any man that has asked you out?" I thought through all of the men who had ever paid an interest in me - Sean Blaster, Gordon, Tim, Gary, Devon and finally Tim again - and then I realised the sad truth. In every situation I had been grateful for the attention. In each case I was just pleased to have been noticed. Not once had I made the decision, or even considered whether they were right for me. With every exposure of my heart, I had dreamt about marriage and family, as if it did not matter who should take the role of my husband. Mine had been a scatter-gun approach - if I dated enough men then someone would want the role.

Uncle P's words came flooding back to me:
"Don't try to be what you're not Annie. I've watched you trying to fit in with everyone else… You are good enough… No one can give you what you already have." I teetered as the revelation sank in. I reached for the wall to support myself. All of this heartbreak, all of these wounds; it had all been so unnecessary.

For the first time in my life I wanted to be single, to establish my foundations. I realised that I could no longer expect others to provide my happiness. If I couldn't make myself happy, then why should I expect them to have the key? This was a time for courage, a time to put an end to my old ways and to step into my future. I picked up the phone and dialled Tim's number.

It seemed an eternity until Wednesday came. My new-found single status had unnerved me a little, but had also released me from a great emotional pressure. I knew that this job offered me a new beginning, an opportunity to start again. I had turned a corner in my thinking and determined to no longer rely on the affirmation of any man to make me feel good about myself. I wanted to succeed now more than ever, but this time for my own sake, and not for the approval and acceptance of others.

I had donned my black and white, checked suit, my black polo neck and had placed my hair up in a bun. I looked in the mirror.
"Professional with a capital 'P'," I reassured myself. I had fully researched AZOIL so was prepared for any questions that they might ask. I could sense a steely grit and determination - this job was mine, I could feel it, and I was not going to let it escape. I called for a taxi to take me to the train station. The game was on!

As I pulled up outside the AZOIL building, I marvelled at its superb structure. The building was in a crescent shape with a circular patch of grass outside. On the other side of the grass was the River Thames. It was a fabulous setting. I imagined that if you were working in one of the higher offices on the protruding arms, then you would feel like you were actually over the water.

"One day I'll be up there," I thought to myself.

"That'll be £5.20, Miss," said the cab driver, interrupting my thoughts. I handed over the money along with a tip. "Thanks very much Miss. I hope you get the job. You look like you'll do well." I smiled at him. His words of encouragement were very much appreciated.

I walked across the grass and became aware of the strong wind blowing in from the river. I was grateful for the can of hairspray that I had discharged into my hair that morning. My bun was like rock - nothing could move it. I turned to the wind and said mockingly,

"You'll have to try harder than that!" No disaster was going to hinder this interview. I was totally aware of myself and my surroundings. I even noticed the cracked pavement tile in time to avoid tripping over it. "Not this time!" I said to it.

I stood outside the rotating doors, put my briefcase on the ground and placed my purse inside. I adjusted my skirt and stepped forward into the rotating doors. I was aware of the wind behind me, assisting with the rotation. Half a revolution later and I found myself inside a marble corridor leading to a huge marble atrium. The AZOIL logo was emblazoned on a central pillar. There was no mistaking that I had arrived at the right address. The splendour was overwhelming. I felt a rush of pride and a longing to be a part of this organisation.

The reception desk, a circular marble doughnut, was on the right. To the left was a long black table with lots of name badges and paper on it. A smart-looking lady in red stood

Revelation and Interrogation

behind the table, clearly awaiting her delegates. I noticed the sign, 'European Oil Convention'. I was impressed.

"Excuse me Miss. Did you leave your case outside?" I turned to see the security guard pointing at my black briefcase on the other side of the doors.
"Oh, yes. I must have. Thank you. I would forget my head if it wasn't screwed on!" I said sweetly, whilst berating myself on the inside. I headed back towards the doors to retrieve the offending article, trying to appear unflustered, but inside I was secretly unravelling.

Once again I stepped into the rotating doors, placed 2 hands on the glass and pushed. The wind, seizing its opportunity for revenge, blew against the other side making all my efforts futile. I pushed again, determined not to be beaten. They moved slightly, so I pushed a bit harder. I felt the pressure release - not as the doors rotated, but as they exploded! The glass shattered all around me and the corridor funnelled the wind and the glass into a tornado-like jet stream; engulfing anything in its path. I was in its path and so was the security guard. We turned and ran for our lives, seeking refuge behind the giant doughnut.

As I peered over the top of the desk, I saw the lady in red leaping into the air to catch her papers, which were blowing all around the atrium. Glass was everywhere.

After about a minute, the wind died down and we all stepped out to survey the damage. My briefcase was still on the other side of the doors where I had left it (amazingly it was still upright, untouched by the wind). I went to retrieve it and was aware of a stinging sensation on my legs. I looked down. My tights were shredded; clearly they had taken the

A Rampage Of Chocolate

main force of the blast. I had a few minor cuts, but nothing significant. Most of the damage was to my pride and my confidence. I wanted to run - to make a hasty exit and to disappear into the background - but I had an interview to attend so I couldn't escape.

I returned to the reception desk and looked apologetically at the receptionist.
"I'm Anne Rosetta Booth. I'm here to attend an interview with Mike Sage." She laughed.
"Well you've certainly made an entrance today!" I smiled at her, not sure as to her underlying sentiments. "Are you okay? I can get a first aider to you if you need one."
"No, I'm fine. I just need to tidy myself up a bit in the toilet." I pointed to my tights. She grimaced.
"Oh! I see what you mean. Bare legs may be better?" I nodded my agreement. Then she whispered, "I've got a razor in my bag if you need." I laughed.
"You're fine! There's no need, but thanks anyway!"

With that I entered the toilet to assess the damage. I removed my tights and wiped the blood off my legs. Thankfully they looked okay. I had a couple of very slight scratches on my face, which I covered up easily with make-up. My hair, however, had escaped unscathed. It was perfect.

I went back to the reception desk and glanced around. A team of 3 people were now busy sweeping up the glass and the lady in red had recovered all of her paperwork and was looking as poised as ever. Normality had returned.

The receptionist looked up at me.
"I need you to sign the accident book; this one needs to be recorded." My heart sank. I wanted this whole episode to be

Revelation and Interrogation

forgotten, but instead it was to be written down on paper for all to see. I took the book and held it as discreetly as possible, so that nobody would see my shame. Just as I was handing the book back over the desk, a tall man with brown hair and blue eyes appeared beside me. He held out his hand.
"Mike Sage. Pleased to meet you. Before we start I just need to know if you're okay. I've had the chairman on the phone to me. He's just heard what happened and wanted to see if you needed anything?" Inside I died and crawled into a hole, but outside I said:
"I'm fine! I'm just very sorry about your doors."
"Don't be sorry, it's a design fault. They're supposed to be shut off in high winds. Obviously we just weren't quick enough this time. It's the second time it's shattered, only last time no-one was in it. You were just unlucky."
"So it really wasn't my fault?" Mike looked at me and laughed.
"Of course it wasn't. How strong do you think you are?" I heaved a sigh of relief and laughed with him. Maybe it was worth staying for the interview after all!

Mike chatted easily to me and led me up to an interview room with a panel of three - Mike Sage (Retail Manager), Suzanne Ford (Head of Personnel) and Lou Beresford (Sales Manager). The panel sat on one side of the table and I was alone on the other. They alternated their questions, sometimes interrupting each other, but mostly just writing. 30 minutes later, I came out drained and convinced that I had failed. I had answered all of their questions, but had received no signs of affirmation. Occasionally they had opted for long pauses, in the hopes that I would elaborate further and expose hidden truths, but this was one day that I didn't feel chatty, so I was willing to sit the pauses out.

A Rampage Of Chocolate

By the time I got down to reception, I felt quite deflated.
"How did it go?" the receptionist asked.
"Erm. I'm not too sure. They didn't give much away."
"Well I hope you did okay. You never know, maybe they'll take pity on you; I'm sure they'd prefer to give you a job than receive a lawsuit from you." It was an interesting thought, but the fact is that I didn't want this job out of pity. I wanted to get the job on my own merits because they thought that I was the best candidate. The receptionist interrupted my thought stream with a wave of kindness: "Let me call you a cab, that way you can go home and put your feet up, with a nice cup of tea and a box of chocolates. You deserve it after what's happened. Don't worry about your interview - Mike's pretty good at letting people know quickly. I also hear he's great to work for; a bit of a soft touch." She winked at me and then picked up the phone.

I stood outside waiting for my cab and looked back at the building (with the broken doors) wondering if I would ever see it again.

Chapter 36

Resignation and Restoration

I received the call at 8am the next day, just before I was due to set off in my car.

"Mike Sage here. I'm just ringing to welcome you to AZOIL. You've got the job!" It took a moment for his words to sink in.

"Really? Wow! Thanks!" was all I could say. He sensed my loss of ability and continued.

"You'll be pleased to know that we aren't going to bill you for the doors either." He laughed at his own wit and then carried on. "So, what d'you say?" I replied with the first thing that came to mind:

"When do I start?"

"You could start as early as Monday."

"Really?" I asked, clearly doubting his calculations. So Mike elaborated.

"I'll get the offer couriered up to you today. The courier will wait for you to read and sign it. Assuming that you

Resignation and Restoration

do, then you're free to resign. In view of the fact that you are transferring to a competitor, ABTEX will probably let you go with immediate effect. That would leave you free to start next week. Or would you prefer to take a week off in between? From our end we should like you to join as soon as possible. This is the third time we've advertised the post and you are the first suitable candidate we've found." My heart soared at the confirmation that I had attained this job on my own merit and not out of a fear of being sued.
"A week on Monday sounds good to me, if that's okay. I could do with the break."
"Great! I'll have the papers to you by noon. Let me know when you've signed them."

My heart raced at the thought of this new start. Mike had sounded genuinely enthusiastic about me joining his team. It was such a welcome contrast to Martin's harsh view. I looked at the clock; I had 4 hours to wait. I picked up the phone and cancelled my appointments for that day and set about boxing everything up. I flicked on the television, but could find nothing to watch - not because there were no good programs on, but because my mind couldn't focus. It flitted between excitement and nerves. Change was something I dreaded, but in this case it was essential. My business phone went. I left it. I was determined not to take any calls before submitting my resignation. It tripped to the answering machine and Martin's harsh, Scottish voice boomed out.
"Hello Anne. It's Martin here. Call me as soon as possible. I have some matters to discuss with you." I smiled.
"Oh I will be calling you soon, but not for the reason you think!" I muttered to myself. For the first time, his voice and words posed no threat to me. I had a new job and he was about to lose all his authority over me.

A Rampage Of Chocolate

At 11.42am the doorbell went. The courier stood there with his crash helmet in hand and a large brown envelope.
"I've instructions to wait until you've signed the documents," he said.
"Sure. Come in." I gestured to him to sit on the sofa. "Make yourself at home while I read and sign them. Would you like a drink?" He shook his head. I handed him the remote control and sat at the dining room table. I took a deep breath and then ripped open the brown envelope. 15 minutes later I took a black pen and signed my name triumphantly on the dotted line. I kept one copy for myself and placed the other carefully back in the envelope. I handed, as if it was the most precious package in the world, it back to the courier, who was deeply now deeply engrossed in an episode of *Neighbours*.
"There you go! Drive safely."

I watched as he sped off down the road, then I picked up the phone to call Mike.
"I'm just calling to let you know that I have just signed the papers. They're on the way."
"Fantastic news! Welcome aboard. In that case I shall see you at head office a week on Monday. Shall we say 10 o'clock?"
"10 o'clock sounds just fine to me."
"Excellent. There's only one thing left for you to do."
"There is?"
"Yes. I suggest that you pick up the phone to your ex-boss!"

What a lovely thought - 'EX-boss'! I couldn't wait to tell Martin the news of his revised position. I thought for a moment about what I would say, but then I decided on a different route, something more victorious. For too long now,

Resignation and Restoration

Martin had made my life a misery. This time I was going to make him sweat. I sat at the computer and composed a quick letter:

Dear Martin,

I hereby tender my resignation. I have accepted a job with AZOIL.

Should you require any further information then please don't hesitate to call me.

Yours sincerely,

Anne Rosetta Booth

I knew that when he received my letter he would want to know what job I was taking with AZOIL. He would immediately want to close down any competitive edge or information that I might impart to them, so he would need to assess my danger level to ABTEX. A Shop Co-ordinator wasn't much of a threat, so I felt that I would make him wait for that information. I didn't want to put him out of his misery too soon.

I started to put my plan into action. I picked up the phone to Emily Worthington.
"Hi there, Emily. Are you okay?" It was a rhetorical question, I wasn't about to wait for the reply, I was shaking too much. "I wonder if you could do me a favour, please? I need to fax something very urgent to Martin. When it comes through, would you get it to him?"
"Of course. What is it?" I paused and then uttered the words that would make it a reality.

A Rampage Of Chocolate

"My resignation." There was a gasp and a pause at the other end.
"I'll do that as soon as it comes through. Good luck, Anne. I hope it all goes well for you."

I put down the receiver and faxed the letter through. A little piece of paper came out at the bottom. It simply stated: 'transaction successful'. The deed was done and could not now be undone. I put in place the second part of my plan - I removed the telephone handset so that Martin wouldn't be able to call me. I entered the kitchen and instigated part 3 of my plan - I poured myself a glass of wine.

For the next 2 hours, I sat drinking wine and using the telephone on my fax machine to call Mum and my colleagues to tell them my news. I wanted the privilege of doing that myself, before Martin banned any contact with me. Everybody was very sweet and they all said how much I would be missed. Finally, I replaced the receiver and waited for Martin's call. It came within 5 minutes; he sounded very frustrated.
"Martin here."
"Hello," I said breezily. This man no longer had any power over me and I felt that freedom. He sounded even more irritated by my light response.
"I've received your letter."
"Excellent." I could feel his tension growing.
"I see that you're going to work for AZOIL. What exactly are you going to be doing for them?" I decided not to surrender any ground; I was enjoying battling from this high place. The freedom and the wine had given me a new found confidence.
"I don't feel at liberty to say. I wouldn't like to compromise

Resignation and Restoration

anything." There was silence at the other end. Clearly Martin had been unnerved by this response.

"In that case, I have no choice but to ask you to cease all work for ABTEX with immediate effect. You are not to contact any of your customers or your colleagues. I shall send someone around to collect all your things within the hour. Please box them up."

"I already have." That was one sentence too far for Martin. The receiver went click with not so much as a 'good bye'.

I was intrigued to see who Martin would send, but I didn't have long to wait. 40 minutes later there was a knock at the door. It was Tim. He stood there shuffling his feet, looking at the floor.

"I'm really sorry, Annie. Martin's asked me to collect all of your stuff." He was clearly waiting for my reaction.

"Don't worry, Tim. I'll be pleased to be shot of it. At least then old Dower-pants can't make my life miserable anymore!" I grinned at him. He seemed relieved. I continued. "Anyway, I'm pleased that Martin chose you." Tim cocked his head to the side, quizzically, clearly waiting for me to expand on my statement. "Yes. I wanted to be able to say goodbye properly. I wanted the chance to put our friendship back on the map."

"You mean you didn't want to bugger off like you did at uni?"

"Ouch! That hurt!" I teased. "That is exactly what I meant. Why don't we put this stuff in your car and then go for a meal to celebrate my new job?"

"I'd like that, except that I have orders to take all of your things to my house for collection this afternoon. Apparently they are having it couriered over to Martin's house so that he can make sure that you haven't damaged or stolen anything."

"Are you serious? That man is even more controlling than I thought! Still, I'm flattered to think that he believes I can have so much impact!" We laughed together.
"Can't say he's my ideal boss either," confessed Tim. "I'm looking around for another job too."
"That's a shame! You're good at what you do. So what about tonight?"
"If it's okay, I'll be back at 8pm. Can I stay the night? That way I can have a drink." I glared at him suspiciously. "On the sofa, I promise! I know my place."
"In that case, yes you can, but no sneaking the television on in the middle of the night… you've got work tomorrow!" I gave him a big hug and then helped him out to his car with my boxes. When he'd gone I looked around my bedroom; it looked very bare, with not one trace of work. I was officially free!

That night we all went out together - Tim, Liz, Tina, Bronie and I. We rang Ben, but he declined, muttering something about a contract that he needed to finish. We headed out to the Mexican restaurant, downing a few cocktails whilst we waited for a table to come free. By the time we sat down, I felt very light-headed. I knew that it was time to slow down, so I decided to stop after one more glass of wine.
"I feel like we need to make a toast," announced Liz over a plate of nachos. We all raised our glasses. "Here's to Annie. Out with the old and in with the new."
"Well that's me out then!" declared Tim. "I'm definitely part of your old scene." I thought about what he said for a moment, before responding.
"Actually Tim, you're part of the new…" Liz looked horrified, clearly worried about the next part of my sentence. "I hope

Resignation and Restoration

to take you forward in a new position… that of 'Great Friend'." Tim smiled.

"I'll drink to that," he declared, clinking his glass against mine.

"In fact, let's all drink to that," I said, raising my glass. "To great friendships and to finding the right partners."

The rest of the evening sailed along beautifully. Tim and I bantered happily together and he dutifully stuck to his side of the bargain by sleeping on the sofa. We had overcome all awkwardness and our friendship was restored. This time I was determined to stay in touch.

Chapter 37

Shocks and Frocks

It is funny how you can change companies and find that the very traits that had you rejected in one organisation are the same traits that gain you commendation in the next. Well that was exactly what happened to me. My easy-going manner, which was so despised by Martin, was lauded by everyone in AZOIL. My personality fitted in easily, leaving me to be judged on my results alone. That left me in the strong position of being branded a 'High Achiever' and 'One to Watch'. After 6 months of this praise I began to believe it myself. I no longer doubted my own ability but instead, for the first time ever, I enjoyed credibility.

The fact that I was single had enabled me to concentrate fully on my career. I no longer worried about seeking the affirmation of men. I was validated by my career and my career was going well.

Shocks and Frocks

I had clearly given off 'stay-away vibes' because even Ben had stopped coming around so much and was now dating a woman called Helen. He only ever joined us for the odd night out. This left me in the unusual position of being the only singleton in the house. Liz and Dean were going from strength to strength and were already discussing things such as children and marriage - sharing their dreams and retirement plans. Tina was busy organising the finishing touches to her wedding plans, which was now only a month away. Bronie and Graham were… well just Bronie and Graham. It was difficult to imagine them ever changing or moving forward. They just interacted over games of chess and if there was any romance or tenderness then it was clearly reserved for behind closed doors.

Occasionally my single status would get me down, as I surveyed all the couples' activities in the house, but for the most part it just inspired me to throw myself into my work. By now I had the reputation of being the most effective person in the field force (mainly gained as a result of the late nights I spent ensuring the prompt return of all paperwork). This had even earned me the right to present to the incoming Managing Director of AZOIL. As an American, he was new to the UK market and had asked for 4 people to present to him. I was one of the chosen few.

I spent 3 late nights perfecting my presentation slides and then sent them off to the graphics department for them to add illustrations. I was to pick them up on Friday, the day of the presentation.

When the day came I popped into Mike's office first. He grinned broadly at me. "Good luck this morning Annie. This is your chance to shine. The new MD is a tough cookie

A Rampage Of Chocolate

- he used to be an interrogator in the Vietnam War - but I'm sure that he'll be putty in your hands." I was reassured by his confidence in me and I liked the way people in AZOIL called me 'Annie' not 'Anne'. It somehow helped to strip the barriers away and made me feel welcome in the organisation. "I believe your acetates are ready for collection now, so I guess you'd better head off."
"Thanks Mike. I will. I'll come back and let you know how it goes."

I shot off down to the graphics department and picked up the brown envelope with my name on it. I looked over my 3 numerical slides and was pleased with their appearance. I checked the detail; all the figures were correct. Then I came to the final slide. This was supposed to portray a new shop concept that I was introducing into the petrol stations - shoe repair kiosks. I had asked for it to be represented with an appropriate picture. Unfortunately the graphics designer had chosen this slide to inject some of his own humour. He had chosen a cartoon picture of someone fixing a boot and underneath in bold capitals had written 'COBBLERS!'

I tapped the designer on the shoulder. He slowly removed his headphones.
"Um. Excuse me," I said nervously.
"Yes?" He looked up.
"You seem to have put the word 'cobblers!' on my slide. Don't you think that's a bit rude for a formal presentation?" He started to laugh.
"Yeah it is. Funny though!" I stared at him in disbelief and then continued, in the vain hope that he would understand the gravity of my plight.
"But this is to present to our Managing Director, who has

Shocks and Frocks

never met me before." He took a bit more time to consider this fact and then offered,

"I'm sure he won't mind. It only means 'rubbish'." I pulled the dictionary off his shelf and opened it at the definition, sticking it under his nose. He paled slightly as he read it.

"Now do you see? My presentation is due in 5 minutes and I really need you to redo this acetate for me. I can't possibly stand before the MD and present this. It would be suicide." He grimaced before replying,

"You're going to have to… The printer's not working." My heart sank.

"But what am I going to do?" He thought for a few seconds and then suggested,

"He's American. He won't even understand what it means. It's probably not rude to him." He had given me a glimmer of hope… but then he removed it with a dash of pessimism: "Worst case, the job pages come out tomorrow." With that he popped his headphones back in. Clearly this conversation was over!

I felt my colour drain as I faced a familiar scenario - this presentation could literally make or break my career and right now the chips were stacking against me. I looked at my watch. There was no way to correct the slide, and I was needed in the board room now.

In the board room I sat nervously twiddling my pencil (I knew better than to chose a pen), waiting for the new MD to come in. The double doors burst open and Lou Beresford walked in accompanied by a very large gentleman with small piercing eyes. I gulped.

Lou stood up and made his presentation, only to be torn to shreds by the MD, Jim Lambert. He glossed quickly

A Rampage Of Chocolate

over one of his slides without referring to his more negative results. Unfortunately for him, Jim was on the ball and immediately spotted the fast pass. He ordered Lou to return to the slide, before interrogating him about his plans to redress the situation. Lou was clearly unsettled by Jim's hawk-eyed approach. It didn't bode well for the 'cobblers' slide, and it was my turn next.

I stood up and walked over to the projector, as a condemned man approaches the gallows. I placed my head in the noose and began. I had confidence in my first 2 slides - my achievements were good and I knew it. He smiled, nodded his approval and then I turned to my final slide. All of the English people in the room went wide-eyed. It was quite clear that in their minds I had crossed the line of offence. Lou smiled, but there was no reaction from Jim, so I decided to brazen it out by announcing the word very loudly, just as it was written on the slide:
"COBBLERS!" I looked at his face; it was quizzical but he had not taken offence. "This is a new concept which I'm looking to introduce into our petrol stations…" I carried on for a few minutes explaining the idea and then waited for his reaction.
"Cobblers! I like it! Well done young lady, I'm impressed! And congratulations on such good results." I was amazed and went back to the table to take my seat. The others looked at me in disbelief and awe that I had got away with it.

When all of the presentations were over Jim left the room. Lou came over to me and whispered,
"Cobblers, eh? Very funny, but don't do it again." He patted me on the back to signify that all was well. I glowed with relief.

When I got home, I was exhausted. The tension of the day had taken its toll. Tina on the other hand was excited - the bridesmaids' dresses had arrived and she wanted us all to try them on. I hadn't given much thought to it when she had asked; we had all been sitting around the breakfast table at the time.

"You're all so special to me. I really want all of you to be my bridesmaids. Will you?"

"Of course we will!" we'd all trilled. What none of us had considered was Tina's concept of style. Now that we were faced with the reality, the idea of publicly wearing such an outfit did not seem so appealing.

Tina had chosen pink for the bridesmaids' dresses. Bright pink. They looked like nightdresses with their puffy sleeves and pleated fronts. The pleats stopped under the bust line and then the dresses flowed to the ground. They reminded me very much of Wendy's nightdress in *Peter Pan*. Unfortunately our humiliation did not stop with the colour: These dresses were adorned with outrageous feather trimming and a rainbow panel, that was only revealed when you walked.

"Aren't they gorgeous?" trilled Tina. "I designed them myself. She's done them exactly how I wanted." I didn't know what to say. It was Tina's day and I didn't want to ruin any part of it for her, but equally I didn't want to lie; so I just said,

"I think it's lovely to have something so original that completely reflects your personality." She beamed at me, clearly interpreting my response as an affirmation of her choice.

A Rampage Of Chocolate

"Well go on then. Try them on!" she urged. I looked at Liz who looked at Bronie. We all dutifully took our hangers and skulked off to my room.

Liz was the first to put on her dress. It slipped over her slender frame (she had lost weight since dating Dean and was now an easy size 12). The style and colour notwithstanding, it almost looked good on her. Bronie on the other hand looked somewhat like a fat, sugar-plum fairy; a Barbara Cartland gone wrong. Finally it was my turn. The dress slipped on easily enough, but the bootlace ribbons at the back wouldn't do up properly due to my broad shoulders. I stared at myself in the mirror. Puffed sleeves and bright pink definitely did NOT suit me! We all burst into fits of giggles
"I can't believe I'm going to have to appear like this in public!" I said, considering the humiliation of the occasion.
"What about me? I look horrendous! I'm like Humpty Dumpty in drag!" declared Bronie. We all descended into peels of laughter again, only to be interrupted by Tina coming through the door.
"Let's see you all!" she said excitedly. Obediently we lined up in front of her, muffling our sniggers. Tina was silent for a while.
"Well?" I asked, unsure of her reaction.
"It's not quite how I imagined it," she said as she surveyed our different heights and appearances. "Maybe a plainer style would have suited you all better."

She focused on Bronie, whose dress was about a foot too long.
"I'll go and get the shoes. Maybe that will help." She shot out of the door and returned 5 minutes later with 3 pairs of rainbow coloured wedges. (Why does everyone always try and dress me in rainbows)? We all slipped them on and then

Shocks and Frocks

stood ready for reinspection. (Bronie's dress was now trailing by only 8 inches and hung a little better due to her sudden increase in stature). A disappointed, "Oh!" was Tina's only reaction.

She stood and surveyed us, clearly looking for inspiration. Finally, she came up with a redemption plan: She approached each of us in turn and started to pluck; until all our dresses were bald; not a feather in sight. The resultant plainer look was much easier on the eye (although still pink). She stood back, surveyed us again and proclaimed,
"Perfect!" And with that she left.

I looked at us all in the mirror.
"Thank God there's no-one at the wedding that I want to impress."
"Only Ben," suggested Liz helpfully. I didn't reply.

Chapter 38

Church Bells and Bombshells

The wedding was to be held in Skegness, near Tina's parents' house. We set off on the Friday in 2 cars. Liz drove Ben and Dean and I drove Bronie and Graham. I put some music on (conversation in my car wasn't exactly flowing well), but felt constrained by the company, so couldn't enjoy my usual car dancing. At one point I started to shimmy behind the wheel, but that quickly ended when Graham asked,

"What on earth are you doing, Annie?" I was too embarrassed to admit that I was dancing, so lied, saying,

"Just stretching my shoulders. They're a bit tense."

"Oh!" he said, accepting my reply. After that I sat rigidly at the wheel and eventually turned over to a more classical station. 2 hours of boredom later, I needed the toilet.

"I'm sorry guys, I'm going to have to stop soon. I'm desperate."

Church Bells and Bombshells

"Sure," was the only response I got. That summed up the conversational flavour of the whole journey.

We had passed many service stations along the way, but as soon as I declared my interest in finding one, they ceased to exist. We drove for miles down the A16, passing field after field and village after village, but there was nowhere to stop. Finally I saw an AZOIL sign.
"Thank God!" I exclaimed. There was a notice across the forecourt. 'Closed for refurbishment. Reopens Sat 1st Sept'.
"You can't go in here it's closed," reprimanded Bronic.
"Oh yes I can. I designed the shop! They know me here and anyway it opens tomorrow." With that I flung my car door open and dashed across the forecourt and into the shop. I ran past Sue, the Manageress, saying "I hope you don't mind, I'm desperate. Don't worry I know where it is." I never waited for a reply. Urgency had overtaken me.

I opened the toilet door, locked it behind me and sat down with a great sense of relief. I had only just made it! It was at this point, of no return, that I heard a shuffling noise from above. Looking up I saw 2 feet poking out from one of the ceiling tiles and then spotted the stepladder in the corner. I was caught in a panic, like a rabbit in headlights. I couldn't change my situation (in the words of one of the greats: 'I have started so I'll finish'). I was committed to my seat. So now I faced a dilemma: do I stay quiet, thus drawing no attention to my predicament below, or do I whistle loudly to alert the workman to my presence, whilst hoping that he doesn't peer down to see who's there? I opted for coughing, flushing and pulling-pants-up-as-quickly-as-possible. I managed to complete the whole transaction in total privacy. His feet didn't move. Much to my relief.

When I emerged, Sue came over to me.

"Did you use the disabled toilet? There's a man working on the electrics in the ladies."

"I was fine thanks. I did spot him." (I didn't like to admit that I hadn't spotted him in time). I changed the subject. "The site's looking good. Are you all ready for the grand opening tomorrow?"

"Definitely!" she beamed. "Pop in anytime to see us, you'll always be welcome."

"Thanks, I will." With that I left, complete with my professionalism and my modesty in tact.

Saturday morning came and we all (Liz, Bronie and I) got ready together. Our outfits were still hideous and were not much improved by the white feathers in our hair or the bouquet of white feathers we had to carry. We each consoled ourselves with a glass of champagne and the fact that we could change our clothes for the evening event.

Tina looked stunning in a long white version of our dresses. Somehow the style suited her better and her feather-trimmed cape, which formed her train, set her dress and figure off beautifully. She had booked a horse and carriage for herself to take her to the church. For us bridesmaids and the remaining guests she had ordered a pink double-decker bus. It was an unorthodox mode of transport to the event, but then this was never going to be an ordinary wedding (with even more transport surprises to follow). My only disappointment was that no clouds turned up to float on!

We arrived at the little country church 10 minutes early.

Church Bells and Bombshells

Tina on the other hand arrived half an hour late, by which time I was frozen and my nose had started to drip. Liz and Bronie, having been hardened by the Newcastle social scene, were oblivious to the elements. The carriage arrived and the driver stepped down to open the door. Tina's father came out first, preceded by his walking stick. He was frail, but proud and stood as upright as a hunchback could be, waiting for his daughter. Tina gracefully descended the little wooden steps and took her father's arm. We set off slowly down the aisle to the tune of 'Moon River'.

We had been placed in height order, with Bronie at the front holding the train. Liz and I walked at the back (somewhat reminding me of the pink security guards at *Highpoints*). As we walked down the aisle, I scrutinised the people on either side. Ben, who was sitting on the end of a pew, sniggered as I went by. I managed to jab him in the ribs without missing a step. I looked to the other side of the aisle. The pews were full of New Age, hippy types and aristocratic gentry. It was an interesting insight into Greg's background. I realised that I didn't actually know much about him and it was now quite clear that he came from a very wealthy family. I should have realised that any person as laid-back as Greg had to have money to accommodate his horizontal position. You can afford to have extreme principles and ideals when you have the finances to support you.

I was amused by the integration of the wealth and the hippy types. In many cases the hippies stood in their floaty kaftans next to their suited and booted parents - headbands next to top hats. As I analysed the incongruity of the congregation, my eyes fell on a tall man with dark hair standing next to Greg's sister. He was in full morning suit and she was in a turquoise silk, Indian trouser suit (a perfect middle ground

A Rampage Of Chocolate

between the 2 camps). The man turned his head towards me and I was shocked to realise that it was Devon. I looked away immediately, but my heart had already missed a beat, quickly followed by a surge of anger. I was annoyed that he had chosen today to pop back into my life - a day when I looked completely ridiculous. It was hardly the triumphant closure that I had sought. I looked back quickly, Devon caught my eye again. He raised one eyebrow and smiled at me, that charismatic, gentle smile that disguised so much guile. I smiled back before I had a chance to control myself and then carried on to the front, where I took my place on the first pew.

The vicar made Tina's father look positively youthful. His tones were croaky, not dulcet, and very monotone. I tried hard to focus on the content of what he was saying, but found my mind wandering. Instead I marvelled at the structure of the building and at the exquisite detail in the fretwork and carvings. There was a painting on the ceiling of Jesus surrounded by lots of angels with a lion and a lamb beside him. I found myself staring into his eyes and marvelling at his smile. It was enigmatic, comforting and safe. I turned my head once more to Devon; his smile offered no such qualities.

Circling the central dome were borders of stone, each with writing on them. I started to read what they said, the vicar's voice still droning in my ears.

'I will praise you, for I am fearfully and wonderfully made. Ps 139:14'

I started to imagine what the 'Ps' was for. Had they forgotten to write something and were trying to add it on after? Or

maybe they had run out of room and had resorted to code. No! It was a secret message. Yes that was it! It was a secret message, only to be translated by those with the codebook. But who was it talking about? I couldn't think of anyone who would fit that description. Who was fearfully and wonderfully made? As I thought those thoughts a man's voice said,
"You are." I looked around but I was surrounded by women. I didn't understand.

I read the words again, contemplating their meaning. Whoever had written them was so confident in their own worth. Could I really dare to believe the same?

It was an awesome concept: to consider myself as a creation that was fearfully and wonderfully made. Someone had meant for me to be just as I am. Not an accidental birth but planned and created. I felt a tear rising in my eye. The thought of being enough just as I am was such an alien concept to me, that to believe it felt like a step too far. Uncle P's words came flooding back to me again.
"Don't try to be what you're not Annie… You are good enough."

I realised in that one moment that I had always viewed myself as a mistake - I had started off as a mistake and had always expected someone or something else to put that mistake right. I had always anchored myself in things that validated and justified my existence. Of recent it had been my career because that was the thing that was going well. Previously it had been my friendships or my boyfriends. It had never been just me. I had never considered myself to be enough to exist in my own right,

A Rampage Of Chocolate

The organist started to play a hymn; we all stood up. I took a deep breath and started to sing, but almost choked on my warbling words. I wasn't sure where to go from here - how to transform the mindset of a lifetime. I looked upwards to read the next stone border. It said:

"For I know the plans I have for you," declares the LORD, "plans to prosper you and not to harm you, plans to give you hope and a future."' Jer 29:11

That was all that I had ever wanted - a hope and a future. It had never been much to ask, and yet I had never found it. I had tried to live out of other people's plans, not my own. And yet here was a carving on a piece of stone that promised me all that I craved.
"Can I really believe it? Is there really a hope and a future just for me?" I said to myself. Once more I heard the voice.
"Yes. There is."

I couldn't explain the voice, but it was firm and authoritative. My whole body responded to it. At the deepest level I knew that the words I had just read were true. My heart surged as I accepted this new reality. I realised that there was a new way for me; a way forward. I didn't know what that way looked like, but I knew that I wanted to find it. From now on I would be a woman on a mission - a mission to fulfil that destiny. No longer did I need to apologise for or justify my existence on this planet; I was meant to be here! The question was... how could I step into that promise?

I spent the rest of the service standing or sitting at the appropriate points. I shed a tear as Tina and Greg exchanged their vows, but mostly I sat distracted, reading and rereading the words on the stone borders. Never had anything so powerfully impacted me. These few words had pierced to the very heart of me and I knew that if I embraced them, then I would never be the same again.

Finally the service was over and we proceeded out into the gardens for the photographs. Various people ran up to Tina to give her lucky horseshoes, charms and chimney sweeps. She held them for a while and then handed them all over to me for safekeeping. Amongst them was a 'lucky dollar' that had been given to her by her American nephew. I looked at it with amusement and then my eyes spotted the words on the back: *'In God we trust'*. I smiled to myself.
"So that's how!" I thought.

The rest of the wedding went very smoothly with a few additional surprises: The elephant arrived on time and whisked (if whisking can be that slow) Tina and Greg down the road to the reception venue. Apart from one small collision in the road, most of Skegness seemed oblivious to the abnormality of an elephant wandering down the street. Tina and Greg, on the other hand, savoured every moment and even managed to avoid the giant puddle of elephant wee as they descended.

The whole wedding was delightful and was designed to nostalgically recreate the events of their engagement, whilst also reflecting the flavour of their honeymoon to come (they were off to India for a month, hence the elephant). Flower petals (which unfortunately stained when wet) were scattered across the guests' seats. Name cards were innovatively created by writing on little, white, wooden elephants. The meal was a replica of the proposal meal - fish, chips and mushy peas followed by banana split.

I found myself seated between Dean and Ben on a table very close to the bride and groom. It was close enough to make faces at Tina, but far enough away not to incur any retribution. It was beautiful to see such a dear friend so very happy. It affected us all in different ways. Dean tucked into his champagne and his meal in a bid to avoid Liz's expectant gaze. Graham sat with his arms crossed for much of the proceedings - a clear indication that he was having none of it. Ben, on the other hand, just went quiet, clearly touched by the magnitude of it all. I just enjoyed being part of Tina and Greg's life for a day. This was their hope and their future, not mine. I wasn't about to build my dreams on their foundations, so I just enjoyed it for what it was.

I spent much of the dinner observing the dynamics between Ben and Helen, his new girlfriend. This was the first time I had actually met her and I was curious. Over the years I had become extremely fond of Ben and without knowing it he had attained a special place in my heart. I admired him so much. He was strong, yet there was a gentleness and sensitivity about him that was quite rare and so beautiful to watch. He deserved the very best partner in life - someone who would recognise him for the treasure that he was and come alongside him to comfort and encourage him. Helen certainly didn't seem to be that woman. She was very pretty to look at, if a little large in body, but her temperament was waspish. With every breath she seemed to want to conquer Ben; like a queen governs a handmaiden. He was gracious, as always, and seemed to accommodate her very public demands without any complaint. I waited to see if he would snap, but it seemed that he was determined not to make a scene. It was impossible to tell whether there were subtler feelings going on beneath the surface, although I did catch a glimpse: I noticed his wry smile when Helen got up to go to the toilet and he spotted the big pink patch left by the rose petals on the back of her dress. He chose not to comment (I think he chose wisdom).

I felt disappointment for Ben. This was the first girlfriend that I had seen him with and she wasn't pleasant. I wondered what Ben had seen in her - they were not well matched and he was clearly not enjoying her company. I felt yet another wave of protection towards him. I wanted to bring him to safety like a mother hen gathers her chicks. This couldn't possibly be the right woman for him. He needed someone kind and fun. Helen was neither. Maybe I should choose his next partner for him, but that thought stung my heart. I looked at his foppish fringe and bluebell eyes and wondered how I'd overlooked such an awesome man. So often the greatest treasures are hidden in our own backyard and yet we drive miles away to find a place to dig. By the time we realise, we return home and the treasure is gone.

When the meal was over, there was time to mingle briefly before going off to change for the evening event. I was stood waiting for Liz, when I felt a tap on my shoulder. It was Devon. This time my heart was solid. I was looking at him through different eyes.
"Good to see you Annie. How've you been?"
"Good! I've been really good."
"I'm pleased. I never got the chance to apologise to you for… for…." I helped him out with his missing words.
"For two-timing me?" I said it gently but truthfully.
"You misunderstood. She was never…" I cut him off from

his lies by placing 2 fingers over his mouth and shaking my head.
"Please don't, Devon. It's the truth that counts. None of it matters now anyway. Your path has gone one way and mine has gone another. I wish you all the luck in the world."

I was just about to leave, when I had an inspired thought, so I turned back to say one last thing.
"Just remember, Devon that every woman you play with is someone who is fearfully and wonderfully made. Don't ever treat them any other way." With that I turned and left. Devon just stood there, dumbfounded.

Chapter 39

New Dynamics

The day after the wedding I was very subdued and thoughtful. I had received life-changing revelation about myself and now I needed to know what to do with it. I felt differently about who I was and about my purpose in life. I wanted to reconsider all things, to reorder my life. There was plenty of time to think on the way home because Graham and Bronie weren't talking. They had argued back at the hotel (something about an illegal chess move) and weren't speaking. So I embraced the silence and thought about my perspectives on life. Part of me wanted to go back and relive my past, to change it, but I knew that forward was the only way from here.

I started to think about our house. We had just begun to advertise for a new housemate, a replacement for Tina (who was planning to move out as soon as she returned from honeymoon). It would change the whole dynamic of our

New Dynamics

house. It meant the closing of one chapter and the opening of another. The start of a new season. Should I stay or should I go? I thought about it for a while.

"I'll stay for this season," I said quietly to myself.

"Where will you stay?" asked Bronie crossly (clearly I hadn't said it as quietly as I had thought). "What season? I need to get home as quickly as possible."

"Oh Bronie, you do make me laugh! You never miss anything. I was just wondering who would replace Tina, that's all."

"So long as they stick to the rota and pay the bills, then I'll be happy with them." She crossed her arms and harrumphed. I chuckled. I saw her mouth twitch into the semblance of a smile, but she held on steadfastly to her crossness.

"When's the first applicant coming around?" I asked.

"Wednesday."

"Oh drat! I'll be in Aberdeen. You'll have to let me know what she's like. I'm returning on Friday, so I should be back in time to meet any others that come round."

On Tuesday evening I set off in the car with my suitcase in the boot and plenty of CDs in the glove compartment. It was going to be a long drive in the dark, but at least I would be fresh and ready for 2 full days of business. I felt more relaxed than I had done for a long time. I knew that I was good at my job and realised that I didn't have to prove it to everyone I met. Somehow that just freed me up to deliver results without the same pressure. I could already feel that it was making me braver. As I drove, I considered a few new concepts that I would like to suggest. Ordinarily I would have concerned myself with the opinion of others and stuck to the safe path, not mentioning them; but these

A Rampage Of Chocolate

made good business sense and so were worth exploring. I smiled as I drove, enjoying my liberation and my renewed thought stream.

Sometimes it seems that when you make progress, the whole world moves against you to put you back into your original box. If you hold fast, then those times are an opportunity to destroy the box and to be free for life. My first opposition came on arrival at my hotel. I was unpacking my suitcase, placing things in the wardrobes and drawers, when I realised my omission - I had forgotten my underwear. All I had to last me for the next 2 days was what I was standing in!

"Oh hell! How stupid!" Then I stopped myself. I had declared that over myself once too often. "Actually, it's not stupid, it's just an oversight. The world hasn't ended. It could've happened to anyone." I stopped rebuking myself and started instead to think of a way around my predicament.

"Okay. So if I wash my knickers in the bathroom and put them on the radiator overnight, they'll be ready for the morning." I marvelled at my practicality and presence of mind and quickly set about my plan. A swift scrub in the sink with soap from the soap dispenser; a quick rinse and wring (followed by some salad-spinning style swinging behind the bath curtain) and my still-sopping-wet knickers were laid out to dry on the rusty old radiator.

In the morning I realised the flaw to my plan... This was a small, privately-run hotel which turned its heating off overnight. My knickers were just as wet in the morning as they were the night before. I gasped in horror. There was only one option now... Commando! Thankfully I had brought a trouser suit, so no-one would know.

My morning meetings went very well; I agreed upon a new

New Dynamics

layout for 2 shops and oversaw the launch of some new chocolate bars. (New chocolate concepts are always trialled in Scotland first. If they succeed in Scotland then they are rolled out to the rest of the country, but if they fail up there then the rest of us never get to know they existed. I really enjoyed being a chocolate guinea pig while I was there). *Clock Off* bars were everywhere and there was lots of advertising on TV. They were flying off the shelves and when I tasted one I understood why. They were heaven in a wrapper!

My final visit for that day was to a petrol station that was being rebuilt. It was due to reopen on Friday and I was there to make sure that it looked fantastic and was correctly stocked. I was feeling particularly proud of this shop. It was the first one that I had designed from scratch and it included all of my new concepts (my favourites of which were the milkshake machine and the chip maker).

I waved at Bill, the Service Station Manager, as I walked across the forecourt. The workmen, who were still finishing off the final touches to the pumps, whistled as I went past. I felt it was rude to treat me that way, but equally I enjoyed the attention. I didn't turn around, but instead wiggled my bottom in acknowledgement. They roared with laughter. I blushed slightly, regretting the exchange, and then walked through the doors into the shop, where I took my jacket off and put it on the counter.

7 people were waiting for my arrival. I called them all around to brief them.
"Thank you so much for turning up today. These next 2 days are vital to the success of this site." They were all hanging on my every word. It was nice to carry such respect. "First

impressions count, so it's really important that we make sure that the entire site is pristine and displayed to the best of our ability." I started to feel tired (I had been on my legs all day), so I sat down on the edge of the chiller cabinet. It was very cold; clearly it had already been switched on. I continued. "I'm going to assign each of you to a section. I want you to clean it thoroughly and then to stock it. I have a plan for each of you to follow and will help you all in turn. Tomorrow I'll come in my scruffs and pitch in wherever you need."

I started to fidget a bit; the cold of the cabinet was really piercing and quite uncomfortable. Finally, it became too much.
"Boy that's chilly!" I exclaimed. They all laughed as I stood up and placed my hands on my bottom to warm it up a bit. It was then that, instead of feeling cotton, I felt my own cold flesh. Clearly something had ripped! I glanced at my jacket. It was out of reach. I looked at the sea of faces in front of me, all of whom were oblivious to what lay behind me. They couldn't see my naked truth and I wasn't about to reveal it to them. There was only one thing I could do: to continue to the end of my briefing, facing strictly forwards, and wait till later to find out the extent of my exposure. I glanced quickly over my shoulder to ensure that there was no reflective material behind me to sabotage my plan. There wasn't. With that crumb of comfort I continued my talk.

Even though no-one could see, I felt the need to cover my bottom, so I sat back down for the rest of my briefing. Apart from my slightly quickened speech, I managed to maintain a calm exterior until I finished talking. Then I handed each of them their instructions. When they had all moved away, I slowly rose from my position of safety, sidled my way along

New Dynamics

the wall to my jacket, covered my rump and dashed into the toilet. There my worst fears were confirmed - my back trouser seam had split wide open. This was one day when going commando was not a good idea!

I looked in the mirror.
"Well you may be fearfully and wonderfully made, but these trousers aren't!" I turned around to survey the view that the workmen must have enjoyed. It was bad! I tried putting my jacket on and found, to my relief, that it covered my entire bottom, unless I lifted my arms (in which case everything was exposed). I rummaged in my bag and thankfully found one safety pin. It wasn't enough to repair the damage, but it was sufficient to stop the seam from gaping wide open.

In the safety of my jacket, I left the toilet with my arms pinned to my sides like an Irish dancer. As I walked, I leaned backwards in the hope of extending my jacket still further. Bill, who is a short man, called me over.
"Annie, you're tall. Would you reach that box for me, please? It'll save me getting the stepladder."
"Which box?" I asked, pretending not to know.
"That box." I looked at the box and I looked at Bill. There was no way that I could get this box down without raising my arms and exposing my all. I stood motionless and tried to buy some time:
"That box?"
"Yes. That box." There was an awkward silence, while Bill waited for me to move. I didn't. "Is there a problem?" he asked.
"No," I lied. I looked between the 2 again. Bill smiled, clearly trying to encourage me into motion. I nodded (it was something I could do without exposing my bottom). Bill looked at me quizzically, surprised by my inaction. I nodded

A Rampage Of Chocolate

some more. He looked even more confused and now slightly irritated. So I took a step towards the shelf in the vain hope that it would bring the box closer. It didn't. The box was still a stretch above my head. Everyone else in the shop was busy with their sections, so it was just Bill and I. I was left with 2 options: the first was to tell him the truth about my situation and the other was to distract him for long enough to get the box down. I had just chosen the latter option when the telephone rang and he left to answer it. With relief and a slight draft to my posterior, I seized my opportunity and grabbed the box. Mission accomplished!

Just then Jan, Bill's wife, called to me from across the room.
"Annie, can you come here and give me a hand please. This is very heavy and Bill's busy on the phone." I went over and helped her to carry a box into the storeroom. (It is hard to carry anything when you're also trying to lean backwards, but I did manage it). We opened the door and went in. "It needs to go up there," she said pointing to the top shelf. My shoulders fell and my mouth dropped open as the same situation presented itself again. I stood immobile as she smiled at me expectantly.

Suddenly the understanding dawned on me. What on earth was I doing? Why hadn't I just admitted to them my predicament? What was I afraid of? It didn't change who I was. This was just circumstance. So I grabbed the bull by the horns and told Jan what had happened. To my great relief she laughed and gave me a big hug.
"Why didn't you say something? I have a sewing kit in my bag. Let's put the box down and then I'll go and fetch it."

Far from being scathing or condescending about my

New Dynamics

misfortune, Jan was supportive and kind. We formed a bond that day which also meant that she shared some of her business concerns with me. She had never done that before, but by exposing my vulnerability to her, she in exchange exposed hers. (Thankfully her vulnerability was a little less fleshy than mine)!

That Wednesday I learnt a very big lesson. There is no shame in showing humility and asking for help, but there is always shame when you try to hide your mistakes. It is not your mistakes that define you; it is what you do about them.

As I drove home that Friday, I thought through my expectations of life. I realised that, even if I was fearfully and wonderfully made, I was still not perfect. To place the expectation of perfection on myself was both unfair and unrealistic. It meant that I would always be disappointed with myself and would therefore always feel like a failure. I decided to change my expectations - to be realistic about my weaknesses and to celebrate my strengths; to be honest about who I am and not to pretend to be something I am not.

When I got home Liz and Bronie were sitting around the table, clearly in deep discussion.
"I don't know," Bronie was saying reluctantly.
"You know it makes sense," Liz was urging.
"Hiya!" I interrupted. Liz looked up, irritated at first and then she smiled as she realised that support may have arrived.
"What's up?" I asked, intrigued. Liz was the first to speak.

"We had the viewing tonight."
"How did it go?"
"Terrible!" Bronie groaned, rolling her eyes.
"Terrible? Why?"
"She was bossy, rude and condescending. She wouldn't fit in at all!" Bronie declared emphatically. I looked towards Liz, who was nodding in agreement.
"It's true."
"Well that's okay because we can just refuse to have her."
"Not exactly…" said Liz apologetically. "Our landlady rang. She said that Catherine was the only person who had applied to the advert, so unless we can come up with a suitable alternative in the next 2 days, she will give her the room."
"Oh!" I said, taking in the enormity of what Liz had just explained.
"So Liz has a plan!" Bronie said sarcastically. I looked at Liz.
"Not so much a plan as a suggestion."
"Which is?"
"That Dean takes the room instead." Liz surveyed my face and saw the surprise, so she tried to soften the blow. "He has to move out of his house at the end of the month anyway, so it makes sense for him. We know him really well, so we know that he'll fit in, so it makes sense for us too."
"He's a man!" protested Bronie.
"Well spotted. Yes he is! Why should that matter?" defended Liz
"This has always been an all girl house and I like it that way." Bronie crossed her arms again in disapproval. There was silence for a moment, then I spoke.
"I always liked nursery rhymes when I was a child, but then I moved on to different music and learned more complicated rhythms, that proved to be more enjoyable in the end. We shouldn't be scared of the new rhythms of life! New seasons,

New Dynamics

by their very nature, demand change. I'm okay with Dean moving in. It seems sensible to me." Bronie and Liz sat there open-mouthed.

"That was very profound! Did you open a jar of wisdom when you were away?"

"Yes. I think I did."

Chapter 40

New Rhythms

The 1st October was a landmark occasion for all of us. It was Tina's last day in the house and Dean's first. Tina arrived the day before to pack all of her stuff. She was very tearful and hardly able to speak. It was difficult to believe that she was moving out, but the boxes were our proof. I watched as she filled box after box, removing her books from the bookcase and leaving big spaces. The house was starting to look bare, like something was missing.

At one point I went in to help her pack, but we both found it too emotional.
"What can I do for you instead Tina?" I asked. "There must be something?" She thought about it for a bit and then replied.
"I think I need chocolate. Something different. I'm not quite sure what." Suddenly an idea came to me.

New Rhythms

"I think I know exactly the thing, if you're prepared to wait a while?"
"Sure. It's going to take me all day and some of the evening. I never realised I had so much stuff."

I needed no more prompting than that. I got into my car and drove. I had been dreaming about *Clock Off* bars all week. They had just started advertising them in England, ready for the launch at the weekend, and it had meant that they were constantly in my mind. However we didn't have until the weekend. We needed them now. So I set off on the hour and a half journey across the border.

I drove and I sang. Sometimes I turned my radio off to speak to a customer. (I was supposed to be working, but I couldn't focus today, not with all the upheaval in the house). I knew that if I took a few calls on my mobile phone then no-one would miss me. And anyway, my friend was in need and I was on a mission to help her.

I crossed the border 90 minutes later and pulled into the first petrol station I could find. I was relieved to see that they still had a giant display of *Clock Off* bars. I grabbed an armful (about 10) and took them up to the counter to pay.
"Any petrol Miss?"
"No. Just chocolate!" I carried my bagful of goodies over to my car and sat down. I couldn't resist opening one bar straight away - I had dreamt of this moment for so long! As I bit into the crispy bar, it dissolved on my tongue. Even my tonsils were chocolate-coated in that moment! I savoured every mouthful. Then I pulled off the forecourt and headed for home. It had been worth the drive.

3 hours after I left, I knocked on Tina's door with a cup

A Rampage Of Chocolate

of hot chocolate and a *Clock Off* bar. She looked suitably thrilled.
"Wow! Where did you get this?"
"Scotland," I said and then walked out.

That night we all went out - the combination of old, current, new and honorary housemates (namely Ben) joined together for a final swansong of unity. We decided to go Mexican. It was our favourite restaurant, the food was always great and the atmosphere totally relaxed. We figured that it would take the edge off our sadness.

We sat around the table, each with a drink in hand. I raised my glass.
"To Tina. You will be sorely missed, but we know that you're going to a better place."
"I resent that comment," said Bronie. I stared at her in surprise, so she explained herself. "It's not better, it's just different. Anyway, you're making it sound like she's died."
"I stand corrected. To Tina! You will be sorely missed, but we know you're going into safe hands." I looked to Bronie for approval. She nodded. We all raised our glasses and said,
"To Tina!"

Dean sat quietly at the table. I thought I would help him out, so I raised my glass again.
"To Dean! The new rhythm in the house." Liz and Bronie beamed, but the others just looked perplexed. They raised their glasses anyway.
"To Dean!" Dean smiled, clearly pleased at his acceptance into the household.

New Rhythms

"I hope that you'll still come and visit us occasionally (as an honorary housemate of course)."

"Oi! That's my role!" protested Ben jokingly.

"No-one's kicking you out, Ben. We still miss you when you're not around." He smiled. Tina on the other hand started biting her lip. She fidgeted and then she spoke.

"Actually guys, I've something to tell you. There are a few more changes than even we expected." She paused. Before she had a chance to continue, Liz gasped and interrupted.

"Oh my goodness! You're pregnant aren't you?" Tina nodded. Liz continued. "I knew it! I was suspicious when you just ordered orange juice. Congratulations!"

I left my seat and went over and gave Tina a hug.

"Congratulations! You will make a fantastic mother. When did you find out?"

"Today. It was a bit of a surprise. Still we have plenty of time to get used to the idea and Greg is really thrilled. Or at least, I think he is… He's so laid back it's hard to tell!"

"Wow! It really is new rhythms for you then - new heartbeats, no less!" Ben quipped. "Congratulations!"

We carried on excitedly throughout the meal, discussing this new turn in Tina's life. It seemed very grown up to have a friend who was married and pregnant. Suddenly it brought home my own reality: without realising it, I had transitioned fully into adulthood. I had arrived!

At the end of the meal we linked arms and walked down the road back to the house. We knew it would be the last time that we would all be together like this, so we enjoyed the moment. We reminisced along the way.

"KFC?" Ben joked as we passed an oh-so-familiar phone

box. We all laughed. We had enjoyed such good times together.

Back at the house Greg was waiting for Tina. He whisked her away, but before she went I gave her a final hug. This time I didn't want to let go.
"You will stay in touch won't you?" I asked.
"Of course!" With that she was gone.

I headed into the kitchen to put the kettle on. I wasn't sure what to do next. I felt lost. A new season was here, but I didn't know how to step into it. All around me leaves were falling and changing colour. I needed to reset my eyes otherwise all I would be left with was the sterility of bare branches. I looked out into the lounge. Liz and Dean were messing about on the sofa, fighting for the remote control. Ben was pacing up and down, and Bronie was trying to rearrange the books on the shelves, so that the gaps weren't as obvious. All of us were trying to redefine the boundaries of normality. This was our new household and like all new machines it would need plenty of lubrication to prevent the cogs from grating against each other.

"Coffee anyone?" I shouted. Everyone readily accepted my offer.
"I'll help!" Ben said hastily and came through to the kitchen. I felt unsettled by his presence. I knew that something had shifted inside of me. Suddenly I understood - my heart started to thud inside my chest and I recognised the drumbeat of love. This time it was different. In the past this feeling had been inspired by a look, a comment, a touch - some gesture towards me, which had made me feel temporarily valued, enough to throw my heart away. Ben had done nothing to generate these feelings inside of me. He was simply being

himself. However our relationship was not expendable; it was too precious. I would not throw it away lightly. We were still friends, but in this moment of clarity I was acutely conscious of how much more I wanted. Sometime between the wedding and this day, I had repackaged Ben. I had moved him into a new box. It was simply marked, 'Partner?' He suddenly seemed so incredibly dear to me and I was scared of losing him. I felt very self-conscious, aware of my every move. I held my breath. I no longer knew his position and the risk of rejection seemed so great.

Ben didn't speak at first. He just helped to get the mugs and biscuits out of the cupboard and busied himself, arranging them several times over into various patterns. I became aware of his every breath and yet I was incapable of looking at him, for fear that my eyes would betray me. I could sense the awkwardness between us. I wondered if he felt it too: all those unspoken feelings bubbling under the surface - neither of us speaking, both of us hiding behind trivial tasks. I felt vulnerable. What if I was wrong? What if he was aware of my feelings and yet no longer felt the same towards me? That thought was too scary, so I grasped at the only conversational straw I could think of to try and make the atmosphere normal again:
"Are you okay?" I asked. "It's just that you seem a bit on edge."
"I'm fine" he said curtly, reordering the teaspoons yet again.
"How's Helen?" I enquired, hating the question. He looked startled.
"She's fine… Or at least, I think she is… I don't know because we broke up straight after the wedding. She turned out to be a bit of a nightmare, so I felt that it was best to end the relationship before it had really begun." My heart leapt

at this revelation and I tried to conceal my smile by focusing on the kettle. Maybe there was still a chance for Ben and I, but how? We had been friends for so long and shared so much. Yet here I stood feeling like I hardly knew how to speak to him. I opted for a lie to break the silence.
"Oh I see. I'm sorry it didn't work out."

Ben spun around on his heel to face me, his cheeks burning red.
"No you don't see, Annie! You've never seen! The truth is that Helen paled in comparison with you. Going out with her was a big mistake." His words hit me with impact, lighting a flame of hope inside; my cheeks started to burn. There were so many questions that I needed to ask him. He must have seen it in my eyes because he elaborated. "I heard that Tim was coming to the restaurant the night you resigned, so I assumed that the two of you were back together. I just couldn't bear it anymore… So I asked Helen out. I shouldn't have… It wasn't fair on her." He hung his head, and then continued. "I've waited for you for such a long time Annie. So often I've gone to ask you out, but then I haven't been brave enough, and instead I've had to watch as you've slipped through my fingers. First Devon, then Tim…" I grimaced at the names.
"I'm sorry!" I said and lowered my head in shame. He caught my chin gently with his hand and raised it back up again, this time directing his conversation straight into my eyes. My heart soared at his touch and then melted at his bluebell eyes. I had never before experienced such a wave of love.
"Do you mean that Annie?" he asked softly. "It's just that I couldn't bear to see you with anyone else again. I love you Annie! I always have. I think you're amazing. I love your disasters and your beautiful quirks, and I love your wisdom and compassion. The trouble is that I can't be just a friend

New Rhythms

to you anymore. It hurts too much. For me this is now or never." I stood rooted to the spot, struggling to hear him over the pounding of my heart. There was no lust in this moment, no needy desperation, just a huge urge to hold and love the man before me. I knew with every cell of my being that I wanted to be with him. I was so wrapped up in this blanket of emotion that I found myself incapable of responding. I didn't know where the next step should be. This was uncharted territory for me.

Ben made the next move - he stepped back and rummaged in his pocket, pulling out 2 small pieces of paper. They were tickets. I could sense his discomfort. He had made himself totally vulnerable in my presence, with as yet no reassuring crumb of comfort. He continued anyway:
"I wanted to bring you something meaningful and this reminded me of you. I would be so proud to take you." He held the tickets out towards me, all the time looking at me with expectant eyes. I smiled - a small handout of hope to reassure him. Then, with more certainty in my heart than I'd ever felt about anything, I reached out to receive my ticket. I knew that in this simple act of acceptance, I was sealing our relationship; fulfilling the desires of Ben's heart. However it was my desire too. I wanted Ben more than I was able to say. Not for what he could give me, but for what I could give him - love.

I looked down at the ticket in my hand. It was for the cinema. The film title said it all:

A RAMPAGE OF CHOCOLATE

I chuckled.

"You know me so well! That sums up my life so far." He gave me a knowing grin.

We stood still, fixed on each others' eyes, our minds reprogramming our relationship. I took down the 'Vacant' sign in my box marked 'THE ONE' and moved Ben into it. The new connections were in place, the process completed. Ben took my hand and smiled at me. I could feel the drawing of our souls. Slowly he leant forward and kissed me for the very first time.

Bronie came rattling into the kitchen and saw us together. She rolled her eyes.
"Not another new rhythm!"

Lightning Source UK Ltd.
Milton Keynes UK
173509UK00001B/5/P